Can you say crazy?
Zaria is over the top and
out of control. Her
outlandish character yanked me
in and never let go! Tell all of
your friends because this book will
surely become a classic!
Miss KP-
Author of The Dirty Divorce Series

Another...
One Night
Stand
THE SEQUEL

KENDALL BANKS

Another One Night Stand

KENDALL BANKS

Life Changing Books in conjunction with Power Play Media
Published by Life Changing Books
P.O. Box 423 Brandywine, MD 20613

Library of Congress Cataloging-in-Publication Data;

www.lifechangingbooks.net
13 Digit: 978-1934230343
10 Digit: 1-934230340

ACKNOWLEDGEMENTS

First, I want to thank my Lord and Savior Jesus Christ. Without You....I am nothing. Then of course there's my mom Roxie, who thinks I'm completely insane for coming up with these characters. She swears I was adopted, but I love her to pieces. Stop hiding my books when the pastor comes over, mama.

Next in line would normally be my significant other, but luckily I caught him in a bad position and kicked him to the curb just before this book went to print. So, I'll just thank my girl Nycole whose been keeping me from crying every night. Thanks for the bottles of Rose. I needed it. I'm still trying to decide if I need to find someone else to keep me warm this winter. LOL.

Now, to all the people who have made this book a success. Let's start with the professionals. Kellie, your designs are to die for. I see why the HBIC for Life Changing Books loves you. Tasha, thanks for keeping our warehouse and all the book orders in place. (Hint. Don't mess up any of my damn orders...LOL) Leslie Allen, just like everyone says, when it comes to these books, you're tough as nails, but the end result makes all your threatening emails worth it. Thanks for all your help with this project. Tressa Azarel Smallwood, thanks from the bottom of my heart for everything you've done for me. I really thought you were gonna kick me to the curb after Rich Girls, but thankfully you gave me another chance to shine. If it wasn't for that, One Night Stand would've never come out or had the chance to become so successful. Because of that, I'm now an advocate of the message, 'never give up'!

Since this story was created from all the people I know

who really have had one night stands- I thank you for sharing your stories. Latoya and Ryan, your stories are really over the top in this sequel. Suggestion-seek help! To Jasmine, Aschandria, Virginia, Lacey, Shannon, and Cheryl thanks for your feedback. I couldn't have done this without you guys.

Shout out to the authors on the LCB label, Miss KP, Tonya Ridley, Jackie D. Danette Majette, J. Tremble, Carla Pennington, CJ Hudson, VegasClarke, Chris Renee, Mike Warren and anyone else I forgot to mention. We truly are with the best urban lit company in the game.

And last but not least to my readers, you guys are awesome. You really know how to make a girl feel good. I love to go on Amazon to read your reviews or simply complain to a bookstore employee about carrying all of my books. By 2013 no one will have to ask, who is Kendall Banks. That's because of you. I love you. Smooches…muah…muah…muah. I truly hope you felt that.

Before I go I want to pay homage to all the African-American authors who've managed to stay afloat through this recession. Let's all band together and refuse to participate. Let's write magnificent stories and get this money vowing to entertain our readers forever.

With love,
Kendall Banks

P.S. Look out for my next hit, Welfare Grind. Coming Soon…

ZARIA

· · · · · · · · · · · · · ·

One

Angry…My adrenaline pumped.

My car hit 80 mph on the dark, New Jersey turnpike. No seatbelt…driving crazy and sitting without constraint. I needed to be free to move about, hoping nothing would pop off to make me snap, stabbing a muthufucka in the jugular. Besides, I needed the ability to rock back and forth in my seat. It calmed me…slightly.

Clutching the steering wheel with both hands, my knuckles pressed tightly against my skin. The highway's white lines disappeared underneath my car in a quick blur as my eyes remained locked on the night's surrounding darkness. The night air splashed my face mercilessly from the opened window, pissing me off even more, but I never budged as it tore against my skin.

"*That sneaky bitch thinks it's a fucking game,*" the voice in my head spat, instigating my actions as it spoke of my aunt Lisa. Just a mere mention of her name made my blood boil like lava. "*But you'll show her ass tonight, I hope…You chump,*" the voice added.

"This is one of them new E350 coupe joints, huh, Zee?" my cousin Kenneth asked loudly from the passenger seat. He tried to project his voice over the newest Rick Ross song playing from the radio. "Ran you about sixty Gs, huh? It had to."

I heard his voice, but was too caught up in my own thoughts to comprehend his questions. From the moment I arrived at his apartment and he told me that my bitch-ass aunt had gone to Atlantic City for some damn slot tournament, I had tunnel vision, seeing nothing but tearing her ass apart. Nothing else held even the slightest interest. Unfortunately, my cousin had no clue of my intent. He assumed I had been in touch with my aunt since she abruptly moved from her place. The only reason Kenneth was with me was because he had refused to tell me what hotel she was staying in unless I brought him along and paid him a few hundred to gamble with. That was no problem. Money wasn't too much of an object for me anymore. The only thing I hated about bringing him was that my true intentions for catching up with his mother would soon surface.

Surely, killing her dead would break his heart and shatter his world just as mine had been when aunt Lisa set this chain of events in motion decades ago. I loved Kenneth and his sister Sonia more than the air I breathed, but spilling their mother's blood tonight *had* to be done. She couldn't walk away from what she'd done.

Although my face masked my anger, adrenaline sharply rampaged beneath my skin and my heart rate thudded loudly and quickly inside my chest. The anticipation of me confronting my aunt was almost unbearable but I remained calmer than the normal Zaria and slowed down a bit, not wanting to get pulled over by the police. That was the last thing I needed since I was already *on the run*. Despite the fact that every single mile seemed to run on forever, I had to stay patient. Revenge would be coming in due time.

"Naw, this muthafucka is fully equipped," Kenneth continued, admiring my platinum colored Mercedes. "What did it run you Zee? Fifty G's?"

"Nah," I muttered.

"You bullshittin a nigga," I thought I heard him say. "Tell me how much."

I've got to take my meds soon, I thought to myself, still too shrouded in my own thoughts to pay attention to Kenneth's ranting. My meds had been holding me down and keeping me calm for the past five months faithfully, causing me to depend on them. They'd been making my life a whole lot more bearable. As long as I took them regularly most of the voices in my head disappeared, and my urge to lash out at people remained tamed.

"What's his name?" Kenneth asked, punching one fist into the other, like he was really thinking hard.

My eyes were on a set of glowing red tail lights in front of me.

"Zee!" Kenneth called, his seat reclined so far back he was nearly laying in the backseat.

"Huh," I answered, snapping back into reality.

"What's the nigga's name?"

"What nigga?" I asked, having absolutely no idea who or even what he was talking about.

Since we'd been on the highway I wasn't sure if I had even said more than three or four sentences to him. My mind had been totally on his mother. My one and only enemy.

"The nigga who got you out here looking like a new person these days," he said as if I should've already known who he was talking about. "You rockin contacts now, hair straight from some girl's head in India... anddddddd you keeping your nails done, and driving a new Benz. I mean damn, nigga. Not to mention this plastic surgery thing you did to yourself. I mean, I know you did it to look better, but I like the old Zee."

"The changes are slight, Kenneth. Just improvements that make females feel better about themselves."

"Yeah...but usually when a woman switches up like that,

there's some dick involved."

"Not necessarily," I told him. "Sometimes a woman just gets tired of trying to make everyone else happy and realizes that it's time to make her self happy."

The answer was more of a belief and philosophy rather than the truth. In all actuality my changes had been made in an attempt to stay low and hidden in plain sight. Too many people knew the old Zaria as a jeans and sneakers wearing tomboy who bit her nails and was always down to kick off her shoes and mop a bitch in the middle of the street. If I wanted to remain a free woman, I had to bury that Zaria and become a new one.

"Whatever," Kenneth said, not believing my explanation. "All that sounds real slick. But get to the part where you tell me the nigga's name."

"There's not a name to give," I lied. Actually there *was* a new man in my life now but under the circumstances I knew that it was best to keep him a secret.

The bright lights of Atlantic City's hotels and casinos began to brighten the night as we paid the last toll. The scent of the aligning ocean filled my nostrils. "So, what hotel is she staying in?" I asked, exiting the highway and pulling onto the main strip.

"The Showboat," he said, pointing me in its direction. "To the left."

Blazing with anticipation and desperate for revenge, I weaved quickly through traffic and pulled in front of the Showboat Casino. Without even waiting for the valet guy, I grabbed my new oversized Chanel Hobo bag from the backseat, opened my door and stepped out into the night. I quickly made my way around the hood of the car and tossed the keys to the young, skinny valet guy who was approaching.

"Damn," Kenneth said, climbing out of the car and admiring the ass of a Puerto Rican girl headed inside. "She got a fat one on her."

I fumbled through my heavy purse. "You sure she's here?" I asked, taking out three hundred dollars and passing the cash to Kenneth.

"Hell yeah," he stuffed the money into his pocket. "Come on. Let's go find her. I'm pretty sure she's still at the slots."

"No-no," I told him quickly. "You go on and enjoy yourself. I'll find her."

"You sure?" he asked.

"Yeah, go ahead. Have fun. I'll text you when I'm ready to roll out."

"A'ight, I'll be at the blackjack table," he said, rushing inside.

Two men admired my frame as I walked through the front doors in my Louboutin red bottom heels and form fitting, black shirt that I wore as a dress. I didn't pay the slightest bit of attention to them or their stares. My mind was completely on finding my aunt as I began to make my way between body after body to the slot machines. Over all the hustle and bustle, I heard my cell phone ring and snatched it quickly from my purse.

"Hello!" I shouted over the loud voices of dealers and gamblers, my eyes never blinking or deterring away from my search.

"Milan," the angry voice sounded.

Damn, now was not the time for me to deal with pretending to be someone else. I needed to be Zaria, so I could be angry and kill me a bitch.

"Milan," Tyson's anger filled voice blared through the phone. "It's two o'clock in the damn morning. Why aren't you here where you're supposed to be? Don't no man want his woman out this time of night!"

"Tyson, I'm in the middle of handling something real important," I said, rounding the end of a long line of slot machines and making my way slowly down the aisle. The machines were making so much noise I thought for sure he would say something about it.

"Unless it's life or death, nothing is supposed to be more important than giving me some pussy right now," he said, not going for my half-ass excuse. "What are you handling at two in the damn morning?"

"Sweetheart, I'll tell you later," I said. "I promise."

"Look-a-here, Milan…"

Just hearing that name always made me wonder why I chose that name as my alias. Of all the bitches I could've chosen to imitate, why her? Was it because she was thin and I wasn't? Was it because she reeked super model status and I didn't? Immediately, my thoughts were interrupted. Tyson was still babbling…but I heard none of his words. I stopped dead in my tracks when I saw her huge frame sitting on the stool several yards ahead of me slipping bills into the slot machine. Tyson's voice on the phone no longer registered to me at all. Nothing around me registered. For ten seconds everything and everyone around me disappeared. All that still existed was me and Aunt Lisa.

My heart rate increased heavily. My breathing excelled. The room began to spin. My mind flashed back to the past. Her words, her smile, her love…it had all been a facade. Her words had been lies. Her smile had been fake. And her love for me *never* truly existed. It had all been nothing more than the building blocks of a scheme she and my father had concocted to get my trust fund money. In reality she never loved me or even cared for me. It had all been a fuckin game to her, a game that she thought she would be handsomely compensated for until my sorry-ass father exposed their secret just before he killed himself right in front of my eyes.

My world had always been a dark place. It had been that way since my mother's death, its torture aggravated by my molestation at the hands of my own father for so many years. I'd always felt nothing could torment me more. Nothing could break me down to my knees any worse. Nothing, until my father told me that my aunt Lisa had been the birth of all my pain.

She'd killed my mother.

I couldn't believe it. Life had always had a way of punishing me for whatever its reasons but I had never been kicked in the stomach by life so hard. The woman I would have died for had turned out to be the devil in drag. And it was time for Aunt Lisa's conniving-ass to receive death.

"Milan!" Tyson called again through the phone, abruptly awakening me to reality just in time to see my aunt slide off her stool and walk her wide frame around the end of the line of slot machines. I wasn't sure if she'd seen me... so I panicked.

"Tyson, I'll call you back," I told him quickly and hung up the phone, tossing it back into my purse.

Immediately, I charged after my aunt, huffing and puffing along the way. When I reached the end of the slot machines and turned the corner, I saw her making her way quickly through the crowded casino to an exit door, never once looking behind her. I gripped the shoulder strap of my purse and chased her like a lion after its prey, determined not to let her get away. She'd eluded punishment for my mother's murder for far too long.

Making my way across the room to the exit door seemed like a lifetime, each step not seeming to get me to it fast enough, although even in heels I was jogging quickly. When I reached the door, I let my body and the palms of my hands slam against it, opening it wide enough for me to charge through without breaking my stride. My heels began to click loudly on the floor of the parking garage, echoing as I caught sight of my aunt Lisa's back ahead of me.

The large garage was filled with only cars, no people or the loud chattering voices we'd just left behind. The pillars and snow white colored walls had quickly become the boundaries of our own world. Only the two of us existed here, no witnesses. Just the way I wanted it.

"Aunt Lisa!" I shouted, gaining on her with each step.

She didn't answer but her speed dramatically slowed second after second, her size making it pretty much impossible to keep up the pace she'd started with.

I was only several feet behind her. "Aunt Lisa!"

She finally stopped and turned to me, realizing that her

weight wouldn't allow her to get away. "Zaria?" she said as if unsure of who I was but fear clearly registering across her face.

I caught up with her and looked directly into her eyes, standing just inches away. Knowing what truly lay behind her pupils sickened me.

"Zaria?" she questioned me again, looking more closely as if wondering if it was really me.

Her days of fooling me were over the second my father blew her cover. I knew that even with my drastic change of appearance she recognized me in the casino. That was why she ran, I was certain.

"Girl," she said, her face brightening with false joy as if she really gave a damn about me. She looked me over from head to toe. "I didn't know that was you. You look so different. What did you do to yourself? You look good, baby."

My eyes saw through her lies easily.

"I missed you," she said, stepping towards me with open arms as if expecting a hug.

Ain't that a bitch?

"Don't touch me," I sneered angrily, my body tensing, and my teeth grinding against one another.

Aunt Lisa stood surprised. "Why are you acting like that?"

"How could you do that to me?" I spat, my heart filled with the pain of her betrayal.

"Do what, Zaria?"

"You killed my mother, your own sister," I said through gritted teeth. My eyes welled up with tears, blurring my vision. It seemed like my heart was breaking all over again. The pain seemed fresh.

"Child, what are you…"

"Bitch, don't try to lie to me!" I screamed, sending hatred flowing through my veins. "My father told me everything. He told me about my mother's murder and the cover up. He told me about Sonia. He told me about the fake psychiatrist, and the attempt to get my money. He told me everything."

Aunt Lisa couldn't speak. She knew it was all over.

"You took my world from me," I said. The tears wouldn't stop falling. "How could you?"

"No, I didn't. You got this all wrong, Zaria. Baby, I've been looking for you."

"Stop it!" I shouted. No more lies. You think I'm crazy?" I asked with hunched shoulders and a deep scowl. "You fled your house and left nothing behind. You know why!" I screamed, "because you knew I was on to you and your fake psychiatric partner."

She began to shake her head. But it was obvious to me that she wasn't shaking it out of sorrow or shame for what she'd done. She was shaking it out of disapproval for my father finally exposing her for the manipulative murdering liar she really was.

"All I had been was a payday for you," I said.

Aunt Lisa smirked. "What do you want me to say, Zaria?" she asked. "That you weren't?"

I stared at her.

"That I really loved you like a daughter?" she continued. Her voice was now full of spite and sarcasm, a far cry from the voice that used to comfort and console me.

My tear filled eyes stared deeply into hers.

"Child, please," she said dismissively, as if genuinely caring for me was nonsense. "No one can love you. Don't you understand that, girl? You're twisted. You're a reject. Who can love a reject?"

The words stung like a swarm of honey bees. Hardy's face flashed throughout my memory. His words, "Third Rate Hoe," echoed in my head along with, Milan's and Jamal's abandonment. It was all just as bad as my aunt calling me a reject. Their opinions of me and what they truly thought of me hurt more than just my feelings and my heart, they hurt my soul.

"And where do you get off judging me?" Aunt Lisa asked, placing her hands on her hips. "You're a murdering bitch! And the police WILL eventually find you for killing that boy and your father. I was hoping they would get you when you went to the bank to withdraw that trust fund money from your account. But they were too slow, too stupid."

Smiley Face. Smiley Face. Can anyone see my Smiley Face? The harmonic and inspirational words began to play in my mind in an attempt to calm the raging storm inside me. But the harmonies clashed with the chanting of that voice that *always* dominated all others as it began throwing gasoline on a burning fire by screaming, "*Kill her, Zaria! Kill her!*"

"It's only a matter of time before the police catch you," she said. "Those contacts and that botched plastic surgery job can't protect you."

My body trembled violently.

"*Kill her, Zaria!*" the voice in my head shouted!

"You're no better than me," Aunt Lisa said, her words sharp as daggers.

Suddenly, the next few moments became flashes and blurs. I didn't even remember reaching into my purse for the crowbar. I only knew that it was in my hand crushing my aunt's skull and repeatedly gashing it wide open like a pumpkin.

"Oh my God, Zaria, what are- are-you- you- d-o-o-o-i-i-n-n-g!"

Her screams and outstretched arms in a pathetic attempt to defend her self were useless. As she fell to the floor, blood poured endlessly from her gaping wounds like a fountain that had been carelessly left running.

"Pleaseeeeeeeeeee!" she screamed from the floor.

The countless memories and images of me sitting on my mother's lap, and the day she taught me how to tie my shoes brightened and then darkened at the introduction of a new image with each swing of the crowbar. The steel repeatedly landing against her back, stomach, and thighs sounded like a boxer's gloves pounding a punching bag. Feeling it land squarely on its mark each time gave me more than immense satisfaction, it somehow gave me freedom. I loved how it felt, never wanting it to fade. I wanted the moment to last for a lifetime.

Aunt Lisa's voice went from screams to moans and finally to nothing at all, mere silence. Her body finally stopped moving, its final breath escaping it a long time ago. Moments later, I finally gained enough control of myself to stop swinging the crowbar. I let my arm drop limply against my hip, my fingertips holding it so loosely it was a wonder that I hadn't dropped it to the ground. Aunt Lisa's blood thickly created a pool around her body, its bitter stench nauseating me. As I stared at her lifeless body my own felt like it was floating. The moment seemed surreal. Suddenly, the sound of the casino's opening door and the laughter of a couple stepping into the garage brought me out of my daze and sent me running once again.

ZARIA
Two

"Oh, Tyson!" I screamed in both pleasure and pain, unable to hold it in. Obviously Tyson was feeling some kind of way about me not bringing this pussy to him last night when he demanded it, and now he was making me pay with each thrust. His sex game was always wild, but...damn. He was fucking me like a lustful savage.

"Take it all!" he ordered, forcefully pulling my body back to his. After my third or fourth attempt; I'd lost count, at backing up against the headboard. It felt good, but a painful good. I'd never been scared of dick before, but he needed to show mercy on me.

"Take all of this dick!" he uttered.

"Tysonnnnnn," I whined, hoping he wasn't tapping my unborn baby's head.

Usually, he made love to me, even if it was rough. Usually, his intentions were to please me. At this moment though, he was intending to fuck the life out of me and my body loved every moment of the punishment. It wanted nothing less than to have multiple orgasms and put an end to my stress.

The soft feel of the sheets and the extravagant look of Tyson's huge master bedroom made me feel like an African queen as he crammed all of himself inside me repeatedly. Its crystal chandeliers, floor to ceiling windows, and marble floors set off something inside of me. Being surrounded by imported classic furniture from critically acclaimed designers like Arne Jacobsen, Jean Prouve, and Garrett Rietveld seemed to increase my ecstasy. It seemed to make me feel like Tyson was dominating me in the center of a faraway palace.

"Fuck me, Tyson!" I gave an order of my own to the beast inflicting destruction on my insides. "Fuck this pussy, damn it!"

I'd never been opened so wide or plunged into so deeply. And my orgasms had never been so intense, damn near sending me into convulsions. No man had ever sexed me or sent my insides into such frenzy like Tyson could do. He was *killing* the pussy.

Moans and groans of pleasure repeatedly escaped my lips as Tyson slammed all of himself in and out of my swollen lips, each stroke taking me to levels of ecstasy I had no idea existed. His tool probed more than just my insides; it probed my entire soul, making the muscles of my throbbing pussy tighten around its entire length.

"Ohhhhhhh shit!" I screamed, then slurped my spit thinking, *damn, this nigga fucks like no other*!

I spread my legs as far as I could, welcoming him and everything he wanted to give. He pounded harder, causing me to dig my nails into his shoulders and hold him tightly. Just like many times before, my eyes roamed and admired every inch of his athletically built body underneath the sunlight streaming through the curtains as he stroked me into orgasm after orgasm.

Too bad he wasn't allowed to see every inch of my body. I wouldn't allow it.

It had been that way for quite some time.

As the sheet began to slide off of my mid section, I

quickly placed it back taking any possible attention off of my stomach. It was a tough challenge trying to hide my pregnancy, but me being knocked up wasn't any of his business. I would tell him in my own time.

My hands glided over his numerous curvaceous muscles, his perfectly chiseled upper body covered exotically with several crazy-looking tribal tattoos. My fingers softly traced the thinly trimmed beard and goatee that lined his chin and razor sharp cheek bones. My nostrils inhaled the naturally intoxicating scent that seemed to stream from his pores in waves, each rush of the current ravaging me. My teeth softly bit into his chocolate skin, savoring its taste.

"Damn, Milan," Tyson moaned through gritted teeth, knowing the pussy was weakening him.

I knew what he needed. I knew that his body wanted to release inside of me. I knew what he craved. He couldn't hide it. "Cum inside this pussy, Tyson," I demanded. "Cum for me!"

My hands traveled to his firm muscular buttocks and pressed him fully into me, not allowing any chance of his dick sliding out. My hips rocked back and forth with the force and rhythm of his own. I began to thrust them into him, taking all that he had to give, and desperate to feel him explode inside of me. Seconds later he granted me what I wished, filling my pussy with his cum until it nearly overflowed.

"Damn," he sighed. "That shit was the bomb."

"I know," I breathed heavily.

He laughed. "Oh, aren't you confident? But I guess that's what attracted me to you. At first I thought it was because you're older than me, but that's not it." He grabbed me like he really loved chilling with me, and just wanted to figure out what had him wanting me so badly.

"I'm only five years older than you," I told him, not wanting to feel like a cougar.

"I know…but there's something about you that got a nigga feigning. I'm not sure what it is." He grinned.

Lying with Tyson and savoring our moment together

would've topped the morning off perfectly, but I had plans for the day. I wrapped the 1200 Egyptian thread count sheet around me and stood from the king sized bed ready to rush off to the bathroom to get cleaned up.

"Why do you always do that shit?" Tyson asked, lying in the bed among the sweaty sheets, completely naked and with no urge to cover him self.

"Do what?" I asked, not knowing what he was talking about.

"Cover yourself with a sheet. It's like you don't want me to admire your body or see how fat that ass is you got back there. Either you're covering up right after we have sex or the room has to be pitch black. You even lock the door when you're taking a shower," he spoke. "What's up with that? I know you're not ashamed of your body?"

I shrugged my shoulders. "It's just a habit, I guess."

"You won't even wear any of those tight dresses I buy you. Everything has to fit loose."

"I'm just more comfortable that way," I replied. "Besides, tight dresses are for bitches that have something to prove or for one's who are trying to catch a man. I already have a man, so I don't have to do that."

Tyson climbed out of bed, stood in front of me, and wrapped his arms around my waist. "Well, don't you think that sheet covering shit is a habit you should get rid of?" He softly pressed his forehead against mine, then looked into my eyes tempting me to push him back on the bed, going for round two. "We've been fucking with each other for a little over two months, I think you should lighten up."

"I will eventually," I said, kissing him and turning to head for the bathroom again.

"Milan," Tyson said, grabbing my hand and jerking me back to him. "Who said I was finished talking to you? Why are you in such a rush?"

"Don't be pulling on me like that," I said, but unable to hide my smile. Hiding it was useless. I liked his assertiveness. It took a nigga like that to handle me.

"You know I'm feeling you a lot, right?" he asked but with a hint of uncertainty on his face. "You know that shit, right?"

"Of course," I responded, as if he should've known the answer already.

"You feeling *me*?" he asked, his face growing serious.

I kissed his thick lips. "You already know I am," I assured him, while knowing that his sex was good, but he wasn't who I really wanted.

Tyson pulled me into his arms again.

I have to take my meds, I thought to myself. I knew that if I didn't immediately, things between me and him would become super complicated. There would be no way of concealing the Zaria I'd been hiding from him. For the past five months I'd been taking my meds faithfully and they'd been keeping me in control of myself. I didn't want to take a chance on slipping.

"Then why don't you move in with me?" Tyson asked. "Let me take care of you." His hands dropped to my ass and pulled me against his chest "You know I got you."

I appreciated the offer. He'd made it several times before. Waking up every single morning to a superstar in the NFL was a dream come true to most. He was the perfect man: gorgeously handsome, rich, famous, and a wide receiver for the Philadelphia Eagles. What woman in her right mind wouldn't want to wake up to that every morning? The problem was that I'd made up my mind to take things slow with Tyson. Although I liked him tremendously and had been spending a lot of time, especially nights, with him since I'd escaped to Philly, I didn't want to rush into actually falling in love again.

My meds had me seeing things a lot clearer now, especially relationships; I wasn't in a hurry to jump blindly into one anymore. I wanted to get to know Tyson first, rather than possibly set myself up for the same pain I felt behind Hardy's lying ass, or Devin for that matter. That shit was for the birds. I still hadn't truly gotten over it.

"Tyson, you know I'm not ready for that yet," I told him. "We've already talked about this before."

"At least bring all of your clothes here and stop living out of suitcases."

"I said I'm not ready yet."

"Well, damn, Milan, what will it take for you to be ready?" he asked, clearly not liking the answer. He was used to getting what he wanted. Hearing the word no was always difficult for him to take.

"Time," I answered.

"Are you sure time is what the problem is?" he asked skeptically.

"What do you mean by that?"

"You know what I mean."

"Tyson, I really don't."

"You never told me where you were until five a.m. last night," he said. "Is there another nigga? If it is, you know he can't compete with me. Tell that broke- ass nigga to kick rocks."

"Tyson, I didn't tell you because there are some parts of my life I want to keep private," I told him. "And 'no', there's no other nigga. You don't have to worry about that."

"You sure about that shit?" He kissed me again.

"I'm sure," I returned, smiling.

Got to take my meds, I thought to myself again. *I've got to get to the bathroom.*

Out of the blue, someone knocked on the bedroom door.

"Tyson," a female's voice called out.

I recognized the voice immediately. It was Tayvia, Tyson's assistant and stylist that I despised.

"How did she get in?" I asked Tyson with an attitude, pulling away from him.

"She has a key," he said, as if there was nothing wrong with it.

"A key?" I instantly got angry. Who the fuck did he think he was playing with?

"Yes," he replied.

"Tyson," Tayvia called again, this time a little louder.

"Hold up!" he shouted. "I'm busy!"

"What does she need a fucking key for?" I shrieked, feeling like he'd just tried to play me with all that damn sweet talk about moving in with him.

"Look, Milan. She's my assistant. Our business relationship is much more convenient with her having a key to my house. That way she always has access to me."

Sounded like a bunch of bullshit to me. "Whatever, Tyson," I said, and jetted toward the bathroom.

"Milan, come here sexy," he said, grabbing my arm.

I jerked away from him, snatched my purse from the dresser and stomped toward the bathroom pissed off. Although we hadn't agreed that we were *officially* a couple, I couldn't help sometimes feeling a little jealous of Tayvia and all the countless numbers of other women who constantly threw themselves at Tyson. They swamped him on a regular basis for autographs, pictures, and conversation everywhere he went. I knew most of them wanted a whole lot more from him though than just his name on a piece of paper.

"Milan!" he called again "Don't walk away from me when I'm talking to you. You know I don't like that shit! I'm Tyson Fennell, damn it! Women don't do that shit to me!" He paused, hoping to get a rise out of me. "And I don't have to deal with this bullshit from no female," he added.

Thank God he didn't call me a bitch. Then the *real me* would have to surface. I stomped into the bathroom, slammed the door and locked it, ignoring Mr. Tyson Fennell.

"Look-a-here, last night didn't I tell you to call before you came by today?" I could hear Tyson asking Tayvia. "You knew I told you that I was gonna spend the day with her. You did that childish shit on purpose just to make her mad."

"Is she your girl now?" Tayvia asked sassily.

What business was that of hers? I wanted to know. The sound of Tayvia's voice angered the hell out of me. I wanted to snatch the door open and sic the *old* Zaria loose on her ass.

"That's none of your business, Tee," he said. "Stay in your fucking lane. I pay your salary. You don't pay mine, remember?"

"You don't have time to be in love, correct? Isn't that what you told me?" Tayvia asked him. "Besides, you've changed since you started dating that bitch."

"Tee, you're gonna fuck around and find yourself replaced if you don't stay the hell outta my personal business," he told her. "Start listening or find yourself a nice spot in the unemployment line. I've heard them shits stretch around blocks in Philly these days."

Ignoring Tayvia's blatant disrespect, I walked to the mirror and let the sheet I'd wrapped myself in fall to the floor. I hated that bitch. She was sneaky and something just wasn't right about her. Soon, I let Tyson's and Tayvia's voices grow distant as my hands began to softly rub my slightly growing belly. I couldn't help but wonder what was growing inside. I looked at myself in the mirror, staring into the beautiful features of the *new* Zaria.

Directly after escaping to Philly five months ago, I managed to successfully withdraw my trust fund money from the account set up to receive the transfer exactly the day of my 30th birthday. I took it all, unsure about who would try to track me down. Quickly, I found a reputable plastic surgeon in the Philadelphia area, and got the third degree burns from my face fixed and altered, along with a nose job, and cheek and chin implants.

Since the police back in New York were looking to send my black ass away for the rest of my natural life there was no way in hell that I was going to make it easy for them to recognize me. If they were going to even have the slightest chance at catching me, they were going to have to truly do their job. It was crazy how stupid they were and how they let me get away from my father's place that night. But hell, I wasn't put on earth to help dummies. I was still on edge though. Police cars still made me nervous whenever they were near, but I wasn't going to run again unless I had to.

Tyson and I met a few months after my surgery and began talking. He loved the fact that I was thirty, making me *five* years older than him. He immediately became infatuated telling me that he loved the fact that I didn't sweat him like most chicks. But I made it clear to him that I'd been hurt too many times before and I had no intentions of getting hurt again, so a relationship was out of the question. If he wanted a chance with me, Milan, he would have to be patient and let me take my time. He agreed.

Immediately after, he began to shower me with jewelry and clothes while also practically moving me into his mini-mansion in the suburbs, taking me away from my efficiency in the hood. No one had ever spoiled me like that before. And I would've probably let his gifts, great sex, and good looks rush me into falling in love if it wasn't for my meds.

I turned on the faucet, grabbed my pills from my purse and swallowed two of them. Being on my medication and sticking to it strictly had me acting and feeling noticeably different these days. Depression and anger no longer dominated my life. The pitch black darkness that had always surrounded my world had faded. Waking up every morning seemed more like a blessing than a curse. And since the doctor had prescribed me with a low dose of meds, I didn't have to worry about them hurting the baby in my stomach.

My cell phone rang. I frowned instantly. Once again, it was Kenneth. I was sure just another attempt to threaten me over the phone. He'd been calling, and leaving death related messages since I left him in Atlantic City, hoping to at some point hear my voice. In my eyes there was no need. He died along with the rest of my family as far as I was concerned. And his threats…let's just say, he would never find me. I smiled and sent his ass to voicemail.

As soon as I hit the end button on my phone, another call came in. I recognized the ring tone immediately. It was Devin. I grabbed the phone from my purse and answered excitedly.

"Hey, sexy," Devin said.

"Hey yourself," I returned, happy to hear his voice. "You ready for tonight?"

Tyson began to bang on the bathroom door, startling me. "Milan!" he called from outside the door. "She's gone. Come out here so we can talk!"

"Shit," I said, annoyed. "Devin, I've gotta call you back," I whispered, not wanting Tyson to hear my conversation.

"I can't wait to see you," Devin said, ignoring my attempt at getting off the phone.

"I can't wait either," I told him.

The doorknob began to twist and turn. "Milan, open the damn door so we can talk!" Tyson shouted.

"I've got to go, Sweetheart. I'll see you this evening," I whispered to Devin, telling him I couldn't wait to molest him. But I hung up before he could say anything else.

Just like that, the bathroom door flung open and popped off the hinges. Tyson stood there, with flexed muscles, resembling the incredible hulk with a crazed look on his face saying, "Look what you made me do Milan, don't lock the fuckin' door no more. There's no such thing as privacy around here."

I just shook my head and brushed past him, leaving him standing there looking stupid. *Crazy muthufucka*, I mumbled to myself.

HARDY

Three

As usual her mouth felt so damn good. Through closed eyes and my head buried into my pillow, the vision of her head bobbing up and down slowly in my lap had me going crazy. The warmth of her mouth made my dick throb and pulsate continuously. Her moans of fulfillment as she greedily crammed all of me into her throat, lodging it tightly, made me bite my bottom lip softly.

She seemed to have absolutely no interest in coming up for air, choosing to breathe through only her nose. Pleasing me to the fullest meant more to her than breathing, and I had no problem with it. I'd always preferred head from women who weren't scared to take the *whole* thing. Bitches who chose to suck only half, thinking they were *really* doing some award winning shit, annoyed the hell out of me. I couldn't get a nut off that way.

I softly placed my hand on the back of her head as it arose, then dropped, turned on by the feel of her soft, wavy hair against my thighs. With my eyes still closed, I focused like a blind man on only feel and sound, both working perfectly for me without complaint.

"Shit," I whispered with pleasure as she gripped my shaft and fed more of me into her throat without choking. She started to suck the life out of me harder and faster. My toes curled and locked underneath the bed sheets.

"Damn!"

"Ummmm," she moaned softly, the taste obviously sending shockwaves of delight to her taste buds and anticipating the thick load of cum I was close to feeding her. I could feel it building inside my balls. In just a few moments, I would release and explode. My body needed it.

Suddenly, the evening news came on the small television. Over its sound were my moans and the sloppy wet sounds of my experienced head nurse's mouth. A female newscaster's voice came over the television with breaking news. A nine year old child had been kidnapped right out of his own backyard in Hoboken, New Jersey.

"Dad, are you coming to get me?" Terrell's fear filled words echoed in my head, the last time he'd spoken to me.

My lover continued devouring every inch of my throbbing shaft. But I was no longer interested.

The newscaster's voice gave way to a distraught mother pleading for her son's kidnapper to return her baby safely. Her tone was filled with worry, sadness, and unspeakable pain. She couldn't stop crying, causing my own eyes to fill with water instantly.

I could feel the woman pleasuring me grip my pole even more tightly than before. She began to stroke hard, desperately wanting me to cum for her. Everything inside of me wanted to as I grabbed the back of her head and began to repeatedly raise my hips into her face with vicious thrusts, strangely out of newborn anger.

Moments later, the missing boy's father began to plead for the safe return of his son on the television, begging with all his heart that his child be returned alive and unharmed. The darkness behind my eyelids was suddenly pierced and blindingly brightened with both the blaze and eardrum shattering blast of a .45. In the gun's flash, for only a fraction of a second, I saw the back of Terrell's head explode and his lifeless body slump limply to the ground of a dark lonely place I didn't recognize. The sight made me open my eyes immediately and push Detective Santiago's face from my lap.

"What's wrong?" she asked.

"The fuck you think is wrong?" I said knowing she should've already known.

Realizing what had just caused me to end our session so abruptly, Santiago grabbed the remote from the bedside dresser and turned off the television. She pulled me close, wanting to hold my body in her arms and console me.

The room became dead silent. Emotions flooded me. Anger, disgrace, repentance, so much more. They each began to take an equal hold of my mind, body, and soul; refusing to set me free. Darkness fell over my world and the faces of those that used to make it shine.

Dana had gotten engaged to Mario, I'd heard. The pain of knowing that she and the man who was once my best friend, and who was the best man at my own wedding, would be getting married soon was killing me... a slow agonizing death. I had always heard that you never truly miss a good woman until she's gone. I never had a reason to even dwell on the meaning of that saying until Dana left me. I understand it clearly now. My heart ached for her presence every second of the day. And just the thought of Mario now knowing the taste of her lips shattered my heart over and over again in millions of pieces.

During nights that I missed her most, I used to call her, usually drunk and out of my mind with regret for not being the man she had deserved and wishing I could have a second chance at making things right. Just hearing her voice would be enough to help me through my personal hell. But she wasn't having it, unwilling to take a chance on letting me compromise her newfound happiness with my ex-best friend. Dana always refused to talk to me, eventually changing her number. When she did that, I began calling Mario's bitch ass and threatening him, believing that he'd probably poisoned her mind against me even though her hatred towards me was well deserved. I had brought it on myself. I was the reason my wife and I were no longer together. And I was the reason Terrell was gone. At some point, I had to accept it.

When Terrell's laughter and smile were taken away from me I died. Like the body of a chicken after its head had been chopped off; my body simply hadn't realized it yet. It had become an empty shell, numb to happiness and joy. And my swagger had vanished long ago, leaving me wearing the same clothes for days at a time, and growing a beard and small afro I never developed the urge to comb.

Weed and bottle after bottle of Grey Goose became my breakfast, lunch, and dinner; its effects the only thing strong enough to medicate my never ending pain. Getting out of bed every morning was dreaded. Just the thought of having to see another sunrise and make it through another entire twenty-four hours without my little man suffocated me sometimes so badly I wanted to blow my head all over the walls of my room in the boarding house I lived in. The only thing that kept me from pulling the trigger was revenge. I couldn't leave this earth, no matter how unbearable my life until I killed the woman who killed my son.

Zaria's face was the gateway to my nightmares. It was the demon that haunted me. I saw it every time I closed my eyes at night, making me wake up in cold sweats. The dream of catching her and seeing the air leave her body one final time on God's earth had become my destiny. The only person who seemed to understand and sympathize with that destiny was Detective Santiago.

The two of us began dating two months ago. After months of me blowing up her cell phone and showing up to the precinct hoping she had a new lead on Zaria she invited me out to a bar for a beer. Our conversations about Dana, Terrell, and Zaria began to spark something between us. A relationship grew from there.

"We're going to find her," she said, bringing me back to reality and resting her head on my chest.

I was so damn tired of hearing those words. "When?" I asked, angrily sliding out from underneath her caress, climbing out of the bed and getting dressed.

"Baby, you know we're doing all we can," she tried to reassure me.

I waived my hand dismissively as I put on my jeans and a pair of Nike Air Max running shoes.

"We are," she said. "But I have to admit that it's difficult. It's like she fell off the face of the earth."

"She hasn't disappeared! No one cares anymore. And too much time has passed! It's now May!" I screamed. It had been over five months since Terrell's murder and the police were still no closer to finding Zaria. I'd grown impatient and frustrated with them a long time ago. "If Terrell had been a white kid, Zaria's face would be on every billboard in the country!"

"That's not fair, Hardy," Santiago blurted, offended by me questioning her dedication to crack the case. "Yes, I agree that a murdered white child would probably get nationwide exposure. But the NYPD is doing everything possible to find Zaria. You know I wouldn't dare let anyone half step on this case. I'm taking this just as seriously as you are."

Her words brought no satisfaction, only more anger. I needed results, not excuses or false promises even she herself probably didn't believe. "This is bullshit!"

Santiago climbed out of bed, slipped on her robe, and walked over to me; placing my face softly between her hands and making me look into her eyes. Calm down," she urged warmly.

Vengeance still raced through my veins. Calming down and standing still was impossible. Hearing that missing boy's parents on television had sparked the unrest inside of me. I snatched away from her and began to pace the floor.

"Damn it, Hardy!" she shouted. "You're letting Zaria

consume you. Look at you. You haven't shaved in months. You drink so much it's reeking from your pores. You call her name in your sleep at night. And that's only *when* you can make yourself sleep. Baby, she's destroying you. Can't you see that?"

Her words were true but I didn't care. Zaria would forever be all I could think about until I finally caught her and could make her pay for what she'd done to my universe.

"I hate to see you this way," she said genuinely. "I hate to see you hurting."

Although I knew Santiago loved me, and it was hurting her to see me in constant pain and torment, I couldn't help it. I needed closure more than anything else in life. That would be my only shot at finding any sort of happiness in life again. Without it, I could only live searching for it. There was no other way.

"Have you thought about what we discussed?" Santiago asked me. "About leaving New York and starting over?"

"Leaving New York is not going to change how I feel," I told her. "Santiago, nothing's going to ease the pain of losing Terrell."

"Hardy, didn't I ask you to start calling me Carmen?" she said softly, walking across the bedroom and taking my hand in hers. "You make me feel like you're one of the guys at work. But you're my man so start acting like it. Look baby, stop worrying, we can move somewhere else and start a new family. You know I'm trying my best to get pregnant. I've been trying every fertility treatment possible. I'm going to give you a child, sweetheart."

Her words infuriated me instantly. "Start a *new* family?" I asked in disbelief. "Terrell wasn't a muthafuckin puppy! You can't just replace him with a new one!"

"I didn't mean it like that, Hardy," she said. "I'm just saying…"

"What!" I shouted, snatching away from her. "What the fuck are you saying?"

"I'm saying that I want to marry you Hardy!"

I fell silent. Her words took me by surprise. I knew she

loved me…and I loved her back, most days. But I still missed Dana and marriage was a huge step. We'd only been together for a few months. She was trying to move a little too fast for me. Marriage, moving to a new city, a new family? I wasn't sure how to take all of that. I also wasn't quite sure if her intentions were genuine or if they were merely an attempt to make me forget about Zaria. She wasn't that type of woman, but my head was twisting in too many different ways to be sure. Whatever her intentions, I didn't want to deal with them right now.

"I gotta go." I snatched the backpack I'd been carrying around from the chair so hard my fully loaded .38 fell out and landed on the floor. I didn't even know the backpack was open.

"Hardy," she said with seriousness. Her eyes were locked on my chrome .38. "Why are you carrying that?"

I ignored her and picked up the gun. I tucked it underneath my belt and headed out of the bedroom.

"Hardy, answer me!" she demanded, grabbing my arm. "Why are you walking around with a gun?"

"Because *someone* has to do your fucking job!" I yelled spitefully at her, snatching away from her grip and looking her in the face. "You're more worried about keeping this good dick than finding the bitch who murdered my son!"

"How could you say that?" she asked, unable to believe that those words had fallen from my lips.

I couldn't believe it either. But I was too angry to meditate on them at the moment. Besides, the good dick part was true. I could always mesmerize women with my sex game but just couldn't keep a good relationship, even if someone paid me. All I could do was storm out of her apartment, leaving her hurt. I rushed outside, down the stairs and hopped into my truck. Before the tires screeched away from the curb my eyes dropped to the stack of wanted posters in my passenger seat with Zaria's face on them.

"You'll stick your head out soon, Bitch," I assured her, looking into her eyes as if she could talk back to me. "And when you do, I promise I'll be there to blow it the fuck off."

ZARIA

Four

The cool mist of Flowerbomb perfume disintegrated throughout the entire room as I sprayed it all over my body, including the v-shaped trimmed hairs above my clit. Mary J. played softly from the expensive hotel room's stereo as I slipped on my bra and panties. I sang along with her, hitting each note precisely while sliding on my expensive Gucci heels.

I'd never felt more like a woman than I did since coming to Philly. I'd never felt more beautiful and sexy. Maybe it was the surgery. Maybe it was the attention that a handsome and successful man like Tyson had showered me with. Or maybe it was simply the fact that I was in a new place where my past and my sickness didn't exist. Whatever it was, my heart was grateful.

I felt free. There was absolutely no more worry inside me about why I wasn't born a shade lighter or how thick my lips were. I no longer dwelled on how wide my nose was. Second guessing my beauty and stressfully wondering if I was good enough had stopped. My mind had placed all of that behind me. Only pure satisfaction for who I was remained. The only thing that seemed to be missing was Devin.

As I sat on my father's bed the night he killed himself and discovered through that phone call that Devin was married, disappointment couldn't explain how I felt. Nothing would have meant more than to have Devin pull me into his arms and assure me that the bitch who called herself wifey was a liar and living a fairytale. My life damn sure wasn't a fairytale. In reality, what I got was an angry call from Devin's wife telling me to stay the fuck away from him. The call devastated me. I had never expected him to be the type who would lie to me.

For weeks Devin blew my phone up. I refused to answer each time. I didn't want to hear his voice, despite the fact that he'd said him and his wife had been separated for several months and he was truly ready to divorce her. After calling me relentlessly and telling my voicemail that absolutely no woman on earth had ever made him feel the way I did, my defenses began to break down. Eventually, I answered his call shortly after my surgery and invited him to Philly for a visit. He'd been in Texas training players from the Cowboys, so I truly believed he hadn't seen his wife. The two of us went out for dinner at the popular Asian restaurant called Buddakan and talked. Ironically, I met Tyson there that same night. Turned out Devin had been one of his trainers until the Jets traded him to the Eagles. He slipped me his number later that night after bumping into me as he was leaving, and I was coming out of the bathroom. He had no idea I was with Tyson. Of course I never mentioned it.

Although I liked Tyson, he wasn't Devin. I'd never, and would never turn down the gifts Tyson constantly laced me with: thousands of dollars in the bank account, my Benz, more clothes than I could possibly be able to wear in a lifetime, and diamonds that shined and sparkled brighter than God's stars. No man had ever done those things for me. It felt great to be wanted, and to know that someone wanted me that *badly*. But still, all the money and gifts in the world, nor the good sex could change the most important thing…Tyson wasn't Devin. Devin had my heart. I couldn't commit to any man, not even Tyson, knowing that I loved and eventually would marry Devin.

During his few nights in Philly, Devin promised me that he was going to divorce his wife once he came off the road. Something inside me believed that tonight would be the night when he would give me the good news. I could feel it. But I wanted to trump it with good news of my own, news that I knew would make him equally happy. I couldn't wait to tell him. That would make the night perfect.

I opened my robe and let my hands travel over my growing belly. Knowing that God had loved me enough to give me a life to be responsible for nearly brought tears to my eyes every time I touched my stomach. Having a life growing inside of me meant the world to me.

A knock came from the door.

I became excited.

I knew it was Devin. My man, my love, my future. I looked at myself one last time in the mirror and ran to the door, anxious to see my baby. As soon as I opened it my body couldn't help itself. It was as if his own was a magnet attracting me to him. My mouth needed the taste of his tongue. My ears needed to hear the sounds of his moans. My pussy needed the feel of his dick. I wanted all of him.

"Zaria…" Devin said, with annoyance in his voice, his hands attempting to push me off of him.

Ignoring his reluctance, I continued on. My hands were underneath his shirt and my lips were all over his neck wildly, loving the taste of his skin. I didn't care who was looking out of their peepholes at us. I had missed Devin so much I wanted to fuck him right there in the doorway, possibly even dropping to my knees to devour his entire dick like a T-bone steak.

"Zaria…" Devin said, even more annoyed now and attempting to pull away from me.

My first thought, *damn did he find out that I didn't move to Philly to teach in a poverty stricken area*? All I did was lie to him. However my pussy was so soaking wet and throbbing like crazy that I didn't care what he'd found out. "Devin, fuck me right here," I begged. "Please, baby."

My hands grabbed his crotch and began to fumble with his belt, knowing that if I could get it out of his jeans, I was going to give him some head he'd *never* forget.

"Zaria, stop!" Devin shouted, startling the hell out of me while grabbing my wrists and planting them firmly against my chest. His eyes were filled with something I had never seen in him before.

"Baby, what's wrong?" I asked, seeing in his face a look that expressed him possibly wanting to hit me. The look scared me.

Devin let go of my wrists and stormed past me into the room. "We need to talk," he said, now pacing.

I reluctantly closed the door, unsure of whether or not I wanted to be alone in the room with him. "Devin, what's wrong?"

"You tell me," he said.

"I don't know. You're the one storming in here like you're crazy." I honestly had no idea what he was pissed off about. I had been expecting a memorable evening, possibly the best evening of our lives.

"Don't lie to me, Zaria!" he shouted taking a step towards me. His nostrils were flared and he was breathing like a big bear.

"Devin, I'm not lying," I said, wondering if I should get prepared to guard my face. He'd never hit me before, nor had he ever gotten upset with me. But he'd turned into someone I'd never seen before, a total stranger. "What did I do?"

Devin reached into the back pocket of his jeans, pulled out a folded piece of paper, and slung it at me so hard I flinched as it hit my arm and dropped to the floor. "You're just going to flaunt that shit right in front of my face, huh?" he asked angrily.

I picked up the paper and opened it to see a printed internet photo of me and Tyson hugged up at a club. My heart sunk. I recognized the photo and remembered when and where it was taken immediately. It had been taken several days ago at the grand opening of a new downtown Philly spot called Club Desire. A fan had taken the picture while we were chilling in the VIP section.

"What made you want to fuck him?" Devin asked. "Was it the money?"

Words couldn't leave my mouth at all. I couldn't speak, knowing I was caught red-handed. What could I say with the proof in my hands? All I kept thinking about was the fact that Devin would possibly confront Tyson and find out that I was going under another name. *All of my mess would erupt in my face,* I thought while fidgeting. All this time I was able to hide my drama from Devin since he'd been staying in Texas and traveling to train other athletes.

"That's who I heard yelling in the background when I called you from the freeway this morning, aint it?" Devin kept badgering, forcing me to listen to him.

My eyes closed, wishing I could change what I'd done.

"Of all the niggas for you to cheat on me with," he said. "You picked Tyson? The nigga *I trained*?"

"Baby, I swear it didn't mean anything," I finally opened my eyes and managed to say, "I only want you."

"Oh, you don't love him," he said sarcastically, finishing my sentence like he'd heard that excuse millions of times before. "You just stop by to get a little dick from him every now and then, huh?"

Once again I couldn't speak. The truth hurt too badly to say a word.

"I thought me and you were supposed to be working out our differences."

"We are!" I threw the photo down and rushed toward him. I was hoping he would let me at least touch him. My heart needed at least that much. "And we can, Devin. We gotta be together, baby. Married…you know…husband and wife."

"Are you fucking crazy?" he said, as if the possibility was ridiculous and stopping me dead in my tracks. "After you fucked somebody you met through me? You're a borderline hoe."

"No, baby, don't say that. It's not like that at all. Didn't you ever see Indecent Proposal baby? It was just one night. I swear it meant nothing!"

"Whatever. It looks like you've been enjoying that nigga." He shook his head. "You're such a liar Zaria. Just like you're probably lying about why you got that plastic surgery. That shit still doesn't make sense."

I knew I had violated, but I couldn't help letting myself become a part of Tyson's world. The money, cars, and attention truly did attract me to him. Plus, his place was a safe haven, away from the average Joe coming and going. I needed that protection away from the police. But I'd never stopped to think that it could possibly end what me and Devin were trying to rebuild. Thank God Devin had no idea I was staying there most nights.

"Devin, I'm sorry," I pleaded genuinely. "I'll stop seeing him. I mean it. All I want is you."

Devin shook his head, refusing to believe anything coming out of my mouth. It was clear that my words were now more of an annoyance and aggravation to him than anything else.

"Sweetheart," I continued, taking another step towards him and hoping with everything inside me that he would give me a second chance to convince him that I was sincere. "I'll do anything. I swear I will. Just let me make things right."

"Don't bother," he said, unfazed and fed up. "I never want to see your tramp-ass again."

Those words felt like bullets riddling my heart as he walked past me and headed to the door. They stung worse than the words of Aunt Lisa and Hardy's did. Tears began to drop from my eyes at realizing I had possibly lost him forever. The pain that I had left back in New York had reared its face again.

"Devin!" I cried, talking to his back.

He ignored me and opened the door.

"Devin, I'm pregnant!" I shouted. "Please don't leave me. I'm carrying your baby! I want us to be a family. Don't destroy us, pleaseeeeeee!"

Devin turned and stared at me straight faced, no emotion

or indication of what he was thinking. With my heart of hearts, I hoped that my words hadn't fallen on deaf ears.

"Please, baby," I begged through my falling tears. They were now falling so heavily I could barely see through them. "Don't give up on us. Don't give up on me and your child." I'd never wanted him by my side more than I wanted him right now.

After what seemed like a lifetime of the most uncomfortable silence I had ever known possible, only the soft vocals of Mary J. overriding it from the stereo, Devin finally spoke. "And to think I was actually going to divorce my wife for a lying bitch like you," he said, each word meant to hurt and destroy.

My mouth dropped as he walked out of the door. My knees grew so weak that I collapsed to the floor, the room spinning and its walls closing in around me. The tears wouldn't stop. I felt completely alone. My head began to fill with chattering as running mascara stained my cheeks. It was then that I realized I hadn't taken my meds. The pain made me unable to care. I raised my head, let the voices in my head grow louder, and allowed a silent rage to build inside of me. I welcomed it.

My eyes spitefully surveyed the room as if suddenly hating its value. My eyes became bloodshot red. Suddenly not even remembering getting to my feet, I began to destroy the room. I shattered mirrors, tossed furniture, and punched holes through walls; screaming at the top of my lungs during every second of its destruction.

When I finally gained control of myself, I was standing in the center of the destroyed room breathing heavily, sweat drenching my bra and robe, and staring into the crazed eyes of the reflection in the mirror's broken glass scattered around my heels. The eyes of a woman with bleeding hands at her sides, hair fallen over her face, and smeared mascara running down her cheeks stared back at me. I tried to bring things back with my chant; Smiley Face. Smiley Face. Can anyone see my Smiley Face?

But nothing seemed to work. I breathed heavily and told myself. Devin's wife would pay.

ZARIA

Five

The chattering voices were back and now a part of me like the skin that laced my bones. The old Zaria was back.

At least a dozen different voices chattered mindlessly inside my head as I sat at the vanity dresser in Tyson's bedroom doing my hair. My nerves were so shaky since Devin walked out on me a few nights ago that sitting still was impossible. I had to do something, finally choosing to do my hair as I rocked back and forth in my chair and hummed another Mary oldie, "I'm going down." *I truly was going down,* I thought to myself focusing on my reflection, never once giving even the slightest attention to anything else around me.

There was no longer too much worry inside of me about keeping the old Zaria hidden or locked away. In fact, her return was slowly becoming more and more wanted and even needed. The new Zaria wasn't built to take the pain of disappointment and a broken heart. She wasn't built to feel her way around in the darkness left behind by losing everything your life revolved around. But the old Zaria had been baptized in it all. It was what her thick skin was made of, and what her eyes had long ago adapted to seeing. If anything, deep down the old Zaria had always expected pain.

Hearing Devin tell me that he no longer wanted anything to do with me or the child we had created together destroyed me. And his now refusing to answer his phone or accept my messages had me crying so much that my eyes were nearly as red as blood itself. Nothing mattered to me without Devin; not my child, my meds, my sanity, nothing.

"Milan, you're really starting to bug a nigga out," Tyson said, worriedly from across the room with his hand under his chin.

He was dressed in a white Jordan sweat suit and matching Jordan sneakers. The nigga loved to wear white like the actress Lisa Raye which seemed so gay.

I hadn't said two words to him since he'd walked in a few hours earlier. I had simply snatched away from him when he tried to hug me, headed upstairs to his bedroom, and sat down to do my hair.

"How are you going to sit up in my house and ignore me?" he asked, walking across the room towards me. "That's some disrespectful shit. I mean women prance around my house naked, hoping I want to even touch them. You feel me, Milan? I mean massaging me when I come through the front door, begging me for dick. And this is the shit I get from you?"

Throughout the sounds of my head's chattering voices, I honestly couldn't hear Tyson. I didn't even want to hear him. My ears had tuned his ass out a long time ago.

Tyson was now standing behind me saying something. His words were muffled. I didn't even know he was behind me. I hummed louder, pretending not to be fazed by the voice in my head. It was finally getting to me.

"*Devin was right, you know?*" it continued, taking pleasure and enjoyment in my pain and my return back to the darkness I'd thought I left behind. "*You really are a trashy bitch.*"

The words struck nerves, igniting anger.

"*A dumb one, at that,*" the voice added.

"Shut the fuck up!" I screamed defiantly.

Suddenly, a hand grabbed my arm.

Out of reflex, I snatched away from the hand holding me, leapt to my feet, and sent a backhand to the side of Tyson's face. The loud echoing sound of skin against skin immediately ceased the chattering voices in my mind and brought me back to reality.

"What the fuck?" Tyson asked in disbelief, staring at me for a brief second like I'd lost my mind. "Bitch, are you crazy? he asked, grabbing my wrists, squeezing them and shoving me against the vanity.

Pain shot through my wrists. "Baby, I didn't mean it," I told him. "I didn't know it was you."

His hands gripped my narrow wrists tighter.

"Owww," I said in pain ready to drop to my knees. "You're hurting me."

"I don't know who the fuck you *thought* I was!" he screamed, looking me directly in the eye. "But don't you ever put your fucking hands on me again! My body is worth millions! Do you hear me?"

"Yes, Tyson," I said quickly, hoping and praying he would let my wrists go immediately. The pain was more than excruciating. I thought my wrists were going to snap at any second like twigs from the force of his hands.

"Damn it!" he shouted, throwing my wrists against my chest and turning to walk away while shaking his head. He still couldn't believe that I had hit him. He began to pace the floor. "The last time I was hit by a bitch, I was in the second grade."

The room became silent.

"Milan, tell me the truth," he finally said. He stopped pacing and stared at me from across the room with immense seriousness written across his face.

"The truth about what?" I asked, ringing my aching wrists in my hands. I had no idea what he was talking about.

"Is there someone else? Tell me now."

"No," I lied. Well, technically it wasn't a lie. Devin was now at least physically out of the picture for the moment.

"There is no one else. I told you that already."

"Well, obviously something ain't right," he replied. "You storm up in my house today like you pay the bills around this muthafucka or something, ignoring me and shit. Your eyes are swollen and red like you've been crying for days. You've got bandages on your hands. I mean, what the fuck, Milan?" His voice was riddled with frustration.

He had a point. Between my feelings for Devin and the fact that I hadn't taken my meds in a few days had my head twisted. I had no idea if I was coming or going.

"Milan, what's going on?"

"Tyson," I said softly, "I just need you to be patient with me."

He sighed with aggravation, placed his hands on his hips, and dropped his head toward the floor. It was obvious that his patience was running out.

"Tyson," I called, walking over to him and looking him in the eye.

"I'm almost out of patience, Milan."

I nodded my head knowing he meant every word. "I know. I've just got a lot on my shoulders right now so I need you to be patient with me okay?"

I needed him to say he would be because I still needed a place to stay.

"What's bothering you?" he questioned. "Tell me what's good so I can help. I can fix anything."

"That's sweet…but I can't tell you. We haven't known each other long enough for you to be all up in my business."

He pulled away from me and turned in anger. The look on his face showed that he was getting completely fed up with my secrets.

"But we've known each other long enough for you to accept all the shit I give you, huh?" He quickly turned to walk away.

"Tyson," I said, grabbing his hand and turning him back towards me. "I know I'm complicated, but say you'll be patient.

Please do that for me."

Getting over Devin was already destroying me from the inside out. Getting over losing Tyson would be too much too soon. It would kill me. I stepped closer and looked into his eyes, wanting his answer.

"Alright, man," he responded halfheartedly. It was better than nothing.

Seconds later, a knock came from the door.

Before either me or Tyson could say anything, Tayvia opened the door and pranced inside pushing a rack full of clothes.

"Oh God, not this skinny bitch again," I blurted loudly.

"Trouble in Ghetto Lover's Paradise, huh?" she asked sarcastically, letting us know that she'd been outside the door listening to our argument. She brought the cart to a stop in the middle of the room. "By the way, Tyson likes skinny bitches. Oh, I'm sorry, he didn't tell you," she sassed, putting her hand over her mouth as if she'd made a terrible mistake. It was at that point that I noticed the tattoo on her neck that had the initials D.T.

"Quit it now, Tee," Tyson charged.

"Yes sir, master," Tayvia mocked.

I wondered just how much of our argument the nosey tramp had ear hustled on. Immediately my body wanted to hop on that prissy bitch and gouge her fake bronze contacts out of her head with my fingernails.

"Couldn't you wait for someone to give you permission to come in here?" I asked, wanting to snap on her. "That's disrespectful."

Tyson sighed.

"Why didn't you fire this no manners having ass bitch after the last time she pulled that shit?" I asked Tyson, definitely wondering what more the two had going on after he had just gotten done asking me if there was someone else in *my* life.

"Milan, you're out of line," he said, pointing his finger in my face. "Don't ever tell me who to fire. Who I employ is none of your business. I'm the one who makes millions and I'm the one who pays *all* the bills around here."

Tayvia snickered softly and stood with her hands on her hips and a cocky look on her face like, *"How you like that, bitch?"*

I just stared at her, amazed at how she looked more and more like Chili from TLC as the days went on. They had the same beautiful cocoa complexion, auburn colored locks and skinny athletic build. Quickly, I turned my attention back to Tyson to check him. "Umm, excuse me, but I do have my own money, Tyson."

"Well, you sure as hell haven't used any of it to contribute to this household, so don't let things concern you that you don't pay for. Understand?"

Tyson's cell phone rang from the dresser.

"It doesn't concern me?" I asked, unable to believe he was serious. I became angrier by the minute.

"Right," he answered. "You haven't even committed to being my lady yet, remember? You're just here every night playing house."

The cell phone rang again.

He had a point, but I still didn't like Tayvia being around him. Her presence made me feel threatened and she knew it. Skinny women made me nervous. I didn't trust them malnourished bitches.

"And regardless," he continued as he headed across the bedroom to answer his phone. "Even if or when you become my lady, no one makes decisions about who I employ but me."

Tayvia stared at me with a smirk.

The voices in my head began to chatter again.

"They're playing you for a damned fool," the dominant voice in my head said, drowning out the others. *"How long are you going to let this shit go on?"*

"The rack is good right there," Tyson told Tayvia as he picked up his phone. "Thanks. I'll call you tonight."

"Pick out just *one* outfit," she told me, placing heavy emphasis on the word "one", as if I was a thief or something. "Your non-stylish ass is probably gonna pick out something big anyway," she continued. "I'll be back to get the rest tonight. I'll just use my key, of course."

Her words irked the shit out of me. And she knew it.

"You sure you don't need help picking out an outfit?" she asked with more sarcasm. "I mean, I don't want you to go to the event looking like a tacky bitch."

Her comment did what it was intended to do…piss me the fuck off. I wanted her head on a plate right now so badly my pussy got wet at just the thought. But out of respect for Tyson's home, I kept a leash on the old Zaria, and continued to be Milan…but only for a while. Now wasn't the time or place to snatch a knot in a bitch.

"Nigga, do I look like an ATM?" Tyson asked into the phone. "Is that all that I am to y'all?"

I knew Tyson was talking to his cousin Nigel. He'd been calling Tyson for the past two weeks trying to get some start up money for a record label. The phone calls from his three siblings and numerous cousins had grown annoying, even to me.

"We're done with you so leave," I sneered at Tayvia, with a wiggle of my hand as if she were a slave and the master was done. The look on my face should've let her know that playing with me wasn't a good idea.

"Alright," she said, flinging her hand at me as if dismissing my presence. "Just trying to help the needy." She turned and headed for the door, unknowing that the back of her head looked so attractive to me right now, attractive enough for me to split it wide open with one of the lamps beside Tyson's bed.

"The answer is *no*, nigga," Tyson said into his phone and slammed it shut. He headed to the bathroom. "It's like all my family sees when they look at me is money. I'm tired of that shit. It's either game tickets or money."

"What event is Tayvia talking about we're supposed to attend tonight?" I asked. My eyes eyed the rack of new, pricey pieces with price tags still on them.

Tyson got new clothes delivered to him nearly every day from expensive stores and designers. Some of the clothes were for him to keep. Others were for him to rock during parties and gatherings as promotion and send back. He had instructed Tayvia to start shopping at boutiques and top stores, getting me new pieces, too.

"The benefit that the Eagles are having to help inner city kids. Me and you talked about this last week," he said, closing the bathroom door behind him. "Pick you out something nice."

The event had completely skipped my mind. I really didn't feel like going. I was still fucked up over Devin and didn't feel much like looking into a bunch of faces all night. "Tyson, I don't feel like it."

"Quit tripping," he said. "Pick something out. I told Tayvia to get you a few of those sexy Herve Leger dresses."

"Why? You already know I don't wear dresses like that."

"Just pick something then Milan and be ready at eight by the time the limo comes."

"I'm not tripping," I told him. "I just don't feel like it."

The toilet flushed. He opened the bathroom door and walked out into the bedroom. "What do you mean you don't feel like it?" he asked. "We made plans for this. I wanted to show you off."

I sat on the bed. "Tyson, I'm not going."

"You sick or some shit? Oh, let me guess you wanna stay home and watch one of those dumb ass movies that you love to look at."

"No, I just don't feel like it."

"You know what, Milan," he said, throwing his hands up. He was frustrated with me all over again. "I don't know what the fuck your problem is, but I'm going to pick my Range Rover up from the detail shop. If you're not ready by the time I get back, I'll find someone else to take. Plenty of broads would love to go in your place."

Before I could say anything else, he was out the door.

I hated ultimatums, had never been too good with accepting them. But I also knew I wouldn't be too good about accepting Tyson taking some other bitch to the event either.

My phone rang.

Without bothering to look at the screen I pulled it from my purse and answered.

"I know it was you, Zee!"

"What?"

"It was you, bitch! The police told me everything. How could I have been so stupid to lead you right to my mother? We were supposed to be family. We took your ass in!" my cousin Kenneth screamed at me. He was crying and sobbing like a bitch.

"Kenneth," I said softly, resting my eyes against my thumb and forefinger. A headache was coming on. "You'll never understand. She deserved it."

There was no need in me trying to lie. I guess after the police found his mother and him in the same city, he told them about me taking him there. It didn't take a genius to figure out the rest. I wished he could understand why I did what I did. My heart wished he could see her for the person she really was.

"She deserved it?" he asked, unable to believe those words had escaped my mouth. "You really are crazy!"

Hearing him say that set off rage inside me.

"You ungrateful bitch!" he shouted. "You know you good as dead, right?"

The words burned. The bond he and I had was gone and it hurt immensely to know that we were now enemies. But the war was on.

"Fuck you!" I screamed at the top of my lungs, jumping to my feet and gripping the phone. "Fuck you and that lying mother of yours! The bitch may be dead, but I'm not done with her!!! When the bitch get's a grave, best believe I'll be spitting on it daily!"

"When I catch you, Zee..." he screamed. "I'm going to kill you! Do you hear me?! I'm going to kill you!"

Unable to take anymore, I slung the phone against the

wall, shattering it. "Try it," I yelled out loud. "Just try it! I'll be waiting muthafucka!"

Under normal circumstances, I would've popped a pill…but I was done with medication and the world needed to get ready for me.

HARDY

·················

Six

Can you say "Never been a fan of the police?" Hell, I've despised the ground they walk on for as long as I can remember. I witnessed them plant guns on my homeboys, swell nigga's heads up as big as jack'o lanterns in project stairwells, shoot unarmed nigga's in the back during foot chases and then swear in a court of law that the nigga was trying to go for a gun.

Shit, this is New York City, home of the most corrupt gang on the entire planet...The NYPD. These are the muthafuckas who shoot you forty-seven times for reaching for a cell phone. The police are devils where I come from. Before Terrell's murder, I'd never talked to them or even looked their way. Where I'm from, you get found in a dumpster with your tongue cut out for carrying on conversations with them. But with Terrell's murder I had to compromise my opinions and put trust in their asses, or at least try to. Santiago was one of the good ones. Although she had that tough cop attitude that most cops have, it was obvious that she took her job seriously and believed in making a positive difference. I guess that's why I gravitated to her so quickly. But for the life of me, I had no idea whatsoever why I gravitated towards the one in bed with me now.

Selena was a homicide detective.

Head bitch in charge.

A crooked one. And a stone cold freak.

One that Santiago had always told me officers in the department stayed away from because she was into everything foul. Unfortunately for Santiago, she'd now moved to homicide and worked under Selena's irrational ways.

The two of us met under crazy circumstances, during one of my visits to the precinct to see if Santiago had any new leads on Zaria. As usual, "Nothing new to share," her words exactly.

"Mr. Hardy, I promise you that we're doing everything possible."

Those words had been told to me so many damn times, pissing me off the more I heard them, that something inside of me snapped. Before I realized what I was doing, I had flipped Santiago's desk over. A dozen officers charged at me from all directions, anxious to bash my skull in. Selena was the first to lay hands on me, locking one of my arms behind my back and gripping me with her firm forearm. I had to admit, she was super strong for a woman. A short one at that. She would've probably snapped my arm at the shoulder if Santiago hadn't told her that everything was okay. Santiago later explained to Selena my situation. From that point forward she was cordial every time she saw me.

Selena wasn't what I would call sexy or cute. She was one of those female cops who tried too hard to prove that she could be just as tough as her male counterparts. Her face was okay to look at, except for the bodacious eyebrows that were drawn on every morning. Them muthufuckas looked just like the Gateway Arch in St. Louis. Even her hair was cut short, into a fade, resembling that freaky bitch, Amber Rose. And she walked a little too hard. Selena had money though...lot's of it, proving to me that she got paper from other avenues, and not living just off of a cop's salary.

The crazy thing about Selena was that she went both

ways. I discovered that one night after leaving the precinct. The rain poured and my truck wouldn't start. Selena's shift had just ended and she was on her way home. She offered me a ride.

I accepted.

Somewhere along the ride her hand ended up on my thigh. She was one of those assertive butches, I realized; the type who liked to take charge of her mates. But it was at that moment that I realized she liked men and women. She asked if I wanted to have a threesome with her and her girl.

Just like with Santiago, our relationship began with a beer at the bar and conversation. But unlike what I had with Santiago, true feelings were never involved, no strong attraction. At least not on my part. It was just fucking. I'd never fucked a butch before so the unknown intrigued me.

Selena was a *boss* freak with a strong sexual appetite. She was into whips, handcuffs, rough sex, role playing, three-somes, etc. She was also into having her fantasies fulfilled. One fantasy of hers was to come home to her darkened apartment, be overtaken by a stranger, and raped at gunpoint. That was some weird shit, for real. But it turned me on. I actually felt somewhat like I was getting revenge for every nigga who'd been dogged by the police as I cuffed her hands behind her, bent her over the dining room table, snatched her by the back of her neck and fucked the shit out of her pussy with her own gun pointed at her head while she moaned and screamed in pleasure.

Everything was cool for the first couple of weeks, but as time passed by, I developed a conscience. Selena and Santiago were so-so friends during work hours. Santiago had even hap-pened to call during a few of me and Selena's sessions. Selena answered once, right in the middle of sucking my dick alongside another dyke bitch, just to say that she was in the middle of hav-ing dinner with a friend and would have to call her back. Now that was foul. However when Santiago brought up marriage the other day, that's when I definitely began to feel like maybe breaking things off with Selena might be best.

I had planned on ending things with Selena tonight, but

when I got to the Westin, both her and another cute dyke jump off with a fat ass, big titties, and cute face were waiting in bed naked for me. As soon as I walked in they devoured a nigga, making me cum three times. My body was completely drained, and so I didn't wake up until now, hearing her friend leave.

"I hope you've had enough sleep," Selena said to me after kissing my dick with tiny, wet kisses.

"I'm exhausted," I told her, my eyes half closed and my body weak.

"I've got a surprise for you," she said, naked and leaning her body against mine.

"Not up for surprises," I said, turning over and ready to drift off again.

Selena stood up. "Turn around," she ordered. Of course like a trained puppy, I did. "I guarantee you're goin' to like this one," she said, placing her fingers into her pussy while slowly massaging her clit.

I ignored her, too tired to speak.

"Well, aren't you goin' to ask what the surprise is?" she asked.

My mind drifted into darkness. For tonight, I didn't care about anything but sleep.

"I found out where Zaria is," she informed.

For a moment I thought I was asleep and dreaming. There was no way she could've said what I thought she did.

"I know exactly where the bitch is right at this moment," she continued, still playing with herself.

My eyes opened on their own. I turned and looked at her dark, chocolate skin, with no nonsense in my stare. Her eyebrows crinkled causing me to think she'd allowed her little sister to draw them on with a brown crayon. "What did you just say?" I asked, having to be sure I wasn't hallucinating.

"You heard me right," Selena replied. "I told you I would find her. I'm the best damn detective our department got."

"How'd you find her? You sure it's her?" I belted.

"Nigga, did you forget I'm head of Homicide?" She

quickly grabbed her purse from off the floor and pulled out something that looked like a garage door opener. "See, high powered tracking devices like this shit here, is just one of the things that I can pull off. I got friends in high places," she smirked. "This device updates every ten seconds and up to thirty miles…you know like that James Bond type shit. I'm good at what I do." Another wide grin followed. "But you know the drill…do for me and I'll do for you."

She bit at her nubby nails bringing attention to a new, expensive-looking diamond she'd purchased. "What do you want Selena?" I blew an annoying breath through my clinched lips.

"A few things," she taunted. "One, I need you to marry the lady from Haiti that I told you about. She already paid me so that's two g's comin' to you, once you kiss your bride."

"I told you hell no, before! Now, where's Zaria?"

"You don't run this show, Hardy! I do, damn it! Now, you fuckin' with my bizness. You want Zaria and I want to keep my customers happy. And I want somethin' else, too."

Leaping from the bed and throwing on my jeans I asked, "Where is she?"

All I could think about was what crooked muthufuckas Selena had hooked up with to find Zaria because I knew the regular, legal way wasn't working. I didn't give a damn about her wanting me to marry some chick I'd never seen just so she could get a green card to stay in the country. That was bullshit and just one of Selena's many money making businesses.

"Where is Zaria?" I asked again, even more serious than before.

"Somewhere," she said playfully. "She's out there."

I quickly slid my shoes on and walked over to her. "Selena, where is she?" I wasn't in the mood for any games. We were face to face.

Selena smiled and stood on her tip toes to wrap her arms around my shoulders. She stuck her tongue out wiggling the jewel that hung from her tongue piercing, making it clear that she wanted more sex.

My reflexes made me spaz. I grabbed her by the throat and shoved her against the door. "Bitch, does it look like I'm fucking playing with you?"

She laughed, turned on.

My grip around her neck tightened.

Her eyes began to redden and water. "Yes," she moaned. "You know I like that rough shit."

"You crazy bitch!" I screamed in her face, letting go of her neck and grabbing her shoulders. I knew I couldn't choke her to death without getting the answer I needed first. "Where is Zaria?"

"How badly do you want to know, baby?" she purred, grabbing my dick.

"Selena, stop playing with me!" I screamed, slapping her hand away from my crotch.

"Who said I was playin'?" She was unfazed by nearly being choked to death. "I've got what you want and you've got what I want."

"What the hell are you talking about?"

"Do you want Zaria?" she asked, wrapping her arms around me and beginning to plant kisses on my chest.

What the fuck is wrong with this nutcase, I wondered.

"Do you really want her, baby?" she asked, now kissing me around the neck. "Tell me you do, Hardy."

If she was telling the truth about Zaria, I could only get the truth out of her by playing her sick ass game. I was certain Selena had paid someone off for the information and now I had to pay her sexually. "Yes, I want her," I finally said with a frustrating blow of the breath.

"Show me how bad you want that bitch," she replied, backing herself against the door. "Get on your knees and eat my pussy."

I wanted to kill her. She could see it in my eyes but it only turned her on even more, soaking her pussy.

"Go ahead, baby," she whispered. "Give me what I want and I'll give you what you want."

Anger filled me as I shook my head and dropped to my knees. I didn't want to eat her shit. Not now. Not later. Not ever. But a nigga would do what he had to do. If she was lying about Zaria, after this was over, there was no doubt, I was going to kill her. I began lapping at her kitty making all sorts of slurping sounds, pretending to enjoy the sounds of her pleasure as much as she did. She moaned like a wounded animal, talking dirty all along.

"Yes….oohh…yes…act like you hungry, nigga. Eat it. Lick it. Fuck it with your tongue."

Minute after minute, she moaned, groaned, and allowed slob to drip down her chin. Her body moved quickly, and in so many positions, I thought she was having convulsions. But I kept licking. Long strokes, then deep strokes.

"Damn, Hardy!" she cried out.

I made quick, short circles with my tongue making Selena climb the walls. I was so good at my craft that the crazy bitch came within no time. After getting herself together, she told me that I ate the life out of her pussy, before finally throwing me a photo.

"See, I can hold up to my part of the bargain sometimes. It's a picture of Zaria and that nigga, Tyson Fennell who plays for the Eagles. They were at some publicity event out in Philly. Oh yeah and she looks a little different,"she told me. "Now, don't forget you're gettin' married on Saturday at two o'clock. Let's get this money."

I quickly glanced at the photo before turning it over and seeing an address written in Selena's handwriting with an imprint of her lips. Knowing the address probably belonged to Tyson was all I needed to see. I shot her a half-ass grin, darted out of the room, hopped in my truck, and hit the highway. That bitch Zaria was as good as dead. *And if her little football playing boyfriend got in the way, he was dead too,* I thought to myself as I took my .38 from inside my waist and stuffed it underneath my seat. Instantly, I grabbed my bag of tricks that I'd gotten from the spy shop; audio recorders that looked like ink pens, wearable spy gadgets like earrings, tiny GPS tracking devices, and count-less other surveillance products. I always kept my shit close never knowing when they would come in handy. But what ex-cited me most was adding Selena's high tech tracking gadget to my collection. No sooner than I'd slipped the audio recorder into my pants pocket, my cell phone rang. I looked at the screen and saw that it was Kyle.

"Yeah," I said, answering the phone while keeping my eyes locked on the dark highway and taillights ahead of me.

"Are you crazy?" Kyle asked.

"What are you talking about?"

"I spoke to Mario today. That nigga said you've been calling over there and threatening to kill him."

It wasn't a lie. I'd called a couple of times just to speak to Dana. But the other night Mario finally answered his phone and stuck his chest out like he was a real nigga or something. He told me some shit about respecting his house and leaving his woman alone. I snapped and threatened to shoot him if I ever caught him on the street. The weak ass nigga got shook and called the police to give me a warning.

"Fuck that nigga," I told Kyle as I changed lanes.

"I know you're hurting, man," Kyle said, "But he's a lawyer. If you kill him, they'll put your ass *under* the jail."

I knew he was right, but didn't really care to hear it at the moment. When I finally got a chance to see Mario's ass, it was going to be on. But for now, my attention was on Zaria. My phone beeped.

Without telling Kyle to hold on, I clicked over. "Yeah."

"Is it true?" Santiago asked through the phone.

"What are you talking about?"

"Tell me the truth about you and Selena," she said with pain in her voice.

I shook my head in annoyance, hung up the phone, and then put it on vibrate. Right now wasn't the time for Kyle's or Santiago's nonsense. I had a bitch to kill.

ZARIA

Seven

When the limo took the corner at a rapid speed, I found myself hurling into Tyson. It didn't matter though, we'd already spent the entire ride to the party arguing, and had just crossed the Walt Whitman bridge.

"Milan, what the fuck is wrong with you?" Tyson shrieked. "I put you in diamonds, a nice car, and take you to nice places. But instead of appreciating it all, you're sitting here snapping on me for any little thing you can think of."

"Tyson, you act like I owe you something," I snapped. "I don't owe you shit. Don't blame me because you're hooked on me like a lil bitch."

In my heart I knew the words were from the mouth of the old Zaria but I was powerless to control her.

"What?" Tyson asked, surprised and pissed off. "What the fuck did you just call me?"

My eyes locked on him with no fear. "I called you a bitch. Bitch, bitch, bitch," I told him straight forwardly.

For three days since I'd been off my meds, I'd been wildin' out on him like crazy.

Tyson leaned in. "I don't know what your damn problem is," he said, "And I'm not hooked on you. I happen to like you. But I can most definitely return the calls of some of the women tryna get at me. But you'd better watch your mouth when you talk to me, Milan."

"Or what?"

Suddenly he reached for my throat but caught himself. He shook his head in anger and looked out the window.

"I didn't think so," I told him.

"Don't test me, Milan," he said, while still looking out of the window. "Don't try my patience."

"Um hum, whateva."

We rode in silence until we got to the hotel's parking lot. When the chauffer climbed out of the car, Tyson grabbed my arm and displayed a serious expression.

"If you expect me to remain patient with you and whatever this relationship is we've got," he said, his eyes still and unblinking. "Don't embarrass me tonight."

The chauffeur opened my door.

"Whateva," I said and stepped out into the flashing cameras.

Flashes from paparazzi trailed me and Tyson from the limo to the lobby of the Marriott as if we were Barrack and Michelle Obama. I should've been loving every second. It should've felt as if in that moment the entire world belonged to me as all eyes were on my every move in envy and admiration.

Although Tyson was looking sexy as usual in a black tailor fitted Armani suit and Bruno Magli shoes, I knew *my* beauty and swagger tonight was top level as well. I was rocking a black strapless Marc Jacobs bubble style dress that concealed my stomach, but still complimented my breasts, hips, and thighs perfectly. My weave was pulled back into a side ponytail, leaving my shoulders to be admired. With a pair of peep toe Valentino pumps showing off my toes, and the height of the five inch heel giving my calves and thighs a solid thickness, I knew *no* man at the party would be able to keep their eyes off of me.

The platinum bracelet full of crushed diamonds on my left wrist along with the matching necklace around my neck flickered amazingly with every shot of the paparazzi's cameras.

It seemed as though my smile for the cameras were more like smirks, immediately followed by the rolling of my eyes. And the constant stopping to pose for them like I was on display or some shit had quickly become annoying rather than enjoyable. I was developing a throbbing headache and the repeated bright flashing lights weren't helping. During each pose for them Tyson could undoubtedly sense my reluctance, but he forced me to pose for them anyway, subtly jerking my body to his own in a way not easily noticed by others. Shit, instead of feeling like I was being led by the hand like a lady, it felt like I was a dog being led by his damn collar.

"What the fuck is your problem?" he asked me several times on the way into the hotel while still keeping a smile on his face for the cameras. He talked only loud enough for me to hear.

I ignored him.

"Can you at least *act* like you're having a good time?" he asked as we approached the ballroom.

"Fuck you, Tyson," I said.

Tyson glared at me as he gave the hostess our invitation at the entrance of the ballroom.

The hostess shot me a glare also, happening to hear me curse Tyson out.

"What is that look for?" I asked her.

"Excuse me?' she said, trying to play stupid.

"Look, Bitch, I saw the way you looked at me. Say what you gotta say," I began to tear into her.

"Milan, stop it," Tyson said, embarrassed.

"Your job isn't to be in my business," I told her, ignoring Tyson. "Your job is to show us to our table. And don't even think about talking about me when I walk away because I will come back and whip your ass."

She was clearly embarrassed. The woman stood frozen like a deer caught in headlights.

"Chop-chop," I told her, clapping my hands twice. "An-delay...Andelay. Arriba," I continued, sounding like the little Mexican mouse on the old Loony Tunes cartoons. "Get on your fucking job and show us to our damn table."

Tyson subtly but forcefully pulled me by my upper arm shoulder to shoulder with him. "Milan, this is not the place for that ghetto shit," he whispered while trying to keep the problem hidden from the guests behind us. "I meant what I told you in the limo."

I snatched away from him. "Quit grabbing on me like I'm your property. You don't own me."

"Then act like you've got some fucking sense."

"Whateva."

Tyson's jaw clenched as he tried to keep his composure.

The hostess began to walk us through the ballroom toward our table.

Alicia Keys' *Unbreakable* played from the speakers. The inside of the brightly lit room looked like the inside of a castle. Chandeliers hung from its two-storied ceilings. Tasseled floor to ceiling curtains covered the windows where a gold lined staircase led to a beautiful second story balcony at the far end of the room. As we followed the bitch past several tables, numerous Eagles players greeted Tyson with daps and hugs, their eyes slyly sneaking a peek at me. I should've felt grateful for the entire moment, I guess. But in reality...

"*Bitch, you're still low class*," the voice in my head said. "*Don't get it twisted. Don't let the surroundings fool you. Don't think for one moment that you're one of these people. You're a simple minded bitch who just got lucky. That's all*."

The voice had been hounding me for the past several days, and wouldn't let up on agitating me and beating me down.

By the time we reached our table, I was totally disgusted. Two stripper looking broads in tight skirts, heels, and twenty-two inch weaves were already sitting down sipping champagne. I turned to see Tyson whispering to the hostess saying he was sorry for how rude I'd treated her. He even slipped her a fifty dollar bill.

"This table is already taken," I told the hostess. "And why are you apologizing and tipping that slow bitch when she can't even do her job right?" I loudly said to Tyson.

"We're okay," he assured the hostess and allowed her to leave. "Milan, chill out. We're sharing this table with my home-boy Eric." He pulled out my chair. "These young ladies are with him."

"*He must really think you rode the short bus to school,*" the voice in my head said. "*And what's even worse is that you're letting him get away with it. Can't you see what's going on, Zaria? It's common sense and simple mathematics. What does this Eric nigga need with two bitches? One of them stank hoes has to be for Tyson.*"

My eyes locked on both of them hood rats and my pressure rose. He was trying to play me for a fool. Besides, I'd heard the stories about Eric Monroe, all his women, and how much of a ladies' man he was.

"*The only way to prove to him that you're not to be fucked with is to beat both these hoes into comas,*" the voice said, giving me a headache. I squinted my eyes to ease the pain.

"Baby, have a seat," Tyson said, trying to keep things de-fused.

"*Don't let him play you like this,*" the voice taunted.

"I want another table," I demanded, with hatred in my voice. I was ready to snap.

The two women looked at each other.

Tyson looked at me like I was crazy. "Why?" he inquired.

"You know why," I stated while looking at him directly.

Tyson's anger and frustration showed but he kept it restrained. He stepped closer to me and whispered in my ear. "Milan, there are some very important people here. You're really pressing my buttons tonight. I already told you that these ladies are here with Eric. Now have a…"

"Which one of them is here to suck your dick?" I asked,

cutting him short. I placed my hands on my hips, and looked straight at both women. "Which one is it?"

"Milan, you're out of line, for real," Tyson said, looking around quickly, hoping the other tables hadn't heard me. "You owe these ladies an apology."

I crossed my arms and defiantly looked at him like he was nuts. The likelihood of me doing that was like a crack-head refusing a rock.

Tyson shook his head. "Ladies, I apologize for that," he told them.

"It's okay," the both of them said, shrugging it off, all along grinning at my man. They hated me and I knew it.

I sat down reluctantly, but not without adding some final words.

"Tyson, you know I'm the baddest bitch at the party tonight. None of these other play-wives, mistresses, or whatever you want to call them are on my level and you know it!"

Steam poured from my veins.

"I know, Milan, I know," Tyson told me, attempting to ease my rage.

"Tyson!" someone called from our left.

Tyson turned to see Eric walking up on him with a bottle of Cristal in his hand. "What's good, Bruh?" Tyson asked, giving his teammate some dap and a shoulder hug.

My eyes were still on the bitches across the table from us. I knew they were talking about me as they repeatedly leaned into each other whispering. I couldn't hear them but I just knew. I wondered which one was for Tyson.

"Eric, this is Milan," Tyson introduced us. "Milan, this is my homeboy, Eric. He plays Safety."

I looked up to see a sexy, athletically built man standing beside Tyson dressed in black Ferragmo loafers, black slacks, and an ugly Robert Graham shirt that I wasn't feeling, but he still looked nice. His head was shaven, completely bald and his skin's bronze complexion seemed to give off a golden glow. His eyes were light brown and slightly slanted. It was obvious that he was mixed with something Asian, maybe Chinese or Japanese. Whatever it was, it gave him an exotic sort of look and sexiness.

"So, this is her?" Eric asked, surprised and with a beautiful smile. "This is the one that's got you wide open, huh?"

Tyson smiled and nodded, trying to get over the hell I'd just raised.

"He talks about you all the time, luv," Eric assured me, taking my hand. "I see why now. It's nice to finally meet you."

"Likewise," I returned. Something about his eyes calmed me, even made my headache weaken. Tyson had always told me Eric had the gift of gab, always knowing the right thing to say to the ladies.

Both Eric and Tyson took their seats. Shortly after, a waiter delivered three more bottles of Cristal to the table. When I asked for apple cider, Tyson looked at me crazily. I simply shrugged my shoulders.

As the night moved on, I couldn't help but sneak peeks at Eric and swore he was doing the same. Eric had swagger, but possessed a touch of hood too that was turning me the hell on. I was actually beginning to loosen up. But as usual, Tayvia had to show up at the wrong damn time. It was now more than obvious to me that her constant poor timing was always well planned. She was really working my last nerve with that childish ass shit.

"What's up, Tee?" Tyson greeted her, standing to give her a hug.

For that short moment that his arms were squeezed tightly around Tayvia, an indescribable jealousy flowed through me as my eyes spitefully wandered her body searching for a flaw. But there was none. Her Indian facial features were top tier this evening, even with only *minimal* make-up. Her long wavy hair hung past her shoulders and the ballroom's fluorescent lights made those fucking fake contacts glisten as beautifully as the diamond pendant around her neck. Her tanned skin was naturally smooth. Her blue dress with spaghetti straps hugged her hips, thighs, breasts, and thin waist gorgeously. Silently, I had to admit that she was a beautiful woman, even more so than Milan had been. *Maybe I'll change my name to Tayvia*, I thought crazily.

I hated the bitch with a passion. Knowing that even with my plastic surgery, her natural beauty made me feel inferior. That shit irked me. She made me even want to be short again, anything to have the attention she was getting.

As Eric hugged her, I lost it. It was a strange hug, one that only another woman could detect. How well did they know each other? And even Tyson developed a questionable glare. Finally, he whispered something in her ear and she just rested her chin on his shoulder, locking her eyes on mine. Something wasn't right about them. I could see it and sense it. Hmm…What was Tayvia up to now?

"Tyson, I can't stay," she said quickly, moving in his direction. "I really need to talk to you about something. It's urgent."

Tyson kissed her on the cheek, groaned and sat down. "No business tonight," he responded. "I'm here to enjoy myself. I don't want to discuss business."

"It's not business," Tayvia said, her eyes glancing at mine with a strange look in them. "But it's real important."

I grabbed Tyson's hand, pulled my chair beside his, and looked up at Tayvia. "You heard him," I told her. "He said he doesn't want to discuss business tonight. So beat it."

Her contempt and dislike for me showed on her face now much more different and extreme than it ever had since the moment we'd met. Something definitely wasn't right. I didn't like it.

"Tyson, it's about her," Tayvia said, pointing at me. "She's not who you think she is. We really need to talk."

Eric and his dates' eyes were darting back and forth from Tayvia to me like a tennis match.

"Look, you damn bugaboo!" I shouted, unable to take anymore of her. "Tyson just said he doesn't want to talk so why don't you go try to fuck up someone else's relationship for a change!"

"Tyson, she's been lying to you!" she yelled. Her face was tight. Tighter than I'd ever seen. "Her real name is not…"

Before I knew it, I was out of my seat and going for her head with a bottle of champagne. As I swung, Tyson jumped up and grabbed me before the bottle could connect with her skull. The bottle dropped, crashing to the floor causing the alcohol to spill everywhere.

Tayvia quickly dropped the papers from her hand, grabbed Tyson's chair and posted up ready to swing. "Yeah, bitch!" she yelled. "I know your little secret now! You lying bitch!"

Eric jumped up from his chair and quickly made his way around the table. But Tayvia had gone wild. She released the first chair in my direction, then reached for a bottle of champagne just as I had. The entire ballroom's eyes were on us. Some spectators even became bold enough to walk right up on us, gathering in a circle.

"You'd better do something about that hoe, Tyson, before I kill her!" I threatened.

Tayvia charged me with the bottle.

"Tayvia, stop!" Tyson ordered, letting me go and rushing to take the bottle from her.

I charged at her ass again. This time Eric grabbed me.

"Man, take her outside for me, Eric!" Tyson said while trying to hold Tayvia back.

"After tonight, back to the ghetto you go, bitch!" Tayvia taunted. "I know your secret and I'm telling it!" For once, her eyes actually put fear in me. I was certain she had information that would ruin me.

"Tayvia, stop!" Tyson screamed.

"Tyson, that bitch is a fraud!" she yelled. "She's been…"

"I don't want to hear it, Tayvia!" Tyson told her. "You've been jealous of her since the first time you met her!"

"Jealous? Her eyes bulged even more. That tramp! What does she have that I don't Tyson, huh?"

Tyson became silent as if he realized everyone knew there was something more between them.

"She's a fraud, Tyson!"

"I told you I don't want to hear shit you've got to say about her!" he yelled.

I kicked and swung wildly trying to get at that bitch, but Eric's arms were too strong. "You fucking bitch!" I screamed at Tayvia.

Out of the blue, Tayvia escaped Tyson's grasp and jumped across the table at me like a ninja on attack. Somehow she grasped the bottle and cracked me across my face leaving me bleeding underneath my eye.

I went wild as champagne spilled over my face and dress. "Youuuuuuu bitch!"

"Eric, get Milan out of here now!" Tyson demanded, now seriously worried.

Eric carried me all the way out of the ballroom as I watched Tyson appoint someone to tame Tayvia and direct her to the door, picking up her papers from the floor in the process. By the time I got to the parking lot, I realized that I'd finally met my match. A bitch who wasn't afraid of me. Tayvia may have been crazy but I'd get that bitch for cutting me.

"Damn, you feisty," Eric said when he got me outside and let me go.

"I hate that bitch!" I screamed to the top of my lungs. "Hate her…hate her…hate her!" My adrenaline was still pumping as I started to pace back and forth. "You should've let me bust her head wide open."

"And what would that have accomplished?" he asked, using the end of his white sleeve to blot the blood beneath my eye.

"I'm not looking to accomplish anything, I just want her dead."

"You'd be in jail right now for murder," he replied. "Besides, we should walk to the front and get a first aid kit. You're bleeding more than I thought."

He was right, but I wasn't in the mood right now to be rational.

"I'd rather go back and stab Tayvia," I told him, with my pain suddenly increasing. I could taste the blood as it dripped down my cheek landing on my upper lip.

"Enough of our black women are sitting in prison right now for bad decisions," he continued. "You're too beautiful to let that become you. You've got to chill with that temper, lil mama."

Just like inside when I wanted to flip out on the bitches at the table, something about Eric's presence and voice calmed me. When he called me beautiful the term of endearment instantly made me stop pacing and look at him. For the first time tonight I could've sworn I saw a glimpse of Hardy in him, the part of Hardy that I fell in love with.

"Are you starting to calm down?" he asked. "I gotta make sure you straight."

I nodded.

"Let's go inside. I think you need stitches," he said, taking his shirt completely off, exposing his sexy six pack, and using it to apply pressure to my wound. "You straight?" he asked again, this time in a more sexy tone.

"Yeah," I said dryly. I still really wanted to whip that bitch's ass.

"You don't sound like it," he said, not convinced. He was now directly in my face, as if we were lovers preparing for a bear hug.

"That bitch just really gets under my skin."

"I feel you," he said, understandingly. "We've all got people like that in our life. But we can't just hit them with a bottle when they don't act right."

I looked at him. The moonlight brought out his eyes. And that damn bald head was to die for.

"You've got a lot of fire in you though," he said, admiringly. "I like that. I see why Tyson likes you so much. He's lucky to have you."

He got closer. As close as he could get, continuing to nurse my eye.

"Tyson doesn't *have* me," I corrected him, but flirtatiously.

"What does that mean?" he asked. It was clear that he'd picked up on my interest in him.

"It means just that. I'm not Tyson's. I'm no man's."

"So, then you're still on the market," he said, smiling and taking a step towards me, knowing that I was intentionally inviting him into my space.

"You can say that." I was turned on by his eyes and the smell of his Tom Ford cologne.

For a moment it seemed like no one else in the world existed but us. I liked how it felt.

"What about you?" I asked. "Where's your woman?"

"Don't have one."

"And the two bitches at the table?"

"They're just something to do."

I nodded.

"And Tayvia?" I asked eagerly.

"Just an acquaintance."

"You sure? She hugged you much too tightly."

"Trust me. It was nothing. We barely know each other."

I still don't know who initiated it. It happened too quickly. I didn't even remember it beginning. All I know is seconds later our lips were releasing each others. My mouth relished the taste of his lips and couldn't wait to get more. We smiled at each other. It seemed so perfect until the two of us glanced over to see Tyson standing at the hotel's entrance way looking straight at us.

Busted, I told myself.

HARDY
Eight

The early morning sun had only been up for several hours and my body was cramping like I'd worked for twelve hours straight. Throughout the past several hours I must've shifted and changed positions in my Tahoe's driver's seat over a hundred times, never truly getting comfortable. My eyelids were heavy and continuing to keep them open had become nearly impossible.

"Damn it," I said, frustrated, banging my fist against the steering wheel. "Where the hell are these two?"

I'd been sitting across the street from Zaria's boyfriend's house since I'd gotten off the highway yesterday evening, anxious to put my murder game down. The hour and a half ride to Philly nearly drove me crazy. As soon as my eyes caught her in my sites I was going to jump out of my truck, run right up on her, and shoot her in the face so many times she would have to be given a closed casket funeral. And if her dude got in the way, I was more than prepared to give his ass the exact same business. I didn't give a fuck. Anybody could get it.

The anticipated murder scene had been playing itself out

in my head. And every time a car approached, my heart began pounding and my adrenaline rushed beneath my skin. I wanted this moment more than anything I had ever dreamed of before.

Throughout the night, I held the gun in my hand, with its cold steel pressed tightly in my palm. The feel intoxicated me even more than the fifth of Grey Goose that I'd been drinking. Behind the tinted windows of my truck I stared at it for hours, not even sure if I had even blinked. All I was sure of was my anticipation of seeing the look on Zaria's face when she saw my pistol pointed directly at her. The fear in her eyes would be priceless.

I stared at Zaria's picture over the past several hours. Just like Selena said, she looked different. That bitch had definitely gotten some work done altering her face, but it was still her. There was no doubt in my mind. I was absolutely sure the woman in the picture Selena had given me was Zaria.

As my eyes spanned the huge home behind the gates, I couldn't help but wonder how she'd pulled it all off. Plastic surgery? A multi-million dollar NFL football player for a boyfriend? A muthafucking huge estate? Zaria had made a serious come up. She was eating well these days. But my wonder was just that, not admiration or envy. If anything more, it was sheer hatred.

While my baby was lying dead in the cemetery, his life taken away from him before he got a chance to have one, this bitch was here in Philly living high like shit was sweet. The thought made me even pissed off at God. How could he reward that child killing bitch for what she'd done; the innocence she'd stolen? The last thing in the world that hoe deserved was happiness and riches. But from the looks of things, that and so much more was what God had given her.

Zaria's success made me so nauseated that I'd opened the driver's door of my truck a few hours ago and threw up everything in my stomach. That bitch literally made me sick. Everything within me despised her.

Suddenly, a silver Jaguar XF appeared in my rearview.

At first I got excited, but then, even at a distance, I could tell it wasn't Zaria or her boyfriend. It was a woman with a head-full of wavy hair yapping on the phone, and driving like a maniac. I became frustrated. I started my truck, ready to pull away to find a hotel, then come back later in the evening when suddenly, the Jag slowed as it reached me and pulled up to the gates of Tyson's house. My heart started pounding again. This was my chance. I could easily just draw down on that bitch in the car and force her to tell me where Zaria was.

But something inside wouldn't let me. Something told me it was best to stay patient. I watched as the girl entered a code into the security system and the gate opened. My eyes watched the Jag closely as it made its way up the circular drive-way to the house. I quickly grabbed my binoculars from the backseat, and pointed one of my surveillance cameras her way. I watched the driver as she climbed out of the car with three bags.

The woman was more than beautiful. She looked to be about 5'3"… maybe 5'4" with beautiful skin. Her frame was slim with a thin waste, but her hips and ass were *bananas*, for real. Absolutely sexy and enough to give me a hard on.

The woman opened her trunk, pulled out more shopping bags, and headed up the mansion's stairs.

Who the hell is that, I wondered as she pulled a set of keys from her pocket and let herself inside. Maybe she was old boy's sister or something. Whoever she was though, she was sexy as hell and had suddenly given me an idea. I tossed the binoculars in the backseat and pulled away from the curb.

******

It hadn't taken me longer than a few hours to go do what I had to. I'd found a nearby Wal-Mart, Foot Locker, and Men's Warehouse. I ran inside each, grabbed a few things, and searched for a hotel. My truck's OnStar led me to a Holiday Inn that was just three miles away. I ran inside to get myself a room. My beard, nappy afro, and wrinkled clothes had the white bitch behind the counter completely shook. It was obvious she thought I was there to possibly rob the place. Her body language couldn't hide it at all. The shit pissed me off, but I didn't have time to get sidetracked or lose focus. I paid for a room, got my key, and hopped on the elevator. When I reached my room, I went inside and got directly down to business.

In less than an hour, I was headed through the lobby past the lady behind the counter, making her do a double take.

"*Yeah, bitch. It's me,*" I whispered to myself, knowing how different I looked now. I looked like a new man...the old Hardy. My head was completely shaved, and my goatee was neatly trimmed. My plain white tee and matching Air Force One's were brighter than those bitches in them Colgate commercials, and my jeans were crisp. I smiled knowing I had my swagger back.

It only took twenty minutes to drive back to Tyson's neighborhood. When I got there, the Jag was still sitting in the exact same spot. Perfect! For a few moments I thought about walking up to the gate and pressing the buzzer. But I quickly realized that wouldn't work. She'd probably think I was a fan or some shit just trying to get an autograph. I was going to have to stay patient and catch her little sexy ass one on one.

An hour later my patience paid off. She came out the door, hopped in her whip, and made her way down the driveway. After she pulled out the gates and made it nearly to the end of the quiet suburban street, I turned the key in my ignition and began to follow her.

I made sure to stay a decent distance behind her so my presence wouldn't be so obvious. Several minutes later she pulled into a Starbucks parking lot and parked. I pulled into the lot, parked my truck several cars away from hers, and watched. She climbed out of her car, talking on her cell phone and headed across the lot into Starbucks. I hopped out of my truck and followed her inside.

Getting directly behind her in line gave me a perfect view of that ass and those hips. Both looked damn good in her tight fitting skinny jeans that immediately made my dick take notice. If everything about my plan worked out, it wouldn't be long before me and my dick would get a chance to sample those goods. But for now, it was about staying focused. There was a job to be done.

I listened to her phone conversation as she spoke, not really expecting to hear too much more than the normal shit women cackled about: clothes, shopping, gossip, nails, hair, etc. But was caught totally off guard when I actually heard Milan's name come slithering out of her mouth. Then as if I hadn't heard her correctly the first time, she mentioned Milan's name again. My ears were on fire at that point. I listened intently, hoping to hear something I could use. She had to be talking about Zaria's roommate which meant Zaria was nearby, too.

The woman said something about Milan being fake, and her real name being Zaria, and that she didn't like how that Tyson nigga was loving the ground she walked on. She called her a fraud several times and believed she should call the police even without Tyson's permission. My ears went up when I heard her say that Tyson didn't come home last night but was expected soon. She hated Zaria profusely and just kept repeating it as she fumbled around in her purse for more money. I was listening so intently that I hadn't even noticed her pay for her coffee. And she herself was so into her conversation that she turned and bumped into me so hard she dropped her phone on the floor.

"I'm so sorry," she said quickly.

"Don't worry about it," I assured her with a smile as I knelt down, picked up her phone, and handed it to her. "No harm, no foul."

"I should've been paying attention instead of yapping on that damn thing."

"Sweetheart, you're good," I told her. "Could've happened to anyone. Must have been a deep conversation though."

"Not really," she replied, shrugging off the cell phone conversation. "Just a little gossip. I'm pretty sure you already know how us women are." She smiled.

I immediately noticed dimples in her cheeks, which I'd always loved in a woman's smile. That's always been a definite turn on. "You have cute dimples," I complimented.

"Thank you," she stated genuinely.

"They go perfectly with your smile."

Appreciation and interest showed on her face. "That's sweet," she said, her smile growing bigger. "Thank you."

"Don't worry about it. I'm pretty sure your man tells you that all the time."

"I don't have one of those," she said.

"Why not, you're gorgeous?" I asked, giving her a look of surprise.

"I have a hectic job," she said somberly. "It's hard to find time."

"Damn, you gotta change that," I said looking at the D.T. initials tattooed on the side of her neck.

"So, if you don't have a man, whose initials are those?"

"Long story. A real long story," she responded with a slight grin.

All of her words and mannerisms seemed genuine. I liked that. Most women, cute like her were usually stuck up. Knocking off sadity bitches had never been a problem for me. But down to earth ones like this one made it easier, less work for the pussy.

"A good man would be grateful with whatever time you could give him," I told her.

"There's a shortage of those type of men though."

"Nah," I corrected her, looking directly into her eyes. "We're out there. You just gotta know where to find us."

She looked at me just as closely as I was looking at her, liking what she saw. I always knew when a woman was interested in me. The dead give-away was in the eyes. The eyes never lied. Hers were definitely saying what I wanted to hear. I extended my hand. "I'm Hardy," I introduced myself.

"I'm Tayvia," she said, accepting my hand.

Minutes later we were exchanging numbers and standing

beside her car, while she sipped on a Caramel Frappuccino. Like a gentleman, I opened the door and she slid inside. As she turned the key we assured each other that we'd get together soon. When I told her don't make me wait too long, I could see her insides light up. While watching her pull out the parking lot, all I could think about was how easy my revenge would now come. But even more importantly, the amount of fun I was going to have with the new plan I'd come up with the moment I first saw Tayvia. It brought a smile to my face. Fuck just killing Zaria. That was too easy, I realized. She didn't deserve a quick death. I was going to make her suffer slowly. And Tayvia would be my key at making it happen.

Suddenly, my thoughts were interrupted by my cell phone ringing. I answered like I was on top of the world since I knew it was Selena. "I owe you my life, girl," I chanted.

"You sure do," she snapped.

"My payment to you for the marriage is now only one thousand. I texted you earlier and told you to meet me to get the marriage certificate."

"Mannnnn, fuck that shit Selena! You know what I'm doing right now."

The bitch started humming. "And Hardy…" She told me in a chilling tone, "I need fifteen thousand from you by tomorrow, or the entire NYPD will think you've been harborin' a fugitive."

"What the …"

The phone fell silent. And just like that Selena was gone. *That bitch was always up to something.*

ZARIA
Nine

I'd been silent for most of the ride home from the hotel. Tyson and I had spent the night and half the day at the Intercontinental Hotel which was just a couple of miles from the hospital. Thanks to the bitch Tayvia, I ended up getting fifteen stitches underneath my eye.

Thank God there was no issue with Devin's seed inside of me.

Tyson was so heated he never even walked with me to the back of the emergency room when they called my name. But after a whole lot of begging and pleading from me he agreed for us to stay the night out, away from any drama. When Tyson caught the end of my kiss with Eric, I thought for sure I was a dead bitch. Out of reflex and quick thinking, I backed away from Eric pretending that he was simply consoling me and my wound.

For a moment, Tyson only glared at us in silence with his arms folded leaving me unable to read him. His non-reaction to what he'd just seen made me nervous. Then Eric attempted to smooth things over, since Tyson hadn't actually seen our lips pressed together.

Things worked out, but it bothered me for hours hearing Tyson say, 'Milan wouldn't last a day with you and what you have going on'." Eric just grinned and left me and Tyson to argue alone.

"Baby," I remembered telling Tyson, looking dreamily into his eyes. "I'm ready to be yours. I'm so ready, sweetheart. I want to stop playing around and be your girlfriend."

The words were lies; all of them. I still didn't love Tyson. In all actuality my heart was still Devin's and I hadn't all the way given up on the possibility of Devin coming back. But I would've been a damn fool to derail the money train Tyson had me riding on.

I begged and pleaded with Tyson until he took me to the hospital and then to a hotel. Obviously, my apologies weren't enough for him though because the fucking he gave me last night was brutal. For hours, although I like rough sex every now and then, he yanked my weave so hard my roots were still sore. He fucked me viciously like I was some hoe off the street, and only stopping a few times to force his dick so far down my damn throat I came up gasping for air each time. When we were finished, I allowed him to cum in my face, knowing I hated that nasty ass shit.

"That truck never been out here before," Tyson said as the limo pulled up to the gates of his home. Those words were the first he'd spoken to me since having his way with my body last night.

I didn't bother to look or say anything about whatever truck he was talking about. I stared out my window glassy eyed, a little ashamed of myself for letting him degrade me like he did. I wrapped my arms around my body.

Eric was also in my head. It couldn't be helped. I had been definitely feeling him last night and was hoping that he'd try to get with me later. Shit, I was feeling him so much that after Tyson fell asleep last night I went into his cell phone and got Eric's number, storing it in my cell under the name Savior. I just hoped that when I finally called, he wouldn't hang up on me.

"Tinted windows," Tyson continued, still looking at the truck. "I'll bet it's a muthafuckin news reporter stalking me over that bullshit *you* pulled last night. That was so damned embarrassing, Milan."

"Tyson, don't start," I said as the limo pulled into the opening gates and headed up the driveway. "I told you I was sorry."

"You gave them white folks a reason to start printing negative shit about me again."

"I made a damn mistake, Tyson!" I screamed. "Leave it alone!"

"First of all!" he screamed back. "Watch your fucking tone when you talk to me!" His voice was so loud it shook the wine glasses inside of the car. "I told you about that shit last night! That's why your face is fucked up now from messing with people."

"What the fuck ever," I said, shrugging him off.

The limo stopped.

Tyson didn't wait for the driver. He opened his own door, stepped out, and slammed the door behind him.

When the driver opened my door, I stepped out and headed up the mansion's stairs with nothing on my mind but lying down and getting some rest. Although it was only a little after six p.m., the pregnancy had given me a morning sickness feel. When I walked into the foyer, I nearly froze at the site of Tayvia staring directly at me while Tyson was sifting through mail. What the fuck was she doing here? I closed the door without taking my eyes off of her.

Tayvia had a spiteful look on her face and her hands were on her hips.

Tyson was still sifting through his mail, ignoring the both of us.

The foyer was uncomfortably silent. Extra awkward.

"She's not who you think she is," Tayvia finally blurted.

"Her name isn't Milan. It's Zaria."

Tyson turned and looked at me like he'd been hit with a ton of bricks. I guess he wanted answers.

"She's pregnant, too, Tyson," Tayvia said, still looking directly at me.

Tyson looked even more surprised. "What?" he asked.

"She's pregnant," Tayvia repeated. "Five months to be exact. That means there's no possible way that *you* could be the father." She folded her arms.

Tyson's face was filled with disbelief. "How do you know?" he questioned her. "And her name is what?"

Tayvia pulled some papers from my last doctor's visit out of her back pocket and handed them to Tyson. She had gotten them from the glove compartment of my Benz.

"What the fuck were you doing in my car?" I asked her, ready for round two. This time she would leave with the cuts and bruises.

"Why I was in your car is the least of your worries," she replied in a sarcastic tone.

I took a step towards her.

"Milan," Tyson said, looking up from the papers angered and heartbroken. "Whose baby is it?"

"Tyson," I said quickly, his question sidetracking me from whipping Tayvia's ass for the moment. "I was going to tell you."

"Whose baby is it?" he asked again, this time his tone more stern.

Tayvia shouted, "Her name is Zaria, Tyson, and we need to call the police. Now!" She turned and rushed into the living room as Tyson scanned the article.

"Baby," I said pleadingly. "That doesn't matter. I want *you* to be the father."

Tyson looked at me like I was a nutcase.

"That's why I told you I was ready for you and me to finally become a couple last night," I lied quickly, trying my hardest to do damage control. "We can become a family."

Tayvia came back into the foyer and handed Tyson several more papers. "This is what I was trying to tell you last night," she said.

I wasn't sure what was on the papers Tyson was looking at but my heart began to pound. I had an idea of what they could be and what they might contain. Even through my anger I could only look at Tayvia now with eyes that begged for her mercy, pleading for her to back off.

Tayvia wasn't having it. "She's had a little plastic surgery," she told Tyson. "But if you look closely at those pictures, it's her without a doubt."

"Tayvia," I begged. "Please stop doing this." Tears ran down my cheeks.

Tyson stared at my Wanted photo in shock. He then looked at the internet printout out of the New York Times article of Terrell's murder. "Oh my God," he whispered.

Tayvia nodded. "She killed that little boy, Tyson."

Adrenaline sparked inside of me.

"*Kill that meddling bitch!*" the voice in my head appeared from nowhere and screamed so loud my eyes squinted in agitation.

"*Kill her now, Zaria!*" it shouted louder than before. "*Do you want to go to the fucking penitentiary?*"

"No," I answered, sounding like a scared child.

Tayvia glanced at me, wondering who I was talking to.

"*Well, that's exactly where your dumb ass is headed!*" the voice shouted. "*If you don't shut that nosey bitch up!*"

I grabbed my head. The foyer seemed to spin. The moment was happening too quickly. Snot trickled from my nose and my chest heaved up and down. I was ready to do a windmill on Tayvia's meddling ass.

"*Kill her, Zaria!*"

I grew dizzy.

Dozens of voices began to chatter inside my head.

"*Kill her now, Zaria!*"

"Smiley Face. Smiley Face. Can anyone see my Smiley

Face?" I began to chant over and over again, hoping the words would calm me. They didn't. I could see Tyson and Tayvia staring at me like I was some sort of nutcase.

Finally, I screamed to the top of my lungs as I charged Tayvia like a line-backer, knocking her to the marble floor so hard the back of her head thudded on it like a bowling ball.

"You bitch!!" I screamed as I snatched a handful of her hair and punched her in the mouth so hard her teeth cut my fist open.

"Milan, Zaria or whatever the fuck your name is!" Tyson called, tossing the papers and grabbing me.

I paused for two, short seconds, realizing that Tyson had called me Zaria. Then I went back to attacking Tayvia.

"I'm going to kill you, bitch!" I threatened Tayvia, letting loose with another punch, this time to the side of her head. She'd managed to protect her face by covering it with both hands. Then suddenly pulled a wrestlemania move on me and ended up on top.

"Tayvia!" Tyson shouted again, trying to pull her off of me.

I had a handful of Tayvia's hair, refusing to let go. "I'm going to murder her ass!"

"Stop it, both of you!" Tyson demanded, finally able to get her off of me, kicking and clawing for more. When I got up, he slammed my back flat against the door and grabbed my wrists. "Stop!" he yelled.

Tayvia staggered to her feet with her mouth bleeding. "She's crazy, Tyson!" she belted. "Call the police!"

I looked Tyson in the eyes and tried to kiss him. "Don't listen to her," I pleaded. "Me and you can work this out." I even stuck my tongue out sexily, letting him know I was ready to suck him off.

"Tyson, call the damn police!" Tayvia demanded, holding her mouth.

"Baby, please don't listen to her," I begged, each word falling out of my mouth super quickly. "Make her leave, Tyson.

Make her leave so you and I can talk. I'll tell you everything."

I was still wildly trying to kiss him but he was still refusing to let my lips touch his face.

"Make her leave, Tyson," I repeated. "And me and you can work things out."

I was desperate.

Tyson let go of my wrists and stepped back. He reached into his pocket and pulled out his cell phone.

My eyes widened. "Baby, no."

Tyson flipped the cell open.

I dropped to my knees in front of him crying so badly my vision was blurry. "Baby, please stop. No police. Pleaseeeee. It's all a lie. Just let me explain."

Tayvia shook her head.

Tyson dialed.

I dropped my head and cried harder than I had ever done before in my life.

"Police," I heard Tyson request of the 911 operator.

My world began to crash down around me. They were going to take my baby away from me and lock me up for the rest of my life. God, I didn't want that. I tilted my head and looked up at Tyson with nothing but pain and sadness preparing to run. "Tyson, they framed me," I whimpered. "I swear they did. I didn't kill that boy." My voice was just above a whisper.

Tyson stared down at me silently with the phone to his ear.

"I didn't do it," I lied, sobbing heavily. "Baby, I swear I didn't. They set me up.'

Still only silence from Tyson.

My hands grabbed the bottom part of his leg. "Please tell me you believe me," I begged. "Please, Tyson."

Finally, Tyson spoke into the phone while still staring down at me "Yes, Police, I…" he said and stopped.

"Please," I whispered. My heart continued to beat like a drum.

The room was dead silent.

Tayvia stared at me from behind Tyson.

Tyson, finally spoke again, surprisingly telling the police that there was a suspicious vehicle parked outside his home and that he wanted them to come and have the driver move. He described the truck and hung up.

I didn't know what to say.

"Tyson," Tayvia said. "What are you doing?"

Tyson didn't answer. His face still had no expression. He placed his hands into his pockets, kicked me off of his leg, turned, and walked out of the foyer.

"Tyson," Tayvia said. "What type of hold does she have on you? I mean this is crazy. Why couldn't you want me the way you want her. I mean wasn't our one night special?"

Tyson walked up the spiral staircase, leaving me and Tayvia alone, ignoring all of her words.

Tayvia looked at me with disgust.

Still on the floor, I looked at her and smiled. "Look at you," I whispered. "I knew there was something between you two. But I had no idea you gave up the ass…One night…just sex…nothing more," I told her. "I bet you're wishing your pussy was good as mine."

Tayvia said nothing but her eyes spoke multitudes,

I stood to my feet and waltzed into the living room to sit on the couch, figuring I would let Tyson be alone upstairs. I had just dodged a bullet and didn't want to take a chance on fucking things up. I sat for a few minutes contemplating how I would take control and throw Tayvia out for good. Tyson and I *would be* together. He just didn't know it yet.

Five minutes later, Tyson made his way down the staircase with two suitcases. He rushed past Tayvia who was still in the foyer with her back against the wall, amazed, trying to make sense of what was going on. I watched Tyson open the door, and toss my bags out onto the lawn. I was devastated. Before I could even react, he jetted into the living room, grabbed my car keys from the table, and stuffed them into his pocket.

"Baby, what are you doing?" I asked, having absolutely

no idea what was going on.

"Get out of my house," he said calmly.

"But, Tyson," I attempted. "You bought that car for me, baby!"

"And now I'm taking it back. So get your child killing ass out of my damn house, Zaria!" he yelled.

I leapt to my feet and tried to wrap my arms around him. If I could just touch him, we could work things out. "Tyson, sweetheart…"

He grabbed my arms, painfully squeezing them, and pulling me toward his chest. Looking directly in my eyes he said, "I can't believe I had a child murderer living in my house. Get the fuck out! I'll do you a favor by calling the police after you leave, since I don't want that much attention on me."

"No, Tyson…call them now!" Tayvia chimed in.

"But, baby," I attempted quickly. "I'm innocent. I can explain the name thing…but believe me, I was framed."

"What the fuck ever," he said, pulling me toward the door.

I let my body drop to the floor like a sack of potatoes and began to reach for anything that I could hold onto, but found nothing.

Tyson grabbed me by the ankles and began to drag me towards the door again.

Tayvia stepped out of the way, of course grinning the whole time.

My nails clawed at the marble floor. "Tyson, please!" I screamed as he continued to drag me. "Please don't!"

The door was getting closer.

"I'm only three months pregnant, Tyson!" I lied, kicking and reaching. "It's yours! I swear the baby's yours! Tyson Junior."

Tayvia shook her head at my desperate attempt.

Tyson wasn't falling for it. He'd had enough of my lies. He drug me out to the stairs, went back in the house, and slammed the oversized door; leaving me alone and crying in the darkness. I felt so defeated. The moment made me feel the same hopelessness I felt standing on my aunt's porch in my nightmares. There was nowhere for me to turn for help. No keys to any car to drive.

Nothing.

No one.

But through my tears I realized that Tyson's stoop wasn't the place to throw myself a pity party as I glanced down the mansion's lawn to the curb and didn't see the truck he'd wanted moved. The police must have already come. However, I wasn't going to stick around and find out if they were coming back.

ZARIA
················
Ten

My hands trembled uncontrollably as I took five hundred dollars from the ATM for the second time within two minutes. This time from an account Tyson funded for me; play money as he called it. I wanted to get more before he'd be able to close out my account in the morning.

With shaking hands, I placed the stack of crispy twenty dollar bills into my pocket and began to make way through the desolate parking lot to the Hertz across the street. Although my heart rate had slowed since leaving Tyson's, it wasn't by much. As I hitchhiked from the mansion lined neighborhood to the nearest ATM my eyes stayed watching for police cars. I wasn't sure if Tyson had maybe changed his mind and decided to call them after throwing me out, but the possibility had me on edge.

Visions of the Lexus I'd just hitchhiked in repeatedly played over and over again in my head. The entire time I sat in the old rich white lawyer's sedan, I nervously rung my hands, unable to stop. My body rocked back and forth in his passenger seat, making him glance at me with a strange look on his face several times.

"Are you okay?" he'd asked twice.

I assured him I was.

"Are you sure you don't need help, or the police?" he asked as he pulled into the plaza's parking lot.

Just hearing the word *police* made me grab my suitcases from his backseat and hop out of his car before it had even came to a complete stop. I wasn't taking any chances. I just hoped he didn't call anyone once I got out the car. It was a little after nine and my nerves still hadn't settled yet.

Fear wasn't the only thing that had my nerves rattled. Anger did also. I couldn't believe Tayvia's audacity. The fact that the sneaky bitch had gone through my car and even ran a background check on me like I was a criminal had me still seeing red. I still wanted to kill her for that trifling shit. What the fuck made her so special that she could search through someone else's past and personal business like she was God or some shit? Funky bitch! I should have gouged her eyes out!

Before long, I'd waltzed into the Hertz rental place and was forced to rent a Ford Focus. Damn-that's fucked up. I went from a Benz, fully loaded, to a cheap ass Ford Focus in only a matter of two hours. This definitely was *not* my night.

After putting my suitcases in the trunk, I stood outside and pulled my cell phone from my pocket to call Devin. It was about the fourth or fifth time that I'd called since being tossed out, but still only got his voicemail. Immediately I wondered if he was with his wife. I wondered if he was fucking her. I wondered if he was holding her. The thoughts and possibilities of what they were doing at that moment drove me crazy and broke my heart.

Nothing meant more to me than to work things out with Devin. I didn't want a Baby Daddy. That was for young broads with no morals, broads who spread their legs for any sorry ass nigga that threw them a little attention. I was better than that though. Me and my baby deserved more. We deserved Devin. We would get him too...if it was the last thing I accomplished on earth.

"Baby, I'm so sorry," I spoke softly into the phone to Devin's voicemail closing my eyes and seeing his face. "I love you with all my heart. And I still want us to be a family. Please call me back, Devin. Please. Me and the baby miss you. We need you."

I hung up the phone, realizing that I had been pacing around the car. With everything in my heart, I hoped Devin would get the message and realize that me, him, and our child was a destiny written permanently in stone. No one would ever appreciate him more than me and our child could. We were the family he was meant to have.

Reality struck me suddenly as thunder sounded from a distance. Where was I going to sleep tonight? Where was I going to lay my head? The efficiency I'd rented was almost an hour and a half away. And I hadn't stayed there in over a month, nor paid the rent, so didn't know if my key would even still work.

Since arriving in Philly I'd been staying in nothing but hotel rooms, knowing it was best to stay on the move each night. I'd never even let Tyson know where I laid my head.

Lightning brightly blazed across the sky.

I had an idea. I opened my cell, searched for Eric's number, and called him. After several rings I got his voicemail.

"Shit," I said frustrated. After hanging up, I called again. As the phone rang, I noticed a car slowly passing by the Hertz parking lot. Eric's voicemail played again. "Damn it," I said.

Thunder loudly erupted across the sky again.

A raindrop fell on my forehead.

The fact that Tyson had put me out and Tayvia was still there began to anger the hell out of me. Fuck his reasoning. How could he do this to me? I thought he really wanted to be with me. If he truly wanted to be my man, why couldn't we work things out?

I began to speak to Eric's voicemail without thinking. "Eric," I said. "Please call me. This is Milan. Tyson beat me up and threw me out of the house for kissing you." The words were coming out of my mouth faster than I could think of them. It was like they had their own mind. I had no idea why I was lying on Tyson. "I'm a good person, Eric, and I don't like seeing any harm come to anyone. Tyson wants to hurt you. Call me so I can tell you what he said about you."

Another raindrop fell.

"I don't know what to do," I continued, my words frantic. "But I can't stay there with a potential murderer. And I don't know anyone else in Philly and I'm all alone. Please call me," I ended after rattling off my number and slamming the phone shut.

For a moment, I stood beside the car still and silent, not knowing what to do or where to turn. Then Tayvia's face crossed my mind. She was the reason for this. Everything was going perfect until she stuck her nose in my business. She wanted Tyson for herself. That was why she decided to search my past and lay everything out for Tyson. She was probably in his bed right now. The thought made me see total red. I blacked out momentarily vowing to go back to Tyson's and put an end to Tayvia. I would slit her throat nice and wide.

I wanted Tayvia out of Tyson's house! Immediately, I told myself. Even though I didn't love him, I wasn't going to let a bitch like her have him. I would kill her first. I would kill her before I let her beat me. I had too much pride for that. My mind started playing ping pong as more raindrops began to fall, each exploding individually on the pavement.

Then out of the blue the same suspicious car that I'd seen before slowly pulled into the Hertz parking lot. Moments after that, I realized I'd left my driver's license and credit card in the rental car place. Cursing at myself for the simple mistake, I opened the door of the Ford Focus slowly, watching the mysterious car approach.

It slowly pulled into the lot, creeping for nearly twenty seconds, then suddenly sped towards me, its headlights nearly blinding me. It screeched to a stop directly in front of the rental. The shine of its headlights made me squint my eyes and struggle to see the driver.

Lightening tore through the sky again and rain began to pour heavily.

The driver's door of the car opened quickly.

My eyes were still squinting. I began to wonder if it was an unmarked police car. I grew nervous. My heart beat rapidly, and my first instinct told me to run. Then I got a better look at the car from a different angle. It was white, fancy and too fly to be the police. It appeared to be a BMW.

The driver emerged from the car underneath the pouring rain and quickly dashed towards me, scaring the shit outta me.

Lightning ripped through the night sky illuminating the fastly approaching man's face. The sight terrified me beyond belief. How did he find me?

"Oh God," I said fearfully, seeing the rage and vengeance in my cousin Kenneth's eyes. He had some short, hard looking broad with him, chewing gum and looking at me with a crazy smirk on her face.

"So, that's Zaria, huh?" she commented, still standing near the passenger's side door.

"You're going to die tonight!" Kenneth screamed, charging around the hood of his car with rain pouring down his face.

I jumped in the Ford Focus and locked the door. My heart was beating like crazy.

Kenneth reached my door and yanked hard at the handle. "Open this damn door, Zaria!" he ordered. "Open it now!"

My body was frozen. The rage in his eyes made him look like a monster, far from the innocent little boy I used to baby sit.

Kenneth began to kick my door so hard the entire car rocked. "I'm going to kill you, Zaria!" he promised. "I swear I'm going to kill you!"

I reached into my pocket, grabbed the keys, and attempted to put them into the ignition. But my hands trembled so badly they dropped to the floor.

"Bitch, open this door!" Kenneth demanded, kicking the door again and yanking at the handle. "You're going to pay for what you did to my mother!" He pounded his fists against the window. "You unappreciative bitch!" he yelled. "I told you I'd find you! Open the door!"

My eyes could only stare at him. I didn't know what to do.

The next thing I knew, glass shattered and Kenneth's arm was inside the car swimming for any parts of me. I snatched the keys from the floor and quickly concentrated on getting them into the ignition. Finding success, I turned the key, put the car in reverse, and backed up like a mad-woman, with Kenneth's body clinging to the side of the car.

"You're dead bitch!" he shouted while grasping a good chunk of my weave, and dangling half his body in thin air.

As I screeched to a stop, the tires slid on the wet cement, and Kenneth managed to bang the rest of the shattered glass from the window. He now had full view of my face along with the plug of hair he'd ripped from my head.

"Zaria!" he yelled, "Get the fuck out the car!"

I slammed the car in drive and took off through the pouring rain, immediately turning on my wipers and knocking Kenneth's body to the ground. As I sped through the lot I looked into my rearview to see Kenneth hop into the passenger side of the car and come after me. "Fuck!" I shouted, knowing that I needed to get my hands on a gun.

My heart thudded loudly as I strained to see through the rain pouring down on the windshield. Each drop poured so hard it was nearly impossible for the wipers to give me a clear view. As I neared the lot's exit I looked into the rearview again to see Kenneth's headlights catching up. When my eyes looked out the windshield again, they were just in time to see into the wide, terror filled eyes of a woman directly in front of me holding an umbrella. I screamed as the Ford Focus violently tore into her, knocking her body over the top of the car and onto the lot behind me. I wasn't sure if she was alive or not, but there was no chance of stopping me. I raced out of the lot into traffic, headed towards Tyson's.

Kenneth and his bitch flew out of the lot behind me and fishtailed, giving me a chance to place distance between us. My foot pressed down so hard on the gas pedal it was nearly touching the floor. My eyes darted from the rearview to the windshield. I darted the Ford Focus in and out of traffic, quickly trying to lose Kenneth. He was about three cars behind me and coming up fast.

My eyes widened at the approaching red light at the intersection ahead of me. Traffic was crossing it.

"Oh shit!" I shouted, gripping the steering wheel even tighter but knowing the rain was coming down to hard for me to even *think* about hitting the brakes. There was nothing to do but go for it.

Lightning and thunder both brightened and rattled the sky.

My heartbeat was in my ears now.

I screamed as I shot across the intersection expecting to die, expecting the car to be clipped or rammed into from the side. Visions of me and my unborn child dying in twisted metal, my bloody body mangled, flashed in my mind. But surprisingly within a fraction of a second the intersection was behind me. I looked into the rearview to see Kenneth's car stopped at the red light, unable to cross the dozens of stopped cars that had spun out and screeched to a stop to avoid me. I quickly made a left and got off the busy street. Several turns later, I was headed straight for Tyson's.

HARDY

Eleven

Even though the rain poured, a brightness shone inside me unlike any I'd felt before. Since Terrell had been gone my insides felt hollow, dark and lifeless. But in just a matter of minutes all that had changed. I felt brand new. I'd just pulled back into Zaria's boyfriend's neighborhood and parked just a few houses down from the mansion. My heart pounded against my chest and I couldn't stop my fingers from drumming nervously against the steering wheel. My eyes raced over and over again from my windshield to my rearview, hoping the cop who'd made me leave about two hours ago wouldn't happen to pull up again.

When I first saw the cop slowly pull beside me earlier, my heart jumped into my throat. I had the gun sitting in my lap and was caught totally off guard. Thankfully my truck sat too high for him to see inside from the driver's seat of his cruiser. He simply told me that he'd gotten a complaint of a suspicious vehicle and that I was gonna have to move.

"No pictures tonight," he'd commented, obviously thinking I was some sort of reporter.

I obliged. But told myself, fuck him and came right back, parking three houses away at a house that seemed to have some kind of get together going on inside. My car didn't look out of place among the cars of their guests.

Before the cop made me move, I'd been parked out front for hours until the limo carrying Zaria and Tyson pulled into the mansion's gates. When I saw Zaria climb out, everything inside of me came to life. The sight of her seemed so surreal. But I knew that my eyes weren't playing tricks on me. It was her. My body began to tremble.

I wanted to murk that bitch so bad it felt like I was going to explode. But I knew I had to wait for the right moment. Out of anxiousness, I called Tayvia, maybe hoping to hear Zaria's voice in the background. We had a date scheduled at nine thirty at a restaurant called Maggiano's on West Avenue and I needed to be sure she wasn't going to stand me up. She was my key to getting into the mansion's gate. When Tayvia answered, she let me know that she was finishing up a few things at work and was *definitely* coming.

Tayvia had pretty good conversation and a sweet personality. Too bad I wasn't going to get the chance to explore it too much. The two or three times we'd talked on the phone throughout the day were simply to find an opening where I could get to Zaria. When we decided on a date, and I saw Zaria climb out of that limo, that was all I needed. Now all I needed to do was wait for Tayvia to leave. It was about seven-thirty then. It was now a little after nine.

My cell phone rang.

Without looking at the screen, I answered it quickly, hoping it was the call that would set everything in motion. "Hello?"

"Where's my fuckin' money, Hardy?" Selena's voice sounded.

"Shit," I whispered, not up for her bullshit right now. "Selena, now isn't the time," I told her. My eyes were still darting between the windshield and the rearview mirror.

"Fuck that!" Selena screamed angrily. "Where's my

damn money!"

"Are you tryna frame me! If so, bitch you didn't do shit that nobody else couldn't have done."

"I found her Hardy! Nobody else did! You owe me nigga and I want what's mine!" She paused. "And my fuckin' credit card is missin', too, you got it?"

Actually, I'd gotten close to twenty-five hundred dollars off her card to buy more surveillance items and the new clothes I'd just bought. I snuck it out of her purse just before leaving her and rolling to Philly. Shit, the bitch owed me, I reasoned. My son's dead and she decided to make me eat her pussy before giving up information on his killer. And she wanted me to marry a bitch so she could make a shit load of money! Fuck that! I had to get some kind of get back in addition to stealing her high powered tracking device.

*Bitches don't trick me…I do the tricking…*I told myself attempting to pump my own self up.

"I don't have it," I told her bluntly.

"Yes, you do!" she returned. "You took twenty-five hundred dollars off of it in just two days. I just called them and found out after discoverin' my card was gone!"

The bitch was getting on my nerves.

"I cancelled the card," she said, and I know where to find you.

No problem, I thought to myself, after hearing some goofy nigga in the background talking shit.

"You hear me, Hardy! I'll make sure your black ass is in jail by Sunday! Cuz nigga you are gettin' married on Saturday. Two more fuckin' days Hardy, so don't forget it! I have a reputation to uphold."

My ears had blocked her out. My focus was on the house.

From the darkness, I watched the mansion and its gates. The wait seemed to drag on, each minute torturing me with fierce anticipation. Each time I looked at my watch I realized only a minute or two had passed, although it had seemed like an hour. The wait was killing me.

"You son of a bitch," she continued. "I'll let them know you're in Philly committin' a damn murder!"

That set me off. "Go ahead, bitch!" I snapped. "And I'll be sure to let them know that you're the crooked cop who gave me the information! How do you think they'll feel about that? How do you think they're going to feel about finding out that you had information on the whereabouts of a known child murderer and kept it to yourself?"

She went silent.

"Yeah, grow some nuts if you want to," I said. "I'll play all those freaky ass phone messages you've been leaving me over the past couple weeks, too!"

Still only silence.

"Don't make threats you can't make good on," I told her. "Fucking with me will get your job snatched, bitch." I left no room for a comeback. I simply hung up.

Just like that my mind was back on Zaria. I wondered what she was going to say when she saw my face. I wondered if she was going to cry like a newborn child and beg me for her life. The possibility intrigued me.

"Yeah, bitch," I could see myself saying, answering her pleas and offers of doing *anything* to save her life. "Get down on your knees."

The vision made my dick grow and stiffen. Seeing Zaria do what I ordered made my balls begin to swell, both full of cum.

"Open your damn mouth, hoe," I could hear myself demanding in my sick, twisted, but revenge filled fantasy. Seeing Zaria open wide made me grab my dick and squeeze, her weak and pathetic whimpers turning me all the way on. "You ready to suck it?" I would ask.

Through spilling tears she would answer, "Yes."

Then I would free my hard dick from my jeans, place it directly in front of her face, and drench her in hot piss. She did-n't deserve my cum or the taste of the head on my dick. However, what she *did* deserve was the humiliation of being on her knees soaked in my urine as my finger squeezed the gun's trigger, sending three or four bullets through her face.

Suddenly, my cell phone rang.

I looked at the clock on the dashboard. It was 9:40 p.m. I answered the phone.

"Didn't mean to stand you up," came Tayvia's voice from the other end. She sounded sorta sad as if she'd been crying. "Something unexpected held me up at work this evening, but I'm on my way to the restaurant. They close at ten so I hope we make it."

"I'll be waiting," I said. This was the call I'd been waiting for.

Tayvia hung up.

Tossing the phone onto the passenger seat, I pulled out the chrome .38 revolver from my waist, made sure it was fully loaded and the safety was off. I slipped on a pair of leather gloves and quickly wiped it clean with my shirt. My heart began pumping dynamite as I stuffed it back into my waist. I climbed out of the car, shut the door, and stood beside it in the night's darkness. Seconds later, the mansion's gate opened and Tayvia's Jag pulled out in a hurry. My feet immediately took off towards the gate to get inside before it closed as Tayvia's taillights disappeared down the street. As the gate closed behind me, my heart and adrenaline pumped intensely. I charged from the car, up the freshly cut lawn, stopping at the door. I began pounding on it with my fist, prepared to kick it in if I had to. Several seconds later, the door was snatched open. I hoped and prayed it was Zaria as I reached underneath my shirt.

"Man, what the fuck are you beating on my door for?" Tyson asked angrily. "Who are you and how did you even get on my property?"

"Where the fuck is she?" I asked, dead serious.

"Where the fuck is who?"

"Zaria!"

"Zaria doesn't live here," he said, after wiping the surprised look off his face. "Now, get the fuck off my doorstep and my property." He tried to close the door.

"You think I'm playing!" I shouted, catching the door before it shut and shoving it open so hard the force knocked Tyson back on his heels. "Where she at, nigga?" I said, pulling the gun from my belt and aiming it in his face.

"Man, are you crazy?" he asked, raising his hands in defense.

"Is she upstairs?" I asked, my eyes darting around the mansion frantically. I was anxiously prepared to search the entire house from top to bottom to find her. She'd probably seen me on a security camera or something and hid.

"Man, ain't nobody upstairs. You got me all wrong," Tyson pleaded, hands still raised in front of him as if they'd be any match for a speeding bullet.

Frustrated with his lies, I placed the gun further in his face. "Quit playing with me, pussy ass nigga!" I screamed on him, even louder than before. "You know who I'm talking about! Now take me to her!"

"Look," Tyson said. "If you're talking about Zaria, she ain't here!"

Fed up, I back handed him to the temple with the butt of the gun, sending him falling to the floor. "I know she's here!" I yelled. "I saw her when she got out of the limo with you earlier!"

Tyson groaned in pain clutching the side of his bleeding forehead. "She was here," he said getting up from the floor. "But I put her trifling ass out my house! She did some foul ass shit!"

Damn, I thought to myself. If he was telling the truth, that meant she must've left when the police made me move. I saw nothing but crimson red at that point. How could I have come so close only to lose her?

"Get her back here!" I ordered.

"What are you talking about, man?" Tyson asked, still clutching his head in pain.

"Call her ass and tell her you fucked up and you need her to come back!" I demanded growing angrier beyond belief.

Tyson suddenly swatted the gun to the side with his left hand. Just as quickly, before I could respond, he caught me on the side of my face with a powerful haymaker that jerked my head and knocked me backwards.

"Muthafucka!" Tyson shouted as he pressed me against the wall while holding both my arms to keep me from bussing at him.

Still slightly dazed from the punch, I raised my knee into his nuts as hard as I could, making him turn me loose. He bent over and grabbed himself while grunting in pain. I backhanded him across the face with the gun, sending him falling to the floor again. Pissed that he would have even thought of trying me I squeezed the trigger. The gun exploded, sending a bullet tearing through his right knee.

Tyson immediately grabbed his knee and let out the loudest scream I'd ever heard. He started wriggling across the floor like a fish in unimaginable pain, blood smearing underneath him.

"My kneeeeeeeee!" he hollered.

"Fuck your knee!" I countered.

Tyson was in tremendous pain. He was still clutching his knee, and now growling like a wounded animal.

I squeezed the trigger again, blowing a gaping hole through his other knee. "You can kiss that million dollar contract good bye!" I taunted over his deafening screams.

There was no compassion left in me after burying my baby in the ground on that bitter freezing winter evening. I felt for no one. The whole world could burn in hell. Without my son by my side anymore, the value of *any* nigga's life was zero, including a multi-million dollar athlete like Tyson Fennell.

"Get on your damn phone and call Zaria!" I demanded.

"Fuck you!" he hollered. The pain and torture in his scream was gut wrenching. Drool ran heavily from his mouth as he clutched his destroyed legs. But I quickly realized that for him to be holding out like this he must still love that crazy bitch.

His eyes rolled into his head.

"Tyson!" someone screamed from behind me at the doorway.

I turned to see Zaria dart past me headed toward Tyson at top speed. She tossed her purse and dropped to her knees never even noticing me standing nearby with the gun. She held his wriggling body in her arms with tears in her eyes, his blood gathering on her clothes.

"Tyson," what happened," she whined. "Oh my God, baby!"

"You brought this crazy muthufucka here!" Tyson winced in pain. "You bitch, you did this. I shoulda never let you into my house."

This nightmare was my dream come true. I stepped to her and pointed the gun in her face. Nothing or no one else in the entire universe existed right now but me and her.

"Tyson, baby," she cried out, cradling him in her arms like I didn't exist. She attempted to console his misery as she rocked him back and forth. She still hadn't looked me in the eyes. "It's gonna be okay," she promised him, "I'm gonna get help! Bitch, don't you see this muthufucka behind you. Turn around!"

"Look at me, bitch," I said through gritted teeth, taking another step forward with the gun still aimed. I wanted to see her eyes before she died.

Zaria ignored me like the crazy chick she was, continuing to rock back and forth with Tyson held tightly in her arms. I looked on intently as she shared with Tyson her famous psycho chant.

"Tyson, all you have to do is chant…Smiley Face. Smiley Face. Can anyone see my Smiley Face? I promise you the pain will go away," she told him believably.

I'd had enough. "Look at me, bitch!" I screamed.

She raised her tear filled eyes from Tyson to me slowly. They widened when they saw my face. "Hardy?" she asked in disbelief.

I nodded.

She was speechless. Her eyes weren't filled with the fear I had hoped for. There was no fear in them at all. Instead, they were over-run with pain for Tyson. That pain and sadness I saw in her eyes for him sickened me immediately. I aimed the gun at Tyson and squeezed the trigger, unloading its remaining bullets into his chest and killing him instantly.

"Nooooo!" Zaria screamed. But it was useless.

I stared at her with no emotion as she shook Tyson's lifeless body, begging him to wake up.

"How does it feel?" I asked her, sickly relishing her pain.

"Fuck you!" Zaria screamed, her face looking bitter and savage like.

"Smiley Face. Smiley Face. Can anyone see my Smiley Face?" she began to chant.

"Fuck that shit!" I told her. "How does it feel to have someone you care about taken from you?"

"Fuck you, Hardy!" she yelled, standing up from the floor, Tyson's blood was all over her clothes. She looked at me with hatred for the air I breathed and the ground I walked on, then charged at me.

"Bitch!' I shouted as I caught her with a strong backhand that sent her straight to the floor.

Zaria laid there dazed.

The sight of her placed jumper cables on my want for revenge. I stepped towards her and kicked her in the ribs, making her yelp helplessly and curl into a fetal position.

"You took my entire world from me!" I shouted as I let loose with a kick to her back, making her scream in more pain and arch her back.

Zaria clutched herself in a ball, crying heavily.

"How does it feel, bitch!" I asked, stomping her thighs. "How does it feel!"

No answers came, only whimpers and moans of pain as she lay near her boyfriend's dead body.

"Get up!" I ordered, hearing approaching sirens.

Zaria continued to lay there crying.

"I said get your ass up!" I repeated, snatching her up by her hair.

Zaria stood defeated, tears running down her face and blood all over her body.

I stared her in her eyes with the gun pointed directly at her face.

I wanted to kill her. I wanted it so badly. But seeing her crying over Tyson's body earlier made me want something more, something worse for her. As she stood staring into the barrel of my gun, I slowly walked towards her until the gun was at her forehead.

Zaria breathed heavily allowing her chest to move up and down vividly. There was no life left in her eyes, only something I couldn't describe. Everything inside her was drained.

At that moment, I could see flashing lights through the window. My heart raced and Zaria's eyes popped from their sockets. Then a buzzer sounded. I panicked, not sure what to do. It took moments for me to make it to the window.

"Shit…shit…shit," I said, seeing the police outside of Tyson's gate attempting to get buzzed in. I knew it was just a matter of minutes before they either burst through the gates with their cruisers or sent some rookie on foot to jump the gate. My time was limited. Quickly, I removed the gun from her forehead, took her hand, and placed the gun in her palm, closing it tightly.

Oddly, neither of us moved knowing the police would be inside within minutes. We stared at each other for only a brief moment.

Out of the blue, Zaria raised the gun towards my face, now holding it with both hands.

I now stared into the barrel.

Zaria squeezed the trigger.

Click.

She squeezed again.

Click.

"You think I'd be dumb enough to give your crazy ass a loaded gun?"

Zaria didn't answer. She simply dropped the gun to her side in defeat. She looked like there was no spirit left inside of her, no fight whatsoever, her world destroyed.

The gate's buzzer rung loudly repeatedly.

She looked toward the door in fear.

"I put all the bullets in your boyfriend over there," I told her, ignoring the buzzer. "And now your finger prints are all over the gun."

Zaria only stared.

"When they come busting up in here and see you with that gun in your hand, they're going to immediately think you killed your million-dollar boyfriend. Your face is going to be all over every news network and every newspaper. And this time you won't get away. You're going to prison."

"I didn't do this," she whispered. "You…"

"Bitch!" I interrupted her. "Do you think they're going to believe a fucking murderer!"

She couldn't answer.

"I didn't think so," I responded. I walked over to her and grabbed her purse from the floor.

The buzzer rang again and more sirens approached.

I placed her purse onto her shoulder. "There you go," I said sarcastically, patting her on the shoulder. "Now you're already for your trip to prison."

Satisfied with knowing I had her right where I wanted her, I turned to the door. "I'll go let the police in," I told her.

After only taking one step towards the door my ears heard what they were hoping for…Zaria's footsteps beginning their dash across the marble floor to the back of the mansion and out the back door into the night. For a second I smiled, relishing the sound. She'd done exactly what I had wanted. She thought she'd escaped.

"Dumb bitch," I whispered. She had no idea that just before I slipped her purse on her shoulder I'd stuffed a small transmitter inside. The game was just beginning, I thought to myself as I turned and dashed through the foyer quickly to the kitchen and out into the darkness. Whatever direction she'd went didn't interest me. I'd find her soon enough for round two.

ZARIA

Twelve

Lightning cracked across the sky, brightening the night repeatedly but only for a brief second each time. The rumbles of thunder sounded like bombs exploding around me and the heavy winds swayed the trees overhead. The pouring rain made my weave stick tightly to the sides of my head, with several strands draped over my forehead. My shirt was so drenched it stuck to my skin, allowing my bra to be seen through it. However, I could care less. I just wanted to keep running as far away from the sirens as I could.

The sound of a barking dog came from somewhere in the far off distance followed by another. And the police sirens were loud and growing even louder every second that quickly passed. I could tell that with each step I took they were getting closer and closer. With each part of the dark woods I dashed through, and the steep hills I had to maneuver down, the red and blue lights continued shining behind me each time.

I took a brief moment to glance back. I had no idea what direction I was headed as my feet loudly splashed through a shallow, running river. All I knew was I was surrounded by an endless, amount of huge towering trees and desperately trying to find my way out. The sounds of police chatter over walkie talkies could be heard somewhere in the surrounding distance. I didn't know exactly where they were coming from, but I could hear them undoubtedly. It was so many of them, they sounded like they were everywhere.

My heels had been tossed a long time ago. I had no idea where I'd thrown them or even how long they had been off of my feet. Both my heart and lungs felt as though they were going to burst at any moment. Each breath I took was more like a heavy gasp for air followed by another and another, no mercy. If anything, the act of breathing had become hard work the more I ran.

My feet and the calves of my jeans were caked in thick mud more and more with each step I took. I wanted to stop running. Every bone in my body ached excruciatingly and needed a rest. But stopping was out of the question. If I stopped, I would be caught. I couldn't see myself doing life for the murders of Tyson and Terrell.

My focus was dead set on escape. I'd never run so hard and so long in my life. I occasionally clutched my stomach, hoping my child was a survivor and fighter like me. But the rain seemed to be coming down harder, making it difficult for me to see ahead of me. But I kept moving quickly, fighting with everything inside me to stay on my feet and run faster.

My body grew weaker, but I refused to stop running. Adrenaline and desperation continued to kick in each time my legs grew rubbery and I thought about giving up. Finally, I came out of the woods and found myself in someone's backyard setting off their motion lights. The backyard lit up immediately but I kept running relentlessly, putting their house behind me in what seemed like only a second. Tears began to escape my eyes but the falling rain washed them away immediately as if it had no sympathy for my pain or fears. I dashed out into the street, immediately blinded by the headlights of an approaching police car as it skidded to a stop. The lights were so bright, I stopped and shielded my eyes.

Both the car's driver's door and passenger's door flew open. "Freeze!" the officers ordered me with their guns pointed directly at me as they leapt from the car. "Put your hands up, right now!"

I wanted to continue running but was scared they would shoot me down like a dog in the street. Out of fear, I closed my eyes tightly and waited for what seemed like forever for them to either kill me or slam me to the ground. My heart raced as the moments passed by. Unsure of what was taking them so long my eyes slowly opened to a different sort of darkness. There was no rain or thunder. The sounds of police sirens were no longer near. My heart and lungs no longer wanted to burst. My body and clothes were still drenched but I was no longer running or filled with fear.

*****

For a brief moment I had absolutely no idea where I was. Nothing looked familiar. But it was only temporary.

I sat up beneath the dingy blanket that covered my body and let my eyes adjust to the darkness, seeing movement around me and hearing voices. I realized it had all been a dream when the heavy stench of urine bombarded my nostrils, causing me to realize that I had been chased by the police but escaped to where I now laid. The smell was strong as ammonia. Bodies laid in cardboard boxes and blankets even dirtier than mine. Their pores gave off thick odors of musk, wine, and cigarettes that grew thicker each time a breeze passed under the bridge we were all gathered beneath. Voices were laced with curse words and filthy depictions of sex.

I placed my arms around myself and began to rock back and forth realizing where I was and that I'd fallen asleep. I was beneath a bridge in downtown Philly surrounded by homeless people. The realization made my stomach turn and my skin crawl but it was the only place I could escape to without getting caught by the police. I pulled my knees to my chest, longing for the comfort of Tyson's mansion or even a motel room.

I'd been in the same spot for nearly five hours. I chose the spot because I remembered Tyson and a few of his teammates coming here twice to feed the homeless and no one really coming out to bother them too often. The faces and clothes of the people around me nauseated me every second. Their skin was covered in thick, black dirt and their clothes were wrinkled and dirty from being worn over and over again. And their breath smelled horribly of cheap wine and decaying teeth. They were lost souls waiting to be buried. Life had passed them by a long time ago and they had eventually grown comfortable with it.

My skin felt filthy as I thought back to all I'd been through just to escape. I squeezed my knees to my chest much tighter at the thought how bad my life had turned out. Once again, I was lonely. Just as alone as I felt when I first arrived in Philly, I felt now. The only friend I had since arriving was Tyson. Now he was gone. The smell of his blood and the explosions of the gunshots would remain a part of me forever. No matter how badly I wanted them to, they would never fade.

Tears began to fall from my eyes as Tyson's last moments played in my head. I could still feel him in my arms as I held them around him tightly, whispering into his ear that he would be okay. Coming to grips with the realization that those words turned out to be a lie was a regret I was finding it so difficult to live with.

Tyson's death made my body shiver. But it wasn't just his memory that had me trembling. It was also the current moment. I'd come up so big only to turn around and fall so hard. It wasn't fair. I knew I had to get out of town as soon as possible now that Hardy had found me and was trying to frame me.

"Fuck going to prison!" I told myself out loud.

Out of the blue, a rat with a long, thick tail slowly approached my foot in search of food. I cringed at the sight of its nasty ass and kicked it making the rodent turn and run off. My feet were still bare, their heels now cut from the shards of broken beer bottles scattered underneath the bridge, but they were good enough to shoo the rat away.

The urge to go to the bank, grab some money out of my trust fund, and get a hotel room pulled at me constantly. But the fear of what could possibly be waiting for me outside of this bridge kept me imprisoned. I had no idea if my face was all over the news. I had no idea if the police believed Hardy's lies. Because of that uncertainty this bridge would become my home until I could figure out my next move. I wasn't even going to leave for food. I'd decided I would starve first.

Paranoia began to keep me on edge. It held me so tightly that sleep was nearly impossible. The sleep I got a moment ago was short, simply not enough. Closing my eyes for a considerable amount of time while surrounded by at least a hundred of society's rejects was out of the question. One of them would probably slice my throat wide open from ear to ear for what they thought was in my purse or for my blanket, the blanket I'd stolen from someone else.

To comfort myself when I first got there I paced the broken glass covered pavement constantly for hours in my bare feet, and wrapped my arms around myself tightly, rocking back and forth, while staring off into space. Either of those things took me far away from here. Sometimes they took me back to the memories of my father teaching me how to ride a bike before he became the sick twisted man who did all those bad things to me. The memories were so vivid I could sometimes smell the baked cookies my mother used to make before Aunt Lisa stole her from me. Those memories brought smiles to my face and joy to my heart, but only temporarily. Eventually I had to come back to my miserable ass reality.

The voice in my head began to laugh.

I wrapped my arms around my body much tighter than before.

The laugh grew louder.

"Smiley Face. Smiley Face. Can anyone see my Smiley Face?" I began to sing, ignoring the laughter in my head.

"*I know you hear me,*" the voice said.

"Smiley Face. Smiley Face. Can anyone see my Smiley Face?" I continued. With my chin on my knees, I began to rock back and forth in the dark.

"How long do you think *this* hairbrained scheme is going to last, Zaria?"

"Smiley Face. Smiley Face. Can anyone see my Smiley Face?" I said louder.

"Do you actually think these people don't know what you've done?"

"Smiley Face. Smiley Face. Can anyone see my Smiley Face?" I sang even more loudly, my body rocking faster and harder.

"Do you really think they don't know who you are?"

As I sang, I snuck glances at the people around me. Some came from underneath their blankets to stare at me. They hated me and I knew it.

"They know what you've done and who you are, Zaria. They're just waiting for the right moment to get the drop on your dumb ass."

I continued to sing, but paranoia began to make my glances more frantic.

Several people began to whisper among themselves.

Were they talking about me, I wondered? Were they discussing turning me in and splitting the reward money?

"*They're going to take you down, Zaria,*" the voice guaranteed.

Tears began to fall. "Smiley Face. Smiley Face. Can anyone see my Smiley Face?" I continued. My voice's volume was now at the top of my lungs.

As a figure stood and began to walk towards me, I placed my hand over the brick that I'd been keeping beside me since I arrived.

The figure got closer.

My grip on the brick grew tighter as the words I sung echoed loudly underneath every inch of the bridge.

"Ma'am," the figure said, now standing over me. I could

tell it was a man who'd had a rough life, possibly even a little sugar in his tank. "We're trying to sleep. Can you…"

"Get away from me!" I roared as my body jumped from the ground to my feet. "I'll bust your fucking head open, you homeless muthafucka!"

The man quickly reached into his pocket and pulled out a box cutter. "You crazy bitch!" he shouted. "I was trying to ask you nicely to shut the fuck up so we can sleep!"

"I'll kill your ass!" I promised him, not caring about his reasons for approaching me. "Get away from me!"

"Fuck you!" he fired back. "I should cut your damn ass from the neck to your belly button!"

"Cut her ass," someone instigated. "Cut the bitch then maybe we can get some damn sleep."

I looked around. "You muthafuckas think you're slick!" I yelled. "You just want to get the reward money! I'll kill all of you muthafuckas before I let you send me to prison!" I screamed, now beginning to quickly turn around in one spot, re-fusing to let anyone get behind me.

The man with the box cutter flipped his hand dismis-sively at me and walked away mumbling something. Each man and woman stared at me like I was crazy and as if they weren't plotting. But I knew better.

"I'll kill all of you bastards!" I promised.

Everything began to move fast.

People continued to whisper and gawk at me like some-thing was wrong. *Ain't that a bitch? They think I'm the crazy one.*

"Which one of you bitches wants to die first?" I asked.

No one answered.

"Try to get that muthafuckin reward money!" I yelled, still turning around so quickly I got dizzy. "I dare you! I fucking triple dare you!"

As I turned, my eyes locked onto another shadowy figure standing several feet away from me. I stopped in my tracks. The stranger hadn't been there before. It was as if they'd appeared from nowhere. Something about their stance and posture made them look as though they didn't belong among the homeless, as if they'd come from the world I was running from. But even more strangely, although the darkness concealed their face, something about them seemed weird. I couldn't put my finger on it though. It was too dark for me to even be able to tell if it was a woman or man, but something inside me definitely felt as if it recognized them. I squinted my eyes, trying to get a better look.

More homeless people chattered around me when the stranger standing ahead raised a hand towards me as if they wanted to shake my hand. I wondered why.

Suddenly, a loud explosion and bright flame came from the stranger's extended hand making me immediately realize they'd been holding a gun. Within a fraction of a second, I felt a bullet tear through my body with so much force it knocked me off my feet and flat onto my back. The air was knocked out of me.

The homeless people nearby screamed and immediately scattered.

My insides began to ache and sting terribly as if something inside of me was burning and tearing. I could feel blood pouring from my body and spreading underneath my back in a thick puddle. I attempted to talk but my body wouldn't allow it. Not even the voices that hung around my head tried to help me. From the ground I slowly allowed my eyes to journey back to where the stranger had been standing. They were now casually walking away in the opposite direction of where most of the homeless were fleeing, never looking back at me, not even once. And not caring that they were leaving me to die.

HARDY

Thirteen

Everything about Zaria and our moment last night enveloped my dream. I could see her, smell her, and feel her as if she was still actually near me. The sight of her tears and the repeated bullets I'd put in Tyson all played over and over in my dream. But oddly, although dreaming, I could sense someone near me, standing over me. I forced myself to wake up, opening my eyes to the sun shining through my hotel window. My body was covered in sweat.

"Must've been a rough nightmare," a woman's voice said, startling the hell out of me. I turned over quickly to find Selena's crazy ass standing by my bed with a cold stare on her face and her arms folded over her breasts.

"What the hell…" I said, sitting up immediately and wondering what she was doing way up here in Philly let alone inside my hotel room.

"You've been tossing, turning, and saying Zaria's name over and over in your sleep for the past hour." Her voice contained no emotion. "You and her must've had quite a busy night," she said sifting through the stack of hundreds in her hand.

"What the fuck are you doing here?" "And how did you find me?"

"I'm the police, Hardy," she stated plainly.

After hearing that answer I knew there was no need in asking her how she'd gotten into my room. I wanted to tell her to get the fuck out but I knew there was no use. "What do you want?" I asked climbing out of bed in my boxers.

"You already know why I'm here," she responded.

"I already told you that I'm not marrying that bitch," I said, immediately realizing what she wanted. It was Friday so there was only one day left. I slipped my jeans on nonchalantly.

"Look, Hardy," she said quickly. "I'm in a bind. I really need you to come through for me on this. I'll up your cut to three thousand."

"What part of the word *no* do you not understand, Selena?"

She charged around the bed. "Hardy, I'll pay you five thousand dollars. The woman gave me ten thousand and she has a sister who wants to do it too once she see's that this shit works."

"Shit," I said, suddenly remembering to check the tracking device. Like an insomniac I'd been up all night watching television and keeping a close eye on Zaria's movements. I didn't feel myself finally drift off to sleep. Before my eyes finally closed for good the tracker showed Zaria was somewhere underneath a bridge downtown. She'd been there for several hours.

"Did you hear me?" Selena asked, now sounding desperate. "I'll pay you five thousand dollars. And just think, you never have to see her again after the weddin'. Just stay married for two years, then get a divorce. Simple…right?"

Ignoring Selena's offer and brushing her to the side, I went around to the other side of the bed to check the tracker. I really needed to know Zaria's whereabouts. The device was in my backpack which hung from the back of a chair.

"Hardy," Selena said, grabbing me by the arm before I

could go in my pocket.

I snatched away. "Get the fuck off me."

Selena grabbed my arm again, this time with force. She snatched me towards her. Her face was now dead serious and her eyes glared into mine with no intimidation. "Don't you ever snatch away from me again," she ordered. "I'm a muthafuckin' cop. Don't you ever forget that."

"I don't give a flying fuck who you are," I told her. "I'm not marrying that women or anybody else. Get that shit through your thick ass skull. Now, can you get the hell out of my room? I got important shit to do."

Selena didn't budge. "You're goin' to do this, Hardy," she said point blankly. "Besides, you owe me fifteen thousand anyway. I just didn't have the heart to turn you in yet." She paused. "I just might want some more dick first."

My cell phone rang. Recognizing the ring tone as Tayvia's, I brushed past Selena to grab it from the dresser. "Hello?" I said, answering the call.

Tayvia's voice was hysterical and full of both pain and sadness as she began to tell me that the police had been called to Tyson's house last night by a neighbor who heard gunshots. When they got there, they found Tyson's body on the floor dead, his chest riddled with bullets. They immediately believed Zaria did it.

Obviously the news wasn't a surprise to me. I didn't know what she was expecting from me though, or of all people why she chose to call me. Preoccupied with Selena, I was ready to tell Tayvia I was sorry for her loss and all that, but I had my own problems to deal with. Before I could get it out though, she said the cops had found evidence suggesting that Zaria hadn't committed the brutal murder alone. They believed someone else was with her.

My body instantly froze.

"Damn it," I whispered as she rambled on. My ears were keyed in on every word at that point. "What kind of evidence do they have?" I asked, hoping she could tell me so I would know exactly where and how to begin covering my ass.

Tayvia said she didn't know. The police hadn't given her that information yet.

"Shit," I said in frustration.

I started to worry, seeing my plans possibly blow up in my face. My heart began to pound a little harder as slight panic set in. Visions of myself sitting in prison for the rest of my life for Tyson's death began to blaze throughout my thoughts. But I forced myself to stay calm. I quickly decided that I would stay connected to Tayvia for a little while and pump her for information until I found out what evidence the cops had. I told her I would meet her later.

"Hardy," Selena said, stepping towards me. "We got shit to talk about. Whatever you and that bitch are discussin' can wait."

"Hardy, who is that?" Tayvia asked through heavy sobs.

I turned my head away from Selena. "It's nobody, sweetheart," I told her.

"Are you sure?"

"Yeah, but you okay, Tayvia? You seem to be taking this hard."

"Hardy," Tayvia spoke with tremendous sadness in her voice. Her world sounded destroyed. "I'm going through so much right now. I really need someone to be there for me. Do you promise that we'll meet up later?"

"I promise," I told her.

"Hardy!" Selena yelled in the deepest voice she could muster.

"I gotta go, Tayvia," I said quickly before hanging up. "Bitch!" I screamed at Selena. "Didn't you see I was on the damn phone?"

"Fuck the phone!" she shouted back. "You and me got business to talk over! Details, damn it. Now, I need you at the courthouse tomorrow by two."

Fed up, I went to the door and snatched it open. "Selena, get the fuck out!"

Selena slowly walked towards me with a spiteful look on her face. She stopped directly in front of me. Looking me in the eyes she said calmly, "I tried to play nice, but that shit didn't work. So now I'm gonna have to be a very, very, *very* mean bitch. I'm givin' you an ultimatum," she said. Her lips were so close to mine we were nearly kissing. "Either you marry that Haitian lady tomorrow, or I'm turnin' your black ass into the police."

"Turning me in for what?"

Selena gave me a frightening smile, a smile with something sick and twisted hidden behind it but obvious at the same time.

"Turning me in for what?" I asked again, definitely wanting to know exactly what she meant. I stepped in front of the doorway.

With that strange smile still sculpted into her face she winked. "Try me and you'll see," she said. "Now, get the fuck out of my way."

Not budging, my eyes stared at her. My fists clenched. I never was the type to take kindly to threats. I wanted to cave her face in.

The smile disappeared from Selena's face.

"I said get-the-fuck-out of my way," she demanded, sliding her hand underneath the bottom of her shirt and resting it on her gun. The look on her face begged for confrontation. "I'm not sayin' it as the bitch you've been givin' dick to for the past several weeks…I'm sayin' it as a cop."

After several moments I moved, realizing I was in a no-win situation. As she walked out, I slammed the door behind her and rested my back against it, wondering what she meant by turning me in. Did she mean once I killed Zaria? Did she know about Tyson's murder yet? Was she going to turn me in for that? Damn, none of this shit was a part of my plan. Suddenly, I remembered Zaria and the tracker. I ran across the room, snatched it from my jacket pocket, and looked at the screen. Hahnemann University Hospital, it read. What was she doing there, I wondered?

"This shit is getting crazy," I told myself.

Moments later, a knock came at the door.

Still trying to figure out why Zaria was at the hospital, I sprinted across the room and opened the door. All thoughts of Zaria disappeared when I saw Santiago standing on my doorstep. The only thoughts on my mind were what was she doing here? And did she see Selena leaving?

ZARIA
Fourteen

I began to shake…attempted to shout.

Someone was headed toward me. And nothing could help me.

No one could change the fact that my killer had a gun.

Then, the gun exploded.

I screamed, wakening from the nightmare immediately. Paranoia made me look around the room frantically.

"He's trying to kill me!" I screamed, terrified that the shooter was somewhere near. "He's trying to kill me!"

Knowing I had to get away, I began to snatch the IVs and other thin, narrow tubes from my arms, causing the machines beside my bed to give off long, stretched beeping sounds.

"I've got to get out of here!" I screamed. "He's got a gun! He's gonna kill me!"

A heavy-set nurse charged into the room as I snatched the sheets off, and attempted to swing my legs over the side of the bed. Strangely, I felt so sore I couldn't get up. It was weird, but I didn't give up. I groaned as I attempted to lift myself again.

The nurse wrapped her arms around me, attempting to keep me on the bed. "Sweetheart, you're safe."

"He's going to kill me!" I told her, attempting to escape her arms and expecting the shooter to appear at any moment, killing us both.

"No one's going to hurt you," she assured me. "You're safe here."

"No, I'm not," I replied while continuously trying to escape her arms.

Suddenly, it dawned on me that I didn't know where I was. My mind began to race. My head swiveled quickly taking in the bland decor.

"Sweetheart," the nurse said, grabbing my shoulders and attempting to look into my eyes. "Yes, you are. You're in the hospital."

"He's going to come in here and finish me off," I stated quickly, the denial rolling off of my tongue.

"I promise, you're going to be okay here," she responded, now looking directly into my eyes. Her tone was filled with genuine concern. "I promise that no one's going to hurt you. You're safe here."

I looked deeply into the nurse's eyes and saw something in them that assured me she deserved my trust. I calmed down.

"There you go," she said softly, easing me back into the bed and under the sheets.

My head lay back onto the pillows.

The nurse pressed buttons on the machines beside my bed and the loud stretched beeping sound stopped.

"You're at Hannehan University Hospital," she informed. "You were brought in last night suffering from a gunshot wound to the bottom right side of your abdomen."

My jaw dropped. I placed my hand underneath my gown and felt a bandage over the wound. Now calm, I could feel the pain. And everything became so clear to me.

"It's going to be fine," she assured me. "You're a strong woman, being shot and then giving birth."

"Huh," I whispered with sadness after hearing her say I had given birth. Immediately, I began to break down. Tears fell from my closed eyes as visions of my dead baby being pulled from my stomach with a bullet hole ripped into its body tortured me, shattering my heart.

"Noooooooooo, pleaseeeeee," I whined, wondering why all this had happened to me. My hands gently caressed my stomach. The life I had grown so used to loving and nurturing was gone, taken away from me by a stranger's bullet.

"Because of the gunshot," she continued, "we had to sedate you for six hours and give you an emergency C-section."

"Oh my God!"

She placed a hand on my shoulder. "Don't worry. Miss, your baby is alive. He was born premature."

My eyes closed tightly and more tears began to form, this time from joy. *Devin would be so proud of me*, I thought to myself.

My eyes opened.

"But…the gun shot?" I questioned, wanting to know how the baby survived.

"He's in our Neonatal Intensive Care Unit for babies. We call it the NICU," she told me. "Thankfully the bullet missed him. But as I said before, he was born premature at only one pound, three ounces, so he's in pretty bad shape. The doctors said you were about twenty-three weeks. Babies born that prematurely will suffer respiratory and digestive problems, and possibly brain hemorrhages. The little fella has got a helluva fight ahead of him."

"Can I see him?" I asked, wanting to hold my little boy in my arms. I attempted to lift myself out of anxiousness, but got hit with some excruciating pain.

"Sure," she replied. "We'll wheel you down there later this afternoon. He's having a ton of tests done on him, so until then try to relax. You just had a C-section and surgery to repair a severe gun-shot wound all in the same day. It's gonna take several days for you to heal properly."

I tuned my fat nurse out and wondered if my son looked more like me or Devin. I wanted to call. I wanted to call Devin and let him know that I'd just had his child and that I was going to name him Devin Junior. He deserved to know. "Can I call his father?"

"Yes," she said. "But before you do, I have to ask you a few questions."

Something told me I wasn't going to like the questions.

"We didn't find any identification on you. We checked your purse and found several names on different documents and pieces of mail. What's your name?" she asked.

"Tayvia Roth," I lied quickly. If the cops were looking for me, the last thing I wanted to do was have them find me here in such a weakened state.

"Do you know the person who shot you?" she asked

"No," I answered.

"So Tayvia, do you know why they shot you?"

I shook my head, ready to get off of the subject.

"Okay," she said, seeing that I didn't want to talk about it. "Well, the police are gonna want to talk to you. They've been here twice already."

The mere mention of the word *police* sent my heartbeat through the damn roof. My body rose up in the bed, disregarding the pain I felt through my mid-section. "No police," I told her quickly. "I don't want to talk to them. I don't want to see them."

"It's okay," she tried to assure me. "They're just going to talk to you and gather enough information to find the person who did this to you."

I wasn't trying to hear that at all, knowing that the police were probably looking for me for Tyson's murder. "I don't want to talk to them," I insisted.

"I'm sorry," she said understandingly. "I know you're scared, but it's hospital policy. We have to notify the police any time we have a gunshot victim. Plus, we need your insurance information now that we have your name, and we need to fill out the birth certificate along with any other forms regarding your son."

While she smiled, my heart was beating in my ears. Visions of me spending the rest of my life in prison, or possibly getting the electric chair had me so scared my body began to tremble.

"Now, just lay back and get some rest." She handed me some pain pills and a cold cup of water. "We're gonna have to keep you for a few more days for observation. Then you should be able to go home."

My body was filled with worry. Resting would be impossible, knowing the police would be walking into my room at any moment. How could a bitch rest with that shit on her mind? If anything, I needed to get the hell out of here as soon as possible. But with a freshly healing gunshot wound and a stomach full of stitches, shit was going to be super fucking difficult. My brain started racing with thoughts.

"When we release you, who's going to come pick you up?" she questioned.

"My husband," I lied, suddenly thinking of Devin again.

"Okay," she said, giving me a warm smile. "Get yourself some rest. And I'll let you know when someone will roll you down to see your son. Now, understand Tayvia, he's extremely small, and there's lots of tubes."

I nodded sadly.

As she smiled and turned to walk out of the room, I spoke up.

"Please tell me that my purse is in here with me." All I could think about was all those homeless people rummaging through my shit.

She opened a small closet door on the other side of the room. "Is this it?" she asked."

I let out a small sigh of relief. "Yes, it is. Can you hand it to me please?"

"Here you go, sweetheart." She said handing me the two thousand dollar bag. "You can hit the little buzzer beside your bed if you need anything." She handed me my purse

"Thanks," I said, before opening my purse.

I was in complete shock that the homeless people hadn't robbed me blind. After the small scene I'd caused I just knew they had it out for me. However, after seeing me get shot and almost dying in front of their eyes, I guess they felt bad. I wondered who called the ambulance as I noticed that all my belongings were still there.

I immediately grabbed the cell phone and looked at the battery life. I had a little bit of power left, so I called Devin, hoping with all my heart he would answer. My hopes turned out to be in vein. After calling him twice, there was no answer. I decided to text him.

Baby, where are you. Call me as soon as u can.
Our son was just born. He looks just like u.
I luv you with all my heart.
Your wife to be- Zaria

Although saddened by not being able to reach Devin, now wasn't the time to sulk over it. My worry about the police was too overwhelming. Desperately needing to get out of here, I called Eric. Surprisingly, after several rings, he answered.

"Eric," I said, sounding like a scared child, "I've been calling you constantly.

"Milan?" he asked, sounding as if he wasn't sure it was me. Loud music blasted from his back ground.

"Yes, it's me."

"Damn, luv. I heard about Tyson. That's fucked up! You straight?" he asked with worry in his voice. I was glad he didn't think I was involved.

"I'm fine Eric. Luckily, I wasn't at his place when all of that happened."

"Damn, luv, I'm just glad you're okay." He sighed like he really cared. "What's up with that crazy ass message you left me?"

"That's not important now. Besides someone may be listening," I told him. "Look, I need you, sweetheart. I just had a child and I'm all alone. I really need you. Please come pick me up from the hospital."

"A child as in a baby? Wait, when were you pregnant? Pick you up?" he said, as if the request sounded crazy.

"Yes, I need you."

"Milan, I'm in the middle of something right now."

I could hear female voices along with the loud music. "Eric, I don't have anyone else," I said, sounding more desperate than before. "I don't have any place else to go and I don't have anyone else to call."

"Milan, I would like to help but…"

"Someone tried to kill me, Eric," I said before he could finish his sentence. "They shot me. I think they're trying to do to me what they did to Tyson."

"What the fuck?" he asked not knowing what to say or do. "Who shot you?"

"I don't know. All I know is I'm scared to death they may try it again. I don't want to die. I don't want to be erased from this earth."

He sighed heavily.

"Please. I need to stay at your place for a few nights, that's all."

"Milan, I don't know about…"

"Eric, please. I'm begging you. If you don't do this you may as well pull the trigger yourself."

"Alright," he said, reluctance heavy in his voice. "Calm down. I got you."

"Thank you, Eric," I said happily. "Thank you so much."

After hanging up, I laid in the bed in utter silence, wondering how my future was going to turn out. Everything was stacked against me and I was facing it all by myself. But with Eric now in it, maybe I would be able to beat this thing. I wasn't sure but I was definitely going to try and use him, his money, and his resources as long as I could. Maybe our relationship would blossom into something so much more.

ZARIA

Fifteen

Suddenly, my cell phone rang waking me out of my sleep. Hoping it was Devin; I turned over in the strange bed, grabbed my cell from the nightstand and looked at the screen. My heart filled with disappointment seeing it was another call from the nurses at the hospital. Weren't they smart enough to realize I'd left against doctors orders, not interested in returning. I pressed the reject button, tossed the phone back on the nightstand, and laid on my back staring at the ceiling. I could hear voices from the television at a low volume from the room across the hall. Someone had been staying in that room that I hadn't met yet.

It had been two days since I left the hospital. Thankfully, Eric kept his word and picked me up in the wee hours of the morning. Because of that I was able to get out of there before the police came back to visit me about my shooting.

I'd been extremely worried about what other questions Eric would ask me about Tyson and what new developments he'd heard. So far so good. The police were at least keeping the media quiet.

Luckily, Eric never even asked if I'd stayed with Tyson the night of the benefit or saw him afterward. He seemed less and less distraught about what happened to Tyson as the days moved on. I thought back to how I'd cried in Eric's arms after being released telling him I prayed the killer would get the death penalty. I truly hoped Hardy did. But I couldn't let Eric know that I knew anything.

Since leaving, the hospital had been repeatedly calling my cell about the baby. I never answered again after telling them that I was waiting on Junior's father. Though I desperately wanted to see my baby and even bring him home when he became well enough. I wanted to wait until I could reach Devin before visiting. In my head, the vision of the two of us walking into the hospital holding hands as a couple played itself over and over repeatedly.

I kept hope and faith that the three of us would eventually leave that hospital together as a proud loving family one day. That portrait even played throughout my dreams often as I slept. The only problem was that no matter how wonderful and memorable the dream, awakening to reality *always* followed. I was always alone in this huge bed in Eric's chaotic home.

Slowly slipping from beneath the sheets, I placed my legs over the side of the bed, and my feet onto the carpeted floor. I winced and groaned a little. The stitches in my stomach from the C-section stung and burned non- stop. My healing bullet wound did the same. Also, my back and ribs still ached from the stomping I took from Hardy. With so much pain flowing through my body and low dose medication to numb it, all of my movements were slow. Sudden movements would put me in so much pain tears came to my eyes.

I opened the door of my bedroom and heard music coming from downstairs. Since arriving at Eric's house, I hadn't truly gotten any sleep. His house was a party spot, with all types of people coming and going. It wasn't a sanctuary like Tyson's had been, but it was still pretty luxurious. I had to remind myself that Eric's salary was nothing compared to Tyson's, but he did manage to afford a three car garage, and five bedrooms. Its living room was nearly the size of my entire apartment back in New York. The double doors of his foyer were glass and two-storied. They reminded me of the ones Tony Montana stood in as he shot Manny in the movie, *Scarface*. The entire home was nicely furnished, carpeted, and plasma screens decked nearly every room, including the bathrooms. It would do for now.

I slowly hobbled my way down the split staircase and into the living room to find some skinny white Brittney Spears looking bitch in only a pair of tight panties sucking off Eric as he sat on the couch with his head back and his eyes closed. I felt so betrayed. Another white bitch in her bra and panties was snorting coke from the table. The scene made me spaz out. For-getting my wounds and pain, I pulled the bitch who was snort-ing coke by her blonde hair.

"Get out!" I screamed directly into her face, while winc-ing in pain.

Eric's eyes opened quickly. The bitch giving him head pulled his dick from her mouth immediately and looked at me.

"You get your tramp ass out of here, too!" I ordered.

"What the hell are you doing, Milan!" Eric asked, tuck-ing himself back into his jeans.

Both white bitches looked bewildered.

"Are you bitches deaf?" I asked, snatching a lamp from a nearby table ready to split some heads wide the fuck open. "I said get your nasty asses out of here! This man is taken!"

Eric jumped and leapt in front of me as both ladies began to gather their clothes. "Milan, you out of line!" he said.

"*I'm* out of line, Eric?" I asked. "*You're* the one up in here getting your damn dick sucked by these Malibu Barbie ass bitches while I'm right up stairs! I'm trying to recover!"

"So what! This is *my* house!" he yelled. "Who I fuck or wherever I fuck up in here is my business!"

Both women scurried out of the room, putting on their clothes as they ran. As they neared the foyer, I launched the lamp sitting on one of the end tables at their backs. It missed by inches and shattered against the wall.

Eric's eyes widened at the sight. "What the fuck is your problem!" he screamed. "Are you crazy? That damn lamp was an antique. It cost me thirty five hundred dollars!"

"Fuck that lamp!" I said, furiously. "Since I got here you've had one groupie bitch after another running through here!"

"That's how I live Milan! Besides, you're just visiting!"

I stopped in my tracks and spit fire through my eyes. "That's hurtful, Eric," I told him with a straight face.

"Milan, you have no idea about what I'm into," Eric replied with a sincere face. "This is all too much for you."

I stood still wondering what he meant. Since my first day in his house he'd been having women of nearly all nationalities prancing through the house half naked, partying, and going in and out of his bedroom like a revolving door. I wanted a better life for Eric. I wanted to change all of that. "I'm just trying to protect our home, Eric."

"Milan, what part of 'This is my house' are you having the most fucking trouble understanding?" he questioned. "I do what hell I want to do in here! And this is not *our* home!"

Tears formed in my eyes as my heart saddened. I knew he wasn't mine, but I couldn't help feeling disrespected. "Even if it means hurting me, Eric?" I asked, my voice growing soft. "Even if it means breaking my heart?"

Eric looked at me strangely. "Luv, what are you talking about?"

"I'm talking about *us*," I told him. "What we're supposed to be building."

Eric looked at me like I was crazy. "Hold up, Milan. Don't get this arrangement twisted. I never said you and me were building anything. You needed a place to stay for a little while, so I'm letting you crash here because I don't want to see you in the streets. That's it and that's all. There's no relationship. You got two weeks, tops."

"But, baby," I pleaded stepping towards him. "What

about our first kiss? Don't you like me?"

Eric took a step back. "Yeah, I like you," he said, "but you're moving too fast. Besides, I'm thinking you may need to get checked out. Postpartum or some shit like that could be affecting you."

Hearing that shit infuriated me so badly that I couldn't think of anything at all to say. I stood there breathing so heavily my breasts heaved back and forth against my pajama top. My fists clenched as chattering voices began to fill my head.

"Yo, luv, you straight?"

I hated the way Eric always asked if I was straight.

The voices in my head multiplied. I had no idea what they were saying.

"Milan," Eric said, reaching to place a hand on my shoulder.

"Don't touch me!" I screamed, ceasing the chattering voices abruptly. My eyes were as wild looking as a group of blood thirsty animals.

Eric snatched his hand back quickly and stared at me with a confused look on his face. I stormed past him and went back upstairs to my bedroom, passing the other bedroom along the way. I still could only hear the T.V. and it was starting to freak me out. I turned the knob, but it was locked. So, I knocked.

When no one answered, I quickly rushed off to my room, slamming the door behind me. I placed my back against the door. My fury and anger suddenly changed to a miserably depressing sadness in only a split second.

A knock came from the other side of the door.

"Milan, you sure you don't have anywhere else to go?" Eric had the nerve to ask.

Tears started falling. "Just leave me alone."

"Okay luv, but you straight, right?"

"Fuck you, Eric!"

Seconds later, I heard him go back downstairs.

My mind thought about the repeated rejection I kept facing in my life. No one wanted me. No one wanted to love me. Everyone seemed to always treat me like I'm never good enough, like I don't deserve to be loved. I guess that's why I truly embraced becoming a mother. I thought the baby would give me the things I was looking for, even more so, I thought it would give me Devin.

I walked across the room to the nightstand, grabbed my cell and called Devin again. "Please, God," I whispered in prayer. "Let him answer this time." My ears listened intently to each ring, hoping to hear the love of my life pick up. "Please, God," I whispered again, closing my eyes as the phone rang again. My hand clutched it tightly.

Despite my prayers, instead of hearing Devin's voice, I got his voicemail again. My heart sunk. My tears ran down my cheeks from behind the darkness of my eyelids. I hung up then realized I had a text message. I clicked a few buttons then froze. It was a message from Devin.

Got your message. Was with a client.
Miss u so much…tell me exactly where u r.
I'll come get you.

Hopping up, I ran to the dresser where I'd seen a Sports Illustrated magazine and looked at the name on the back. Realizing the publication was addressed to Eric, I texted back so quickly, I thought my fingers were having a seizure. I breathed heavily while sobbing with joy as I typed in Eric's address. I knew it was foul to have him pick me up from Eric's spot, but Eric had violated the trust in our relationship. And even though I pressed send, I decided to call Devin anyway. I needed to hear his voice. Once again, I got the voicemail.

"Devin, I'm so glad you texted back. I'm so glad you're coming for me. Just call me baby to let me know when," I whimpered. "Our baby is at Hahnemann University Hospital in the NICU. We've got to go there. Devin, I know I screwed up. I'm sorry. Sweetheart, I'm *so* sorry. But don't take it out on our child. He needs you. He deserves a father. And I'm so glad he'll have you in his life."

I spilled my heart to Devin desperately until the voice-mail clicked me off. With my eyes closed I just stood there with visions of Devin, me and our child being a family keeping me calm. Above my utter silence I could hear the television across the room still at a low volume. I opened my eyes, looked at the plasma screen and gasped at what was on it. My eyeballs grew to the size of watermelons and my heartbeat took off. A frightening feeling held me captive.

"Nooooooo," I whispered, shaking my head in disbelief at the photo on the six o'clock news about my cousin Kenneth. He'd been murdered and found in an alleyway behind a meat market downtown.

My body was totally frozen in one spot as the newscaster spoke. He was standing at the murder scene. Yellow caution tape could be seen roping off the area behind him. I couldn't believe what I was seeing and hearing. Suddenly my name and picture appeared on the screen as a possible suspect.

"Oh, shit," I mouthed just before letting my jaw drop.

My knees grew so weak I fell to the bed. The room started spinning around me. I wondered if Eric was watching downstairs, or even the nurses at the hospital. What about Devin? Would he find out and decide to leave me here? My heart felt like it was going to explode through my chest.

Philadelphia had been my safe haven. It had been my reason for escaping my past for this long. But now everyone in Philly was going to know who I really was. There would be no where in the entire city for me to hide now.

"Oh, God, no," I whispered. "Oh, God, no."

HARDY

Sixteen

With one final upward thrust I exploded, filling her pussy as she straddled me. The amount was so much and the feeling was so intense my body felt like it had released my entire spirit, instead of just my energy. It totally drained me. The climax did the same for Tayvia also, causing her body to collapse onto mine. The both of us breathed heavily. Our heartbeats matched each other's and within moments both of us were asleep.

I woke up two hours later and drowsily looked over at the digital clock on the nightstand beside the bed. It was six o'clock in the evening and I needed to get back to the hospital.

Alone.

Slowly, I slid from beneath her head, which had been resting on my chest, which I hated. Trying to move as quickly as possible, I began to put my clothes on glancing at her every now and then, hoping not to wake her. The pussy had been okay... but the last thing I wanted right now was conversation. After getting dressed I grabbed my keys from the nightstand and slowly tipped towards the door.

Her body shifted among the sheets. After coming to a

comfortable position her arm reached out for me expecting my body to still be lying beside her own. When Tayvia didn't feel me, her eyes slowly opened. Not seeing me in bed she looked towards the door just in time to see me reaching for the door knob.

"Baby," Tayvia said from the bed. "Where are you going?"

"Shit," I whispered as I turned to her. I hated the fact that she called me baby when we'd only known each other a week. Her clingy type personality reminded me too much of Zaria. "I've got to go handle some things."

"You were going to leave without telling me?" she asked, sitting up in bed with starry eyes.

"Oh, you were sleeping peacefully, so I didn't want to wake you up. I was going to go handle my business real quick. Then come back and wake you with some of your favorite, Chinese food."

The truth was that I had no intentions of coming back. She'd given me the pussy, easily. She'd been tagging along for days since Tyson's murder and the police wasn't giving her any info about their evidence. So the last thing I wanted or needed in my life right now was a committed relationship. Crazily, that's what Tayvia thought we now had after one mediocre night of sex. She had to be cut off.

Tayvia climbed out of bed and walked completely naked towards me. "Your business can wait, baby," she said, wrapping her arms around me and kissing me on the neck. They were wet. Lovingly wet. "Come back to bed, baby."

Growing annoyed I began to back away. "No, Tayvia," I said with frustration in my voice. "It can't wait."

"What can be more important than me?" she asked, still clinging to me and damn near spitting on my back.

"Tayvia, I've got to get back to the hospital and check on my newborn son," I finally admitted.

Her eyes lit up and a smile stretched across her face like a child at Christmas. "Why didn't you say that in the first place?" she asked. "Let me get dressed so I can come with you. It'll only take a minute."

I sighed as she turned to grab her clothes. "Look, Tayvia, I'm going to go by myself."

"Hardy, don't worry," she said, sliding her panties on and reaching for her jeans. "I don't mind coming with you."

The goofy bitch was acting like she hadn't heard me. "Tayvia," I said loudly. "Did you hear me?"

Ignoring me and continuing to get dressed she began to ramble. "I bet he looks just like you. And I'll bet he has your eyes and everything." She paused. "Baby, how come you haven't let me go inside the hospital with you yet? I've been with you too many days now."

"Please Tayvia, enough," I told her.

"Hardy, I can't wait for us to bring him home."

Us, I noted silently. What did she mean by *us*? We had only known each other a week. "Tayvia," I said again.

"I'm going to spoil him," she continued. "As soon as he's home I'm going to buy him so many clothes and toys. I'm going to smother him with kisses. Hardy, I promise that he's never going to have to worry about anything. We're going to give him whatever he wants."

As she spoke it was as if Tayvia was in her own world, I couldn't help but notice. It was as if she'd exed everyone else out, including myself. The shit seemed more suspicious by the minute. But more importantly, all this shit about *us* and *we* was sounding like I was caught in the twilight zone.

"I can't wait to take him out and show him off," she said slipping on one of Tyson's old Jerseys. She had been wearing a different one each day since his death. "I'm going to take him to the park, the ice cream parlor, and anywhere else he wants to go."

Silently I watched her ramble on. The fact that she was making plans for *my* son like she was his mother or like we'd even discussed her being a part of his life had me contemplating on smoking her ass right where she stood. I wouldn't relive the

Zaria bullshit again. Besides, where was all this coming from?

The two of us had been kicking it with each other since Tyson's murder, but it wasn't serious, at least not to me it wasn't. And it definitely hadn't been serious enough for me to allow her to go back into the NICU to see my little man. I still couldn't believe that she still wanted to be around me after I told her I'd recently discovered that I had a newborn son in the hospital. The last thing I expected was for the bitch to become his adoptive mother after one afternoon of good sex.

"It's going to be so wonderful," she said, looking somewhere into space dreamily.

Her mannerisms sent chills down my spine. "Tayvia," I interrupted.

She continued rambling to herself.

"Tayvia!" I shouted.

She finally stopped and looked at me.

"You're not going," I said sternly.

"I have to," she answered, looking as if what I'd just said was silly. "If we're going to take care of him, I need to meet..."

"Tayvia, there is no *we.*"

She looked at me as if she didn't understand.

"Look, you're seeing these past several days for more than what they are. I'm not interested in a relationship right now."

She looked at me in disbelief. "But after Tyson's murder you promised me you would be here for me," she responded. "You told me when we first met that you were one of the good ones."

"I know but I can't do this. I'm sorry."

Her eyes dropped to the floor as she fell to the bed. The look of sadness she had on her face was much too extreme for the end of a five day relationship. It looked more like the one a woman would wear after a ten year one.

"We can still be friends, Tayvia."

She sat in silence. Her eyes never blinked as they continued to stare at the floor beneath her.

A part of me felt sorry for her but I didn't acknowledge it. "I gotta go," I said and headed for the door.

"Hardy," Tayvia called.

I turned to her as I opened the door.

Her face chillingly had no expression as she raised it to stare at the wall. Her right foot was now patting the floor. "You shouldn't make promises you can't keep," she said, her voice just as emotionless as the look on her face. She never turned to look at me. "And you shouldn't tell people you're something you're not."

Her voice had an eerie tone to it. But even more so, there seemed like there was something threatening hidden inside it.

*****

As I drove to the hospital my mind was totally focused on the tiny baby lying in NICU. He'd been on my mind relentlessly, his face dwelling inside my head since seeing him for the first time four days ago. I was even seeing him in my dreams. His presence was constant and welcomed. And I wished with all my heart he would grow to be healthy. Finding out that he'd been born prematurely and had countless issues broke my heart.

As I thought back even more to the first time I saw him after going to spy on Zaria in the hospital, I got emotional. I had no idea exactly what I was going to do, if anything. All I knew was that I had to work on framing Zaria some more, and needed to figure out why she was in the hospital.

When I got to the information desk and asked if there had been a patient there named Zaria Hopkins recently, they said no. I knew something wasn't right because the tracker had definitely indicated that she had been there up until an hour before I arrived. After asking a nurse to check a second time and getting the same answer, I got irate.

"I know she's here," I remembered carrying on.

"No, she isn't," two women announced at once.

"Yes, she is," I shot back.

I ended up pulling out one of Zaria's wanted posters from my back pocket and showing it to the two ladies at the desk and the security guard they'd called on me. Luckily, another nurse passing by recognized her immediately. She said that Zaria had given another name after being brought in for a gunshot wound. She said that Zaria had also given birth and had just been released an hour ago against doctor's orders.

I remembered going ballistic and out to the parking lot to think for a second, wondering who had shot her and why. But her words were truly holding my mind captive. The fact that the nurse said that Zaria had been a little over five months pregnant made me sick to my stomach. Five and a half months ago was around the time we'd had sex. There was no ignoring the obvious. The child could've been mine.

Knowing the hospital wouldn't be allowed to give me the information I needed, I called Santiago. We'd just had a serious argument back at the hotel. She'd discovered that me and Selena were fucking and came all the way down to Philly to let me know. Although she had stormed out of the hotel room screaming she never wanted to see me again, I knew she was the only person who I could trust to help me. I called her and pleaded for help. Reluctantly she turned around on the highway back to New York and came to the hospital, making it absolutely clear she was only doing it for the baby, not for me. She ordered a paternity test. *Police orders.*

Just as I thought about the police. I heard sirens. WHOOP-WHOOP!

The sound snapped me from the memory. I looked in my rearview to see an unmarked car.

"Damn it," I said, pulling my truck to the curb.

After putting the truck in park, I looked in my side view to see the car's driver's side door open. A second later, Selena stepped out in heels, a tight fitting skirt, and a breast hugging cropped shirt. She had a Louis Vuitton bag on her shoulder and applied lip gloss as she walked toward me. She looked totally different from the dyke bitch she always carried herself as. I jumped out of my truck.

"What the fuck?" I asked angrily as she stepped in front of me and folded her arms over her breasts. "Didn't I tell your crazy ass we're done?"

"Hardy, I could give a damn about that," she said as cars passed by. "I'm here because we had a deal."

Damn, I thought to myself. "Look, I was going to call you about that," I lied. "I just found out Zaria…"

"Was pregnant with your baby boy," she said, finishing my sentence before I could.

"How the hell did you know?" I asked, staring at her strangely.

"I'm the police, Hardy," she answered. "There's not too much I don't know. I even know who shot the bitch."

"Who?" I asked.

She smiled devilishly.

"Who damn it?" I really needed to know.

"How much money you got?"

"What? Bitch please. Who shot her?" I repeated.

"You got any drug dealers I can rob?"

"You know what Selena? You're one crazy bitch. I'ma ask you one more time…"

"Me," she admitted, cutting me off. "I shot her."

My face squinted for seconds. "Why?" I wanted to know. "You did that for me?"

"Hell no! I shot the bitch because she has been ruinin' my business and my sex life. If you weren't obsessed with lookin' for her everyday of your life you could be screwin' me and givin' me good dick nightly."

Anger took over me. I'd just processed it all. "Are you fucking crazy?" I screamed on her. "Do you know the bullet was only inches away from hitting my son! And do you know that's why she had to have him prematurely!"

"Fuck you and fuck your son!" she shouted back while reaching in her purse and pulling out a walkie talkie. "I told you that I wasn't playin' nice with you anymore. I told you that if

you didn't show up for the weddin', there would be conse-
quences!"

I stared at her, not liking where this was headed.

"You missed the weddin', Hardy!" she yelled. "Now, it's
time to pay for it!"

"What are you talking about?" I asked. "What conse-
quences?"

"You're about to be arrested for murder," she spoke with
a spiteful look on her face. She spoke into her walkie talkie, re-
questing for back up and telling the dispatcher where she was.

I stepped back nervously. My heart started pounding.
"Selena, what the fuck are you talking about?"

"I'm talkin' about the first degree murder of a man
named Kenneth McCoy."

"I don't even know a Kenneth McCoy." I took another
step back, ready to break and run at any moment. "I didn't kill
him!"

"Oh, I know you didn't kill him," she said nonchalantly.
"I killed him myself."

I looked at her in shock.

She smiled. "But of course I made it look like you did
it." Once again she got on her walkie talkie sounding like she
desperately needed help. The dispatcher told her back up was on
the way.

"I told you not to try me, Hardy, but you wouldn't listen."

I turned and dashed to my truck, not caring if Selena shot
me in the back. I would've rather died than to be able to see my
son again. Hearing Selena laughing loudly behind me told me
she wasn't about to shoot. I hopped in and sped off, causing two
cars to swerve and slam on brakes as I darted out in front of
them. Everything in me was in panic mode. My plan for revenge
on Zaria had blown up in my face. I didn't know what to do. My
mind was going in a hundred different directions. I couldn't go
to jail now. And who the fuck was Kenneth, I wondered. And
why would Selena try to frame me for his murder of all people?

Suddenly, I realized there was only one person who could possibly help me out of this situation. I pulled out my cell phone and dialed Santiago's number once again.

ZARIA
. . . .
Seventeen

The loud noise woke me from my sleep. My eyes opened and looked at the television, then toward the bedroom door. The voices on the other side were so exotic sounding, like something out of a movie. I then realized they were coming from the hallway just outside my bedroom door. I'd never heard them here before. Their Jamaican or Haitian accent was so thick I couldn't understand if they were in joyous conversation or confrontation. While listening closely I could also hear Eric's voice, but lower than the others. Then everything changed, the tone, the volume, everything.

"What the hell is going on in my house, Eric?" I shouted from the bed. I waited for him to answer, but he never responded.

Something about the sound of the conversation going on outside my door gave me the creeps. The words were so heavily accented I couldn't quite understand what exactly was being said, but something about them just didn't sit right with me. Their mere presence gave me a threatening vibe, like warriors in a jungle plotting on harming their enemy.

I slid from underneath my sheets and winced immediately clutching my side. I slowly climbed out of bed, hoping my pain would go away along with the chaos in the hall. After only taking two steps towards the door, my cell phone rang. I turned and grabbed it from the nightstand. Answering it without looking at the screen, I was greeted by a nurse from the hospital who recognized my voice immediately.

"Ms. Roth," she called out.

"Yeah."

"We've been trying to reach you over the past four days."

I sighed in aggravation. "Yeah, I'm aware." Her voice reminded me that Devin still hadn't called. Even after now knowing that we had created a beautiful baby boy, he was still being too selfish to see beyond his anger and forgive me.

"May I ask why we haven't heard from you, Ms. Roth?"

"No, you may not."

"Excuse me?"

Who the fuck did this bitch think she was, questioning me like I was her child or something? "I'm grown," I told her, "I don't owe you an explanation."

"Ms. Roth," the nurse said after a quick, heavy breath. "There's no need to get disrespectful. You haven't been to see your child since the day you disappeared. We just figured…"

"Don't figure shit," I told her, interrupting her sentence. "You don't know enough about me to be figuring anything."

After a sigh the nurse said straightforwardly, "Ms. Roth, due to your baby's premature birth, there has been some complications. We're gonna have to operate on him immediately."

I wasn't even paying attention to the nurse as she explained Devin Jr.'s health problems and the doctor's reasons for having to operate. I'd walked over to the bedroom door and was trying to hear the conversation taking place on the other side of it. Something about it had taken me for a loop. I heard the words, "Or you'll die," which now had me fearful.

"Ms. Roth," the nurse called out.

My focus was still completely on trying to decipher what was going on in the hallway. My ears hadn't heard the nurse say my name or anything else that had come out of her mouth.

"Ms. Roth."

"What," I answered, annoyed at her interrupting my attempt at being nosey.

"Ms. Roth, I just told you that your child is sick and will need surgery. Don't you even care?"

I sighed. With knowing that my face had been on the news, there was enough stress in my life. I loved my son but really didn't want to deal with whatever health issues he was going through at the moment. "Yes, I care," I told the nurse, "but I have other things I have to worry about right now."

"They're other things more important to worry about than your baby?"

"Look!" I had grown aggravated and knew the bitch was trying to look down on me. "Do whatever you gotta do."

"Excuse me?"

"What part of what I said, didn't you get? I know all you bitches at that hospital have been talking about me since the day you met me."

The nurse sighed in both defeat and disbelief. "Well, Ms. Roth, I guess from this point forward, since you don't seem to have a genuine interest in your child's well being, we'll rely on his father to make all decisions."

"What are you talking about?" I asked. What did she mean by the *child's father*?

"The child's father," she repeated. "He's been visiting regularly."

"Father?"

"Yes, his father."

My world lit up like a decorated street on Christmas. "Devin's been visiting?" I asked.

"Ms. Roth, I don't know who Devin is. The name of the man who has been visiting the child is Gerald Hardy."

My world was over taken by fury. "What the hell do you

mean Gerald Hardy has been visiting my child?"

"I mean simply what I just said. Since he's the father, he has a right to visit."

"He's not my baby's father. Stop saying that shit."

"Ms. Roth, we had an expedited paternity test done. It proves that he is the child's father."

I couldn't believe my ears. I didn't know what to say or do. All this time I had honestly thought Devin was the father. My heart wanted him desperately to be the father. So in my eyes, he *is* the father, I told myself.

"Well, Ms. Roth, I just called to notify you about your child's condition and his need for surgery. We're hoping we'll see you here soon. You have a good day."

The line went dead.

My mind was frozen in thought. What the hell was Hardy up to? Suddenly a loud scream pierced my ears from the hallway. Before I knew it, I'd snatched my bedroom door open only to find a woman crying with both hands tied together in front of her as grey tape was slapped over her mouth.

She stood between two men.

Horrifying men whose appearance immediately made my blood run ice cold.

Both men were Jamaican. One of them, dark skinned and had dreads draping his shoulders, damn near hanging to his elbows. His right eye was covered with a black patch and a gruesome scar ran down the same side of his face from his eye to his chin. He was dressed in a pair of dirty jeans, and a wife beater that allowed his muscular arms to display an array of tattoos. I could only focus on the one on his upper shoulder displaying an axe splitting a head wide open.

The other man was just as chocolate and his dreads hung just as long, except they were tied back into a ponytail. He wore all white and his eyes were an exotic but frightful shade of green. Something sinister and deadly hid behind them, something that made me nervous as they stared at me.

Each man, including Eric was now eye-balling me.

"Where you been hiding tis one?" the man with the patch asked Eric, eyeing me from head to toe. His appearance made me nauseous.

I looked at the woman. She was light skinned, pretty, in her early twenties, and wearing a tight fitting dress. Her feet were bare and her tearful eyes were filled with terror. It was crazy how she stood outside the same door that I'd been curious about.

"Eric, what's going on?" I asked, now wishing I'd stayed my nosey ass in the bedroom.

"Just handling some business," he said nonchalantly, as if having a woman standing in his hallway with tape over her mouth was normal.

"Honey, I thought we discussed having too many people in the …?"

The Jamaican in all white stepped towards me causing me to stop mid-sentence. He began to circle around me, his green eyes inspecting every inch of my body as if I was on display. He made me uncomfortable.

Very uncomfortable.

"That one's not for sale, Dauby," Eric suddenly announced.

For sale, I thought. *What the hell did that mean?*

The guy that I now knew as Dauby laughed as he stood in front of me. "Everyting in tis world for sale, Mon. Everyting have price tag."

"But I can't sell that one," Eric said.

"Eric, what the fuck is going on?" I asked, stepping closer to him but keeping my eyes on the Dauby and his piercing eyes.

"Why not she for sell?" the Jamaican with the eye patch roared, his expression looking as if being told no was a surefire way to piss him off. "Dauby, tell tis boy, me no play games today."

"She just had a baby, so it'll be at least six weeks before she can make you any money. Also, more importantly, I just saw her face on the news this morning. She can bring a lot of heat to what we're doing. The police want her for killing a nigga."

My heart dropped. Eric knew about me! But why couldn't he have just said I was his lady?

Both Jamaicans smiled as they looked at me.

"Murderah," Dauby commented as if in admiration of what he had just heard about me.

"Jamaica filled wit murderahs." The Jamaican with the eye patch gawked at me even more before continuing to speak. "Da bitch will fit right in. No one will notice. And just maybe tis the universe's payback."

Jamaica? My payback? I thought fearfully. Hell, I was just here by coincidence, giving Eric a chance to be with me until Devin got himself together. "Eric, baby," I said quickly, "I'm innocent. I didn't kill anyone. I swear I didn't. Someone's setting me up."

Dauby nodded to his partner. With speed, his partner pulled two stacks of money from his pocket and handed them both to him. I was still explaining myself to Eric, my mouth running a mile a minute when the money was handed to Eric. Dauby stepped closer to me. Something told me to run, but I couldn't. My feet were frozen.

Eric had an invisible question mark on his face as he looked at the money. "This is twenty thousand. Why twenty?"

I was suddenly snatched by the arm. "Ten K each," Dauby said, referring to me and the other woman. "We take both."

I tried to pull away, but his grip was too strong. "Get the fuck off of me!" I demanded.

"I really don't think she's a good choice," Eric announced nervously. "Her being wanted by the cops for murder might come back to bite us all in the ass later on. Plus, she was never a part of any of this. Why don't you take the one I showed you earlier downstairs in the basement? She's young, white, and Italian. She just graduated from college, too. A smart biddy."

Dauby held my arm and nodded approvingly. He had

made his choice and was satisfied. "Tis one here will do perfectly."

My heart rate accelerated. "Eric!" I screamed, fighting to get to him. "Don't let them take me away. Baby, I'll do anything. I swear to God!"

The Jamaican jerked me towards the stairs, causing me to slap him across his face. He immediately returned a vicious one of his own, knocking me to the floor, and causing spit to escape from my mouth. Through a heavy daze, I watched him pull a gun from underneath his shirt, kneel beside me, and shove it underneath my chin.

"I body bitches for fun," he warned. "You ever put your hands on me again, I murdah you."

I was scared to death as he snatched me to my feet and began to lead me down the stairs. The slap still had me so dazed my legs felt rubbery, making it difficult to keep my balance. When we reached the bottom of the steps and headed towards the door with the other goon wearing the eye patch, I began to cry.

"Please don't do this," I begged. "Please."

Each step towards the door felt like my last on earth, rather than my last in America.

"I have a child," I cried desperately. "A newborn baby boy. Please don't take me away from him. He's sick. He needs me."

The Jamaican paid no attention to me. He had no sympathy for me as we finally reached the front door.

"I'll do anything you ask!"

All I could think about was what these guys were into. It seemed as if they were selling women. I'd seen that movie *Taken* before and was wondering when Devin would show up to get me back. The torture and horrendous life that awaited me had me terrified beyond words.

When the front door opened, I knew I had no chance of remaining at Eric's. It seemed that I'd never see Eric or Devin again. But what greeted us at the doorstep made us all stop in our tracks. Our mouths were speechless. The only thing I could possibly fear more than the trip to Jamaica stood staring me in the eyes.

"Zaria Hopkins," the voice called out.

My eyes popped open, and so did everyone beside and behind me.

We were all fucked.

HARDY

Eighteen

The police.

The Swat team.

Or anyone else they could get was probably on my tail by now. I was certain there was an APB put out signaling my name. With every glance in my rear view mirror, I expected to see them behind me. And with every passing intersection, I anticipated seeing them appear from nowhere.

As my truck darted through traffic, street after street the only thing that occupied my mind was the possibility of spending the rest of my natural life in prison. Seeing myself trapped in a cell scared me shitless. I had plenty of homies and family who were doing time, many of them still going in and out prison's revolving door. But no matter how much they seemed to think of it as some idiotic ass way to prove how hard they were, I knew prison definitely wasn't the place for a nigga like me. Seeing myself sitting in that four by four for a half a second scared the hell out of me, let alone a life sentence. I just couldn't do it, I told myself picking up speed and turning a corner so fast I was now on two wheels. Whatever was gonna have to be done to keep my ass on the street, I was down for, I concluded as I sped through an alleyway like Mario Andretti.

If I was gonna have to spend the rest of my life on the run, I would.

If I possibly had to kill a cop to avoid arrest, I would.

Shit, if putting a bullet through my own head turned out to be the only way to avoid that miserable Hell on Earth, I would.

Whatever it took, I'd do it in a heartbeat. I was feeling just that scared and desperate.

"Fuck!" I shouted angrily as I banged my fist against the steering wheel.

Car horns blew as my Tahoe recklessly swerved in and out of traffic, making them swerve and slam on brakes to avoid hitting me. One lady swerved then hit a fire hydrant, but I didn't care. All I could think about was Selena.

"I can't believe that devious bitch!" I shouted to myself, seeing Selena's face in my mind, especially those eyebrows, and that hard walk. My heart was beating unnaturally fast as I thought about the foul shit she had just pulled. "Fucking scandalous slut! Why the hell did I get myself involved with her? Why?"

From the corner of my eye, I noticed a car suddenly ride along side me, keeping up with my truck easily. I panicked, feeling my breathing pattern pick up tremendously. Expecting it to be the police, I sighed then pressed on the gas as far as it would go ready for someone to start firing. But there was nothing. I reluctantly looked up, ready to make an upcoming right turn. I thought about slamming the truck against their car, trying to kill their ass if possible. But when I looked at the driver of the car, shockingly my eyes couldn't believe who was driving. It was Tayvia. What the fuck?

She eyed me as she maneuvered her Jag. As houses, people, and buildings whizzed by the both of us in quick blurs, her eyes remained on me as if crashing into someone's car or even running someone over was the furthest thing from her mind. The bitch wasn't even blinking.

As I repeatedly glanced from her to the street ahead of me, I wondered what the hell was going on. Where did she come from? How? And Why? It was as if she had just dropped down from the sky out of nowhere.

Tayvia began to mouth something while pointing past my truck. I couldn't understand what she was saying, nor did I care. But after a few attempts I was finally able to read her lips. She was telling me to pull over. I had no idea why though. Did she want to argue about earlier? If so, now was definitely not the time. Suddenly, she sped up a little and jerked her car directly in front of me, narrowly missing my front bumper.

"Damn, crazy bitch!" I shouted as I slammed on the brakes fishtailing my truck. After skidding nearly half a block, I stopped and hopped out of the truck with a ferocious scowl on my face.

"What the hell is wrong with you?" I screamed, quickly walking up on her car. The bitch had me so pissed off I wanted to snatch her narrow ass out the car.

"Get in the car!" Tayvia blared, her face showing no emotion just like back at the motel room an hour ago.

"Are you crazy? I don't have any time for this right now."

"Do I look crazy?"

I wanted to tell the nutty bitch my true feelings but suddenly heard sirens approaching from the distance. Just the sound of them made my heart move to my throat. *Damn*, I thought. They didn't sound too far away and growing closer. Thoughts of prison filled my head again, causing me to get extra antsy. Suddenly Tayvia's invitation didn't seem too much like a bad idea any longer. If the police were really after me, Selena had most likely given them a good description of my truck so getting far in it would be impossible. Fuck it, I concluded, and quickly hopped inside.

As Tayvia pulled away from the curb, I looked in the rear view. The distant sirens were growing louder but I didn't see any police cars. I leaned back in the seat, wondering if all of this was payback for the way I'd treated women in the past.

"Tayvia, I'm in trouble. The police are after me for murder."

Tayvia didn't react at all in the way I'd expected. Instead, just like her unblinking eyes were dead focused on me a few moments ago as we drove seventy or eighty miles an hour side by side, they were now just that focused on the street ahead of us. But strangely the expression on her face was almost blank. It was as if she wasn't exactly staring at the road but at something in a far off distance.

"Did you hear me, Tayvia?"

She simply nodded.

"Look, this crazy bitch I fucked with has penned a murder rap on me just because I wouldn't go through with some little green card selling scheme she has going on. Even worse than that, the bitch is a damn cop. A *fuckin* cop! That means it's my word against hers."

Tayvia turned and stared at me, her eyes becoming watery.

Why did I have to fuck with Selena, I wondered in frustration, wishing I could go back and change it. Why? Santiago told me about her. Another mess I let my dick get me into. I swore to God that if he could somehow get me out of this one, I would never let my dick do the thinking ever again.

"I want to tell some people higher up in her department," I continued. "Maybe go in with a lawyer and explain the marriage scheme she's been running; let them know exactly how crooked a cop she really is. But I doubt…"

"What's her name?" Tayvia asked plainly and interrupting me while still staring ahead.

"Huh?" I asked, a little caught off guard by her finally saying something.

"What's her name?" she asked again.

"Selena."

Tayvia's jaw clenched. A look of bitterness flashed

across her face but disappeared. "Have you been seeing her while you've been seeing me?"

"Ahhhh…. Kinda. I mean we haven't been seeing each other. We just met days ago, right?" I turned to look behind us making sure there were no sign of the cops or Selena.

Tayvia sighed but still didn't look at me.

"But I broke shit off with her," I said. "That's why…"

"Do you love her?" she asked, cutting my explanation short.

The way she was still staring ahead as she drove was freaking me out. She looked like a damn robot. "No, I don't love her," I said, wondering what the hell that had to do with anything. "I never did. It wasn't that type of relationship. We were just fucking."

"For how long?"

"A few months. Now I regret the shit." I shook my head.

Tayvia placed a hand on my thigh. "We're not just fucking, right?"

"Ahhhhh…" I paused.

"Don't worry about her, baby," she responded. "I can make you happy, even if it's making you cum ten times a day."

I looked at her like she'd lost her mind. "What do you mean don't worry about her?" I asked in disbelief. "Haven't you been listening? I'm facing a damn murder rap because of that bitch. I *have* to worry about her. And I'm not interested in sex right now."

What's with this broad, I wondered. *Is anyone home in the honey comb hideout?*

For the first time since I had gotten into the car, Tayvia finally looked at me. "Baby, I'm just saying calm down," she said with a warm smile. "Let's not let her destroy what me and you have."

Me and You, I thought to myself. Where the fuck did that one come from? Wasn't the bitch listening when I told her ass back at the motel room there was no me and her? Was she deaf or some shit? Or had I really met another Zaria? I swallowed hard thinking about the signs. They were there. *Another bitch who didn't know the difference between love and a one night stand.*

"Look, Tayvia," I began, ignoring what she'd just said, "I think Selena may have had something to do with Tyson's murder also. She may have even killed Tyson herself. You should call the detective in charge of the case and let him know."

Obviously I was lying but I really needed to do something to get back at Selena. Maybe I could set her up for Tyson's murder.

Tayvia didn't react at all the way I'd expected. She had just heard me tell her I knew who killed Tyson and she showed no surprise at all, just the same weird stare ahead of her as her hand still rested on my thigh. Damn, she was crazy.

"I'm serious, Tayvia. Call the detective and tell him what I told you."

She smiled and placed her hand softly to the side of my face. "Okay, baby," she said unconvincingly. It sounded as if she was simply trying to pacify me.

Before I could say anything else, my cell phone rang. I answered, seeing my newborn son's hospital on the screen.

"Mr. Hardy?" a female voice asked.

"Yeah."

"Mr. Hardy, the doctor discovered a terrible infection in your son's intestines. This infection is early signs for a disease called Necrotizing Enterocolitis or simply NEC, which is when bacteria attack the intestine walls. He's gonna have to have surgery immediately. We've scheduled him to go into the O.R. in one hour. I have to be honest Mr. Hardy, this is a very serious surgery."

My world went dark. "How serious?" I asked, dreading her answer.

"Life threatening. He only has a fifty-fifty chance of surviving. You should get here as soon as possible."

Tears began to fall down my face as I hung up. My lil man hadn't been on earth long at all and was already having to face struggle after struggle for survival. It wasn't fair. Suddenly, my own problems disappeared. They no longer mattered. All that mattered to me at that moment was my son.

After telling Tayvia to get me to the hospital, I called Santiago. With pain evident in my voice, I told her about what Selena had done to me. Of course she took a few minutes to tell me that she'd warned me about her. I then told her about the baby's emergency surgery. Santiago told me to remain calm and prayed up for the baby's sake. She seemed reluctant at first acting as if she wasn't there for me, but then told me she was hopping on the freeway to Philly immediately. Of course she threw in the fact that she'd been traveling back and forth between Philly and New York all because of my bullshit. I just said thank you a hundred times hoping she'd forgive me for everything I'd ever done to her.

When I hung up, I could've sworn I had heard Tayvia mumble something underneath her breath about killing Santiago. But I disregarded it, knowing I'd get rid of Tayvia as soon as I got to the hospital. All I could think about was my son, although for a brief second I wondered if Selena knew about the operation. She always seemed to know everything else. I wondered if she was going to be at the hospital waiting for me. If so, it was a chance I would have to take.

"Step on it!" I told Tayvia.

"I will...my love," she told me lovingly.

I simply shook my head.

ZARIA
Nineteen

My eyes wouldn't leave the gun. For long stretched moments we all stared at it, expecting it to go off at any second. Fearfully, I anticipated the pain its bullet would give me as it tore through my flesh, especially at such close range. But even worse, I feared the anticipation of death.

We were still standing frozen in front of Eric's front door as the woman that now held my life in the palm of her hand hummed a few words.

"Hmm ump humph."

What the hell was that all about? And why had my life turned so chaotic? I'd done nothing to deserve anything that was being dealt to me. I just wanted to give love and get a little back in return, I thought.

Her stare was cold and her eyes were filled with a mixture of rage, anger, and fury. She was thirsty for my blood. It was obvious. I could only remain speechless.

"What the fuck?" the Jamaican holding my arm said. "Who is tis bitch?"

Both Jamaicans pulled their guns instantly, locking on

the woman's head standing on the door step. Then verbal chaos broke loose as the Jamaicans began to quickly demand answers from Eric, shouting and waiving their guns back and forth from him to the strange woman. I just prayed someone would drive by Eric's well hidden home and notice all the chaos.

Eric raised his hands in front of us all defensively. "I don't know this bitch," he said quickly. "I swear to God I've never seen her a day before in my life."

For several moments, which seemed more like hours, each man yelled threats in the open air as their guns continued to wave back and forth. Throughout the confusion I was terrified that at least one of the guns would go off and kill me. I didn't know what to do. Something inside me was screaming for me to run but a gut feeling forced my feet to remain planted where they were. The voices in my head began.

No one wants you to live Zaria. No one. Not this woman, not Eric, and not even a bunch of islanders who traffic women for a living.

"Who the fuck are you?" Eric asked the woman, snapping me from my thoughts. His hands were still raised defensively in front of him as if they would be able to stop a bullet.

"I'm Kelsey Taylor," the woman finally said, while staring at me in a way that said I should've recognized her.

The Jamaicans looked at Eric, their guns still pointed and ready to squeeze off.

"Man, I told you I don't know the bitch. I swear it." His heart appeared to be pumping wildly as sweat poured from his forehead. "What the fuck do you want?" he asked the woman.

"*She* knows what I want," Kelsey said, pertaining to me.

"What? I've never seen this bitch a day in life."

The Jamaicans now eyed me but I had no answers for them. I was in just as much suspense as everyone else.

"Look at me, bitch!" Kelsey ordered. "Look at my damn face!"

I stared at her, hoping she wouldn't shoot me.

"I'm Devin's wife."

My face tightened and my heart stopped beating.

"That's right. Let me say it again, Devin's wife...the love of his life, the one he fucks regularly," she told me, quickly cocking the gun while still keeping it aimed at me. I noticed her finger wrapped tightly around the trigger.

My eyes widened in sudden anger. I was face to face with the tramp who had been standing between me and Devin. Immediately, I wanted to snatch her ass up but couldn't with her gun aimed directly at my face.

"You messed with the wrong bitch's man," Kelsey spewed.

"Fuck you!" I spat back. "He doesn't love you. If he did, why did *I* just give birth to his baby?"

Kelsey didn't answer, only seethed with growing anger, an anger capable of boiling over any minute.

"Yeah, bitch," I taunted her. "He's going to divorce your weak pussy having ass. Trust me on that. Then me, him, and *our* child are going to be a family."

"He already has a family," Kelsey retaliated. "One that you won't get another chance to break up. You've been stalking my husband for too long. Now it's time I put your trifling ass to sleep!"

"Well, do it, bitch!" I screamed, stepping closer to the gun and placing my hands on my hips like Super Man. "What the fuck are you waiting for? Do the shit!"

Suddenly, Dauby charged Kelsey, knocking me to the pavement, and yanking her inside. Somehow he was able to grab her hand and jerk the gun away from her all at the same time, ending with a ferocious jab to the jaw. It didn't take long for all of the women to be forced back inside and led to the couch like kindergartners. Even though Kelsey was the one bleeding from the mouth, the other women were having multiple anxiety attacks. Both Dauby and his side kick were now in panic too, screaming and cussing at each other, unsure of what to do next.

"The police are on their way," Kelsey stated boldly from

the couch, holding her bleeding mouth in pain. "I called them just before I got here. They're definitely on the way."

Eric was pacing back and forth.

"Shut up!" the Jamaican with the eye patch shouted to Kelsey.

Kelsey looked at me. "They're coming to get you for that little boy you killed back in New York," she said spitefully.

"Shut up!!" the Jamaican shouted louder, his patience wearing far too thin.

"It was me who texted you, not Devin," Kelsey continued. "It was me that you gave this address to. Now the police are going to be here soon. All of you sons of bitches are going to jail."

The Jamaican stormed across the room and smacked Kelsey across her face with the gun so brutally she spat two teeth onto the floor. "I said shut the fuck up!" he yelled.

Eric held his head and began to pace back and forth even faster than before while nervously talking to himself. He was a total wreck.

The Jamaicans loudly spoke to each other, trying to figure out what to do next. Their language fell from their mouths at rapid fire speed and in a barrage of panic filled sentences. They repeatedly waved their guns as if for emphasis.

"I can't believe this shit," Eric was saying over and over again to himself as he paced.

Finally the Jamaicans came up with a solution. They quickly tied Kelsey up and decided to take her, myself, and the other woman to a safe house while they figured out what to do with Kelsey. But before leaving, they both agreed one loose end needed to be tied up first. Both men forced Eric to his knees in the center of the living room.

"Oh God, Please!" Eric loudly pleaded. Tears fell from his eyes. "Please don't do this!"

A gun rose in the air and was aimed directly at Eric's face.

I closed my eyes and turned away, unable to watch what

was about to take place. I could hear the other women whimpering from their taped mouths.

"Please, guys!" Eric screamed. "I'll do anything you want. Just don't kill…"

"Ya put shit in the game now. No witness, boy."

A lump formed in my throat as I listened to the words no witnesses. That's what I was. Smiley Face. Smiley Face. Can anyone see my Smiley Face?

Two gun shots went off, immediately silencing Eric's pleading cries. I heard his lifeless body tumble to the floor along with the muffled screams of the other two women. My eyes wouldn't open. They were refusing to, as if in fear of the sight that would be awaiting me if I did. I could imagine Eric's once sexy and handsome face now destroyed, two gaping bullet holes grotesquely torn into it. I could picture him lying flat on the floor, what remained of the back of his head resting in a pool of blood and thick patches of his brain. Just the thought of it all was enough to make me keep my eyes closed. Suddenly, my ears heard the Jamaican's footsteps rush towards me. I felt one of them snatch me up from the couch by my arm.

"Let's go," he ordered.

I finally opened my eyes as me and the other ladies were being forcefully led to the door. The Jamaicans snatched it open, pushed us outside, and forced us at gunpoint to a tinted out, black Suburban on chrome rims in the driveway. As they opened the doors, suddenly a police car sped down the street with its sirens blaring loudly and screeched to a stop directly in front of Eric's house. I nearly fainted at the thought of being saved.

Two more cars quickly appeared from the other direction and screeched to a stop also. As the cops jumped from their cars and pointed their guns, more police cars quickly flooded the street. In a matter of seconds there were at least two dozen cars in front of Eric's house.

"Drop your weapons!" the police ordered. "Drop them right now and put your hands up!"

Both Jamaicans raised their guns as if they were surrendering but quickly began shooting. I jumped into the backseat of the truck like Rambo, hurting from my belly down to my feet. I laid flat as gunfire erupted. The truck's windows began to shatter and drop down on me as bullets tore through them. My heart pounded furiously as I heard the Jamaicans screaming foul accented words I couldn't understand. I watched as they let off shot after shot at the police, dead set on going out like gangsters.

The repeated explosions from the guns were deafening. My ears were ringing louder and louder with each shot. After what seemed like an eternity, bullets finally tore through the head of the Jamaican wearing the eye patch, leaving him dead beside the tuck. The other Jamaican took several shots to the chest and died on the front lawn like some alien that refused to die.

I laid still as the gunshots stopped and the cops cautiously began to slowly approach the dead bodies. After being assured they were dead, an officer opened the back door of the Suburban with his gun aimed at me.

I threw my hands up. "I'm not with them. They were trying to kidnap me. Thank God you're here!"

"Zaria Hopkins?" he asked.

The situation had me trembling and too rattled to say anything else.

Other officers approached the truck, each with their guns still drawn.

"Zaria Hopkins," the officer said. "You're under arrest for murder."

Damn!

HARDY

Twenty

"Why? Why me?" I shouted with my hands now clutching the sides of my aching head.

Both my mind and heart worried for my son. He was all I could think about or wanted to think about. I'd give anything to take his place, to take his pain and suffering away. He didn't deserve the terrible hand life was already dealing him. He deserved to be in my arms, knowing without a shadow of a doubt he was loved.

I lost track of time as I paced the floor of the hospital's waiting room nonstop. The only thing that ran neck and neck with my worry was my paranoia. The fear of being arrested for murder wouldn't go away. I kept expecting to see Selena burst through the door at any moment leading a pack of trigger happy police officers, each anxious to either take me in or shoot me down in the center of the waiting room. Either way, it wouldn't be a good look for me at all.

Suddenly that annoying voice sounded. "Come over here so I can comfort you."

"Damn, how do I keep getting myself into these wild ass situations with women?" I asked myself while still pacing the floor. "Why don't I ever fucking learn?"

Hatred and disgust built inside of me as I glanced at Tayvia. My fists bashed against the sides of my head in anger. "How do I keep getting myself into this shit?" I asked myself.

Tayvia stood from her chair and reached out in an attempt to console me. My body snatched away. The last thing I wanted right now was the touch of a muthafucking woman. My eyes didn't even want to see one. Bitches had caused me entirely too much pain and torment lately. Their presence nauseated me and pissed me straight the fuck off at the moment.

"Baby," Tayvia said softly, attempting to reach for me again.

"Don't touch me!" I honestly wanted to haul off and slap the hoe even though she hadn't done anything to me but be a nuisance.

"Sweetheart, I just want to help." Her words were genuine and compassionate. "I just want to be here for you."

"I don't want your help." The words sprayed viciously from my mouth before I knew they'd even come out. The anger inside me had spoken them. It spoke from its own heart. "I don't want you to be here for me," I told her. "Don't you understand that?"

"Hardy, you're just hurting," she rationalized. "You don't mean what you're saying. I know you don't."

My eyes locked onto hers. "Who the fuck are you to tell me what I don't mean?" I hated the sight of her. My nostrils were disgusted by the scent of her perfume. My eyes were yearning for the sight of watching her just walk away.

Fuck a woman! Fuck all of them! They could all go to hell!

"Hardy, I'm just saying…"

"Tayvia, you were just a damn fuck. That's all. You were nothing more, nothing less."

Tayvia shook her head in disagreement. "Don't say that,"

she pleaded. "I don't believe that."

"Well, believe it," I spat, my words meant to deliberately sting and hurt as badly as possible.

Women had been the cause of my pain and suffering. They had created the pitch black darkness my life was so shrouded in. Now, I wanted get back. I wanted nothing more than to hurt them.

"I never cared about your ass," I admitted. "In fact, meeting you at that Starbucks wasn't by chance. It was by plan."

Tayvia looked at me with uncertainty. Her eyes stuck out from their sockets.

"I wanted Zaria."

Tayvia was silent, her stare questioning.

"That's right, Tayvia. I wanted Zaria, not you. I just used you to get to her."

"But why?" Tayvia asked saddened by the truth. "And how do you even know her?"

"For revenge. That heartless bitch destroyed my entire universe. She killed my son."

Tayvia looked as though her own world was spinning, her own heart breaking. She placed her hands on the back of a chair as if to brace herself. "You used me?" she asked, unable to truly believe it but unable to deny that she had heard me correctly. The pain of accepting it all was overwhelming.

"Yeah," I told her spitefully, taking satisfaction in her pain. "We used to teach together. I took her out one night, knowing I'd get the pussy. That's all I wanted, but she wanted more…more than I had to give. That's what men do, Tayvia," I spat, seeing that she still didn't get it.

But I didn't care. Tayvia was the enemy. I had no love for her. She was just like the rest of them once a month bleeding out the pussy ass bitches. If I didn't hurt her and kick her sorry good for nothing ass to the curb first, eventually she would find pleasure in doing it to me.

"Hell yeah, I used you. Call it a one night stand if you want," I went on. "So, now that you know the truth and you know that I don't want you, why don't you do us both a favor and get the fuck up out of here. Your job is done."

Tayvia stood still and quiet while staring at me. Resentment and something more than anger began to spread across her face. "You lying muthafucka," she whispered.

I only stared at her, satisfied with the hurt I had inflicted.

"You lying muthafucka," she repeated, now a little more loudly and shaking her head.

I folded my arms across my chest noticing a fine ass nurse walk by. I made a mental note to introduce myself later. Tayvia began to pace the floor mumbling something beneath her breath. She wrapped her arms around herself tightly as she paced. Sweat began to run from her forehead and she began to breathe faster and harder while her mumbling began to grow louder and louder.

As she continued to have a conversation with herself, my cell phone began to ring. Quickly pulling it out and looking at the number, I displayed a small grin when I noticed Kyle's number. I was so glad he decided to call me back.

"What's good, Kyle," I answered.

"Nothing man. I got your message, and I'm on my way. I can't you go through this shit alone."

That's what's up, I thought to myself. Despite all the shit going on between me, Dana and Mario, Kyle was still a good friend.

"Bet. You have the name of the hospital, right?"

"Yeah," Kyle responded.

"Cool. See you when you get here."

"I can't believe this shit," Tayvia said as soon as I hung up.

Well, believe it bitch, I thought. I still wasn't in the mood for her ass.

Suddenly, Tayvia screamed as loud as her voice would allow her to, causing my eyes to immediately widen. "You're just like all the rest! Men aren't shit!" At that moment, she ran up to me and began pounding her fists up against my chest. "I thought you told me you loved me!"

"I never told you anything!" I fired back. As I pushed Tayvia away I saw a nurse behind the desk grab the phone.

"I'm calling security," I heard her say to her co-worker.

"Yes, you did Hardy. You also told me that we would get married!" Tayvia roared. She tried to attack me again, but I kept pushing her away.

"What the hell are you talking about, Tayvia?"

She picked up a chair and threw it directly at my head. Luckily, I had quick reflexes as it hit the wall behind me.

"You guys need to get here really quick," the nurse said into the phone.

"Stop lying!" Tayvia kept taking steps toward me. I knew I could take the bitch with one punch, but her intimidation game was on point.

"Tayvia, you need to take your ass home." Once again I couldn't believe that I'd let myself get involved with another crazy ass female.

"I'm not going anywhere!" Tayvia looked around the room like she was searching for something else to throw.

"Tayvia, leave now!"

She looked at me vengefully. "You," she said pointing directly at me. "You did this. You used me Hardy."

"Tayvia, look it was just all in fun."

"Fuck you, Hardy! Tell me you love me now!"

This bitch is crazy to the tenth power.

I began taking backwards baby steps away from her. Before I knew it Tayvia had done the unthinkable. I watched as she'd pulled her shirt over her head, quick like a Wonder Woman move. Next, it was her bra. I couldn't believe she was stripping in the middle of the hospital waiting area.

"Tayvia, what are you doing?" I questioned.

"I know what it is, Hardy. You don't remember what my body looks like. I'll show you right here and then you can apologize and profess your love to me," she said unzipping her jeans.

Suddenly, security officers burst through the door. The sudden sight of them, and Tayvia's constant screaming gave me a migraine. The officers backed Tayvia into a corner and grabbed her with her boobs jiggling like jelly in their faces..

"Get the fuck off of me!" she screamed. "I have to see my step-son. He's in surgery. Get your hands off of me!"

I couldn't believe my eyes. Tayvia looked like a naked, wild savage as she kicked and screamed at the top of her lungs.

"Get off of me!" she kept screaming. "I hate you, Hardy. I hate your fucking guts!"

The officers finally wrestled her to the floor, giving her several ultimatums along the way. As I watched, I didn't notice the doctor come out of the same doors security had just come out of.

"Mr. Hardy," Doctor Sebrill called, walking towards me.

A lump formed in my throat immediately. Tayvia's screams turned to whimpers as she wrestled beneath the weight of the officers' knees buried in her back. "I need to talk to the doctor about my son," she cried from the floor.

I shook my head, then focused on the doctor nearing me. Seeing his face filled me with fear. His expression was far too solemn. I knew something wasn't right. As he approached me, the entrance doors to the fifth floor slid open. Santiago quickly rushed inside.

"Mr. Hardy, I've got some not so good news." His voice was filled with regret.

As Santiago took her place beside me, Tayvia exploded verbally from the floor again. "That's the bitch?" she screamed as the police still tried to wrestle her and get the handcuffs on. "Is that the bitch you played me for?"

Both Santiago and the doctor looked at Tayvia strangely. I felt ashamed, knowing I'd brought this drama to the hospital where my son was fighting for his life. Talk about ghetto.

"Answer me, Hardy! Is that her?" Tayvia belted. "She's not even prettier than me Hardy!"

The doctor escorted Santiago and I to a nearby hallway.

Santiago glanced back at Tayvia as we walked, obviously wondering what was going on. I could tell all sorts of thoughts played around in her mind. She wanted to interrogate me about Tayvia but couldn't. When we reached the hallway the doctor spoke.

"Mr. Hardy, your son is in recovery right now. He made it through the surgery, but barely. It's still too early for us to know if the procedure was a success. By him being so small and weak, we're not sure if he has the strength to fight through recovery."

Santiago looked just as worried. She wanted this baby just as much as I did. And I knew she'd be a good mother to him even though it wasn't her biological child. My heart was breaking. Could I be losing a second child? I couldn't take the loss of a second one. I wouldn't make it through that.

"All we can do now is to watch him closely. We'll keep you posted on any changes," the doctor continued.

My head dropped to the floor.

"Mr. Hardy," he said while placing a hand on my shoulder. "There's a chapel on the third floor. I don't know if you believe in God, but whether you do or don't, praying is the only thing any of us can do for him right now." He squeezed my shoulder and walked away.

I tried to slide my hand into Santiago's to comfort her, but she wouldn't allow it. I turned to see her look me in the eyes. As a tear fell from my eyes she wiped it away softly.

"Everything's going to be okay," she promised, knowing I needed to hear those words. "You just need to pray. And not just for your son," she warned.

At that same moment we could see the security officers picking Tayvia up from the floor. I'd forgotten all about her. As they drug her away, she screamed she hated me until her voice finally became faint.

"So, are you ready to tell me who that is?" Santiago questioned.

Out of shame my mouth stayed closed. I couldn't tell her.

My eyes could only look into hers with regret for hurting her over and over. She'd stayed down with me despite everything I had taken her through. But the only way I could always seem to repay her was by breaking her heart. Shame overtook me.

Santiago read my eyes and began to slowly back away in regret. "I need to hear the truth…and from your mouth only."

My eyes told her what she needed to know. "It just happened baby. I was depressed."

"No, Hardy," she said in disbelief. "Another one? Do you even have the ability to stop cheating?"

I reached for her. "Santiago, I'm sorry." My words were honest. I was really sorry for breaking her heart. Just one last chance was all I needed. If she would give it to me, I was ready to do right by her. "Just give me another shot. I promise I'll do right. We'll raise this baby together."

"No, you're not sorry," she replied, shaking her head. "You're only sorry I found out." Her expression showed me that she'd tried to toughen up that quickly to deal with me and my ways.

"Santiago…"

"Save it, Hardy."

"But, Santiago…"

"I'm done, Hardy. I can't take this anymore."

As she continued to back away I knew she was right. I really was selfish. But at that moment I really wanted to change. I really wanted to be only hers.

"Santiago, please don't do this. Don't walk away. I need you." Each word shook as it fell from my lips.

"Goodbye, Hardy," she said as tears began to fall from her own eyes again. "It's over."

As she turned and walked away, I wanted to plead for her to stay. I was willing to drop to my knees and beg, but in my heart I realized at that moment there was no use. She was too good of a woman. And just like I had done with Dana, I had let my selfishness push another good woman out of my life.

I deserved to be alone.

I deserved to die.

ZARIA
· · · · · · · · · · · · · ·
Twenty-One

Over the cursing, shouting, and loud conversations coming from each cell I could hear the jingling of keys and the thudding of footsteps coming down the hall. A gnawing feeling in my gut told me they were coming for me. I stopped pacing back and forth and backed myself against the wall at the far end of my cell, scared and trembling. The same officer that had escorted me to my cell when I first got to the precinct several hours ago appeared. This time he was accompanied by a man and woman, both wearing suits and smirks. The officer slid the key into the lock, turned it, and loudly slid the steel bars open.

"Put your hands out," he ordered, stepping inside and pulling a set of handcuffs from his belt.

The woman who accompanied him folded her arms across her breasts and eyed me. She thought I was nothing…trash. I could tell. Why did everyone look down on me? Why was I never good enough for anyone to think good things about me.

"What's going on?" I asked, wishing I could run.

"Just put your hands out, Ms. Hopkins," he repeated, his

facial expression as hard as stone.

I slowly raised my hands in front of me, dreading the feel of the thin bracelets wrapping around my wrists and rendering me defenseless. The officer clicked them around my wrists tightly and escorted me out of my cell to the hall.

"We'll take her from here," the man dressed in a suit announced.

The woman grabbed me by the arm and snatched me away from the uniformed officer so hard I almost tripped and fell over my own two feet. Roughly, she escorted me down the hall with the coldest look I had ever seen on a woman's face. She looked like a witch, with the long, frizzy, black hair and all. We made a left turn and passed two small rooms. When we reached the third, she opened the door, snatched me inside like a rag doll, and pushed me down into a chair. Her partner walked inside behind us and closed the door, making me super nervous.

The room only had a table and two chairs. It was tiny and dimly lit letting me know it was their interrogation room resembling the ones I'd seen in movies. The paint was peeling from the walls, and on the far right side of the room was a dark window impossible to see through. My thoughts…two sided. I was no fucking dummy. They brought me here to frame me, I told myself, realizing the room had given me the creeps.

"I'm Detective Berkowitz," the evil looking woman said, carelessly dropping her badge down on the table. She was a tall, skinny, white woman with mangy hair swept back off her face. Her eyes were a stale shade of blue and her skin seemed brittle and dried up. She took off her suit jacket and placed it on the back of her chair. Underneath her left arm was a gun tucked into a black shoulder holster.

"This is Detective Spears," she said, quickly pointing at her partner as he dropped a manila colored envelope on the table, then sat a small tape recorder beside it, and backed away. Spears was a tall and huskily built black man. He looked to be in his late thirties and had brown hair greasily slicked back. His eyes and expression weren't as menacing as Berkowitz's but they weren't welcoming or compassionate either. Both cops had me feeling much more uncomfortable than the situation itself.

"We're with Philadelphia Homicide," Berkowitz told me as she sat down across the table from me. She pressed a button on the tape recorder, and looked me straight in the eyes.

"That was quite a blood bath back at your friend's house today, huh?" she asked.

The coldness of her eyes made my body shake. My own dropped to my cuffed trembling hands.

"*They're going to fry your black ass like barbeque at a family picnic,*" the voice in my head teased.

My eyes closed, plunging me into darkness. "Can…can I please make my phone call?" I asked, my voice shaking. "They didn't let me have one."

BOOM!!!

My eyes jerked open quickly at the thundering sound of Berkowitz's hand slamming down onto the table. She was now towering over me from across the table.

"A phone call is the least of your fucking worries, sweetheart! What happened at your friend's house today? How exactly did Eric Monroe come up with half his face blown off?"

"I didn't do it," I said quickly, scared to death.

"*Shit's getting good now, huh, bitch?*" the voice in my head asked sarcastically, loving the predicament I was facing.

"But it had something to do with you, didn't it?" Berkowitz asked, refusing to let up, her eyes burning through me like branding irons.

"I didn't even know those people. I swear…"

Berkowitz leaned across the table. "Your little innocent routine doesn't work with me. You're gonna have to try much, much harder."

"But I'm telling the truth."

Her hands slammed down on the table again even louder and harder than before. "What happened!"

I was too distraught and scared to speak.

Detective Spears walked over and placed a hand on his

partner's shoulder. The two gave each other eye contact. Berkowitz gave me a glare then reluctantly walked across the room and leaned against the wall with her arms folded and her eyes still glued on me. Spears sat down and pulled a pack of cigarettes form the inner pocket of his suit jacket.

"Cigarette?" he asked.

I shook my head.

"You sure?" He extended the pack to me generously. "It's okay."

"No, thank you."

"You mind if I have one then?"

I shrugged my shoulders. For a moment I thought I saw two heads on Spears. I closed my eyes then reopened them knowing that my symptoms for my schizophrenia were getting worse. I knew once the hallucinations began, things would only get worse.

He took one from the pack, lit up, and exhaled deeply as if it were the absolute best cigarette he'd ever smoked. "I've been wanting one of these all day long," he said, exhaling smoke to the ceiling. I know it's a bad habit but I just can't seem to stop. One of these days I will though."

I just stared at the detective, not quite sure of how to take him. He seemed nice and polite.

"By the way," he said, placing his cigarette in the ash tray, "as soon as we're done in here, I'm gonna make sure you get your phone call, okay?"

I nodded thankfully. Then I let a slight smile slip from the side of my lip. I could tell he liked me. He'd probably been checking me out from the moment they brought me in.

"So, what happened back at your friend's house today?"

My eyes glanced at Berkowitz who had moved directly next to the glass mirror. She was still looking at me like a blood thirsty Pit Bull ready to charge at my throat at any moment.

"It's okay," Spears said, seeing my fear. He placed a hand softly over mine and leaned close. "She scares the hell out of me sometimes, too," he whispered as if it was just our little secret. "I'm not going to let anything happen to you though. I got you."

I was waiting for him to tell me something mushy and romantic like in the movie, *Diary of a Mad Black Women* when Shemar Moore's character, Orlando told Helen all she had to do was wake up and he'd take it from there. But I knew that wasn't about to happen with Berkowitz staring down our throats. The bitch had something to prove...but Spears was feeling me.

I loosened up a little.

"So what happened?"

I told him everything that happened from the moment I stepped out of my bedroom to the moment I was arrested. He nodded in understanding and never blinked even once as he listened to every word carefully rubbing my hand along the way.

"Wow," he said with surprise when I was finished. "You were damn lucky. The police got there just in time. If they hadn't got there when they did, there's no telling what those bad guys would be doing to you right now."

The possibilities sent a shiver of fear through my body.

He took another puff of his cigarette and placed it back in the ashtray.

"Do you think they had anything to do with Tyson's murder?" he asked with uncertainty.

I looked at him.

"I mean Tyson was your boyfriend, right?"

"Yes, well sorta...I mean, yes. But it didn't have anything to do with what happened at Eric's or at Tyson's."

"Oh, well tell me what happened with Tyson's death."

My nerves started getting bad again. "Can I please make my phone call now," I practically begged.

Berkowitz sighed in annoyance.

"In a minute," Spears said, his voice still friendly. "How did Tyson die?"

"I don't know."

"When was the last time you saw him?"

"*You're going down like the Titanic, bitch,*" the voice in

my head uttered.

"Stop it!" I shouted.

"Who me?" Spears looked at me strangely, then at his partner. He repeated the question. "When was the last time you saw Tyson Fennell?"

"I can't remember," I lied.

"Was it a few weeks or a few months?"

"Months."

"You sure?"

I nodded, hoping he would believe me.

"You're a fuckin lie!" Berkowitz screamed. "We have a reliable witness who says that you saw him the evening he was murdered. They said that the two of you argued and he put you out."

Tayvia's face popped into my mind.

"Is that true, Ms. Hopkins?" Spears asked.

Tears started to fall from my eyes as memories of Tyson started to fill my head. "It's true," I admitted, "but I didn't kill him."

"It's kind of hard for me to believe that," he said sympathetically. "We've got your fingerprints on the gun that killed him."

My heart started pounding. I grabbed my head and started rocking back and forth. I remembered tossing the gun on the floor. How could I have been so stupid?

"Ms. Hopkins, I understand you're scared. I really do. And I want to help you. But I can't if you won't tell me the truth."

"*You're a dead bitch now,*" the voice in my head teased. "*You're so very dead.*"

"Was it self defense?" Spears asked. "Did he attack you?"

"I didn't kill him. I swear I didn't."

"Then how did your fingerprints get all over the damn gun!" Berkowitz yelled. "We're not stupid!"

My mouth wouldn't open. Her yelling and screaming had

me terrified.

"Ms. Hopkins, we know that you were involved in his murder," Spears said quietly. "We also have strong reason to believe you were involved in the murder of Kenneth Hopkins."

"Kenneth was your cousin, wasn't he?" Berkowitz asked.

My hands dropped to my lap as my body continued to rock back and forth. The mentioning of Kenneth's name made my heart pound.

"Wasn't he!" she asked loudly.

I nodded reluctantly. Our childhood memories together began to play. Smiley Face. Smiley face. Can anyone see my Smiley face, I began to chant softly to myself.

"Did you say something?" Spears asked.

I kept chanting.

"You ready to confess?" Berkowitz chimed in. "You should just go ahead and stop wasting time."

I kept chanting and my rocking back and forth intensified.

"You want to tell me what happened to your cousin?" Spears asked.

I stopped rocking. I looked him in the eye and told him the truth. "I don't know what happened to him. I didn't do it." Tears were drenching my face. They wouldn't stop falling.

"Oh, so it's just a muthafuckin coincidence that each of these people that had some sort of a relationship with you wound up dead?" Berkowitz asked, her patience at the breaking point. She stepped to me. "That's a bunch of bullshit. You killed both of those men and you're going to get the chair for it."

I was horrified. Everything was overwhelming. I could barely breathe.

She leaned in closer. "They're going to fry your ass so bad people will be able to smell your skin cooking for miles."

The vision sent horror through me. I didn't want to die that way. I didn't know how burning flesh smelled but just the mere thought had me scared to the core. The vision of my skin in flames wouldn't leave me at all.

Spears leaned in towards me. "It doesn't have to be that way, Ms. Hopkins. I can help you if you tell me the truth. Just tell me what happened."

"I didn't kill them. I loved both of them."

A knock came from the door.

My head snapped. I wondered who it was? "Can I get my phone call?" I yelled out as Berkowitz opened the door.

She and whoever was at the door began whispering. I couldn't hear what they were saying and I was too scared to turn around. Seconds later Spears stood from his chair and joined his partner at the doorway. After several moments Berkowitz walked back into the room. She grabbed the manila envelope, her jacket, and the tape recorder. She smiled wickedly at me and said, "Trust and believe we'll finish this conversation a little later."

I closed my eyes and began to pray as she walked out of the room. I heard the door close, but someone was still in the room with me. Footsteps came from behind me and a woman came into view as I opened my eyes. She seemed familiar. I recognized her but I couldn't remember from where. Wherever it was, I did know that being in a room alone with her had me feeling uncomfortable. My eyes immediately fell to the floor.

"I'm Detective Selena Hill," of the New York Police Department."

"New York City?"

"New York, period. You know…next to New Jersey." Her voice seemed extra serious.

I just wanted the moment to disappear. If it couldn't, having Detective Spears in here with me would help a little. He seemed genuine like he really cared for me, of course wanting something to erupt between us.

The Detective placed a hand underneath my chin and forced me to look at her. "You know what I'm here for, don't you?"

Strangely I did. I knew it was for Terrell.

"Why did you kill that little boy?"

The sound of the gun that killed Terrell filled my head and ears. The sight of me burning in the electric chair did the same.

"What little boy," I attempted.

She placed her hands on her hips. Her back was to the dark window on the far wall. "Why did you kill Terrell, Zaria? Don't play with me."

She looked like she wanted to hit me. I looked into her face. She looked so damn familiar to me. I racked my brain. Suddenly it came to me. She was with Kenneth the night he attacked me at the rental car place. I gasped. But there was some place else, I just couldn't put my finger on it.

"Oh shit! That's where…that's where," I repeated a few times after realizing where I'd seen her.

The Detective figured by the look on my face that I recognized her, but said nothing while Detective Hill placed one hand on the back of my chair and the other on the table. She leaned her face down so close to mine our noses were nearly touching. "You look like you think you know me from somewhere," she whispered threateningly. "Do you?"

I was frozen by the vicious look on her face. And her thick, eyebrows frightened me to the core. Her teeth gritted.

"Do you?" she whispered angrily.

Her message was clear. I was to say nothing. "No, I don't," I answered, knowing she would somehow probably kill me if I told her I recognized her face. It was so weird knowing that the person who'd probably shot me was now in the same room with me and I couldn't tell anyone. There was no one who could protect me from such a nasty savage.

She backed away and my eyes dropped to the floor as I realized she was with Kenneth when he chased me from the rental car place. She was there, riding with him. And now the bitch was out to get me.

"Now tell me about Terrell's murder." She began to circle me.

My eyes were still looking at the floor. "I don't…I…I

don't know anything about his murder."

"So, are you trying to say you didn't kidnap him?" She was still circling me. "Are you going to lie about that, too?"

"I...I..."

"I isn't a fuckin answer, Zaria! You kidnapped him, didn't you?"

"Yes," I admitted shamefully. "But I didn't kill him."

"Then what happened to him? How did his body wash up on the banks of a river?

I didn't know what to say.

She stopped circling me and placed her hands flat on the table. "We know you brutally killed that little boy. We also know that no matter what happens to you here for the murders you've committed in Philadelphia, you will immediately be extradited back to New York City. And I'm gonna make absolutely sure you get the chair."

My body couldn't stop shaking. Visions of myself sitting in that chair made the room seem smaller.

"I've seen executions, Zaria. I've witnessed them."

My body began rocking back and forth again.

"Your skin literally cooks until smoke rises from it."

I rocked faster.

"Your eyes bulge so far from out of your sockets they can't be pushed back in."

"Stop it please, stop it," I whispered.

"The pain is so excruciating you bite your tongue in half and choke on your own blood."

Tears fell from my eyes again.

"It's gruesome, Zaria." Detective Hill's voice was cold. "And the smell..."

My tearful eyes zoomed in on the detective. "I don't want to die," I pleaded.

"Then help me help you. Why did you kill Terrell?"

The truth wouldn't come out. I wanted it to but it just wouldn't. I could only look at her with sadness.

The detective recognized the hurt in my eyes. "Did you

kill him *because* of someone?" Did you kill him *for* someone?"

My head dropped again. Silence was all I could give.

"Is that someone the same reason you killed Tyson?"

Still only silence as Hardy's face appeared in my thoughts and my heart.

"Is it, Zaria?"

So many visions of Hardy flashed. None of this would've ever happened if he would have loved me.

"Was that person possibly involved?"

I couldn't speak.

Detective Hill sighed in defeat. "Oh well," she said. "If you want to burn in the chair, fuck it. I tried to help you." She headed for the door.

"He killed Tyson right in front of me." The words finally spilled from my mouth as the tears poured endlessly.

A grin appeared on the detective's face. "*Who* killed Tyson in front of you?" she asked, stopping to turn to me. "Who?"

I exhaled.

"Who, Zaria?"

My eyes closed. "Hardy," I answered. "Gerald Hardy."

She walked back to me. "Are you sure?"

I nodded. "Yes."

"Is he the reason you murdered Terrell?"

I nodded again. "I couldn't help it. I loved him so much but he wouldn't love me back."

Another smirk appeared on Selena Hill's face as she knelt in front of me. I hated the fact that she had a boy's haircut, yet carried herself as if she thought she was the shit. Something sinister and sneaky was in her eyes.

"You know you just fucked up, right?" she asked, re-minding me of the movie, *Menace to Society* when Bill Duke kept questioning O-Dog and Caine. "You know that, don't you? You just fucked up!"

Nothing but hatred formed inside my heart for her.

Fuckin bitch!

Selena stood and turned to the window. "Now you got your answer, boys," she said. "Go get 'em."

My entire body felt emotionally drained.

Selena walked to the door and opened it. I heard the voices of Berkowitz and Spears as their footsteps dashed quickly past the interrogation room, no doubt on their way to pick up Hardy. Strangely, I felt like I had betrayed him. I wished at that moment I could take back my words. Now that Hardy was my baby's father, we shared a bond. A bond that none could break. I was willing to forgive him for all the wrong he'd done to me. I knew he would forgive me, too. Now maybe we could start over for the sake of little Devin.

"Oh, by the way," the detective stated, walking back toward me. She leaned into me ear and whispered, "For $4,500.00, I can try to get your time reduced back in New York, maybe even lose a little evidence."

Fucking conniving bitch! I thought. She'd get hers if it was the last thing I did.

ZARIA
....

Twenty-Two

"Damn it!" I shouted, slamming my cuffed hands on the table of the interrogation room and monitoring the crowd of detectives in the hall outside the door.

I couldn't believe that sneaky bitch had the guts to ask me for forty-five hundred dollars after she had just talked me into sailing my own ass up the river without a paddle.

The fact that Detective Hill had most likely shot me and had possibly been the last to see my cousin alive had me boiling to the core. By the evil look she'd given me when she noticed that I'd recognized her, it was safe to assume that she'd probably done much more than just being one of the last to see Kenneth alive. The bitch had probably killed him, one of my last remaining relatives. The possibility angered me. What gave her the right to judge and convict me if she had blood on her own damn hands?

There was also a huge amount of sympathy in my heart for Hardy all of a sudden. I couldn't help feeling like I'd betrayed him. The voices in my head attempted to make me feel stupid reminding me of all the grimy things he'd done to me…the way he treated me…and the way he threw me away like trash. But, no matter how angry I was at him for his treatment of me and for killing Tyson, there was still love in my heart for him. Shit, a part of my heart was still his, and always would be his. The last thing I wanted was to see him spend the rest of his life in prison. No matter what he'd done, I didn't want to see that.

Hearing several voices in the hall behind me I leaned back in my chair and listened. Even as whispers my ears could recognize Berkowtiz's and Spears' voices easily among the other officers. I wondered why they were still outside the door after they'd dashed out a moment ago to get Hardy. For nearly ten minutes the voices chattered at a low volume, making me wonder what was being discussed. Something didn't seem right about it.

Did the detectives already know where Hardy was? Were they strategizing? Was my admission that Hardy had committed Tyson's murder somehow running into some sort of problem? What was taking them so long to go and get Hardy?

Footsteps came from the hallway towards my back. Detective Spears appeared in front of me. He had a puzzling look on his face as he walked around to the opposite side of the table and looked at me again. Both his hands were in his pants pockets.

"Ms. Hopkins," he said looking at me carefully. "I need you to be completely honest with me about something."

"Okay," I told him.

He took his hands from his pockets and folded his arms. "Ms. Hopkins, do you know Detective Hill?"

My heart jumped into my throat. Although I hated the bitch's guts, I knew better than to open my mouth and tell what I knew about her. She was probably on the other side of that dark window just daring me to tell so she could kill me, gutting me like a pig. No mistakes this time.

"No," I lied.

"Are you sure?" His expression told me he suspected I

was lying to him.

I nodded. "Yes, I'm sure."

He didn't look at all convinced. He didn't even look like a cop anymore. If anything, he now looked like a worried friend wanting to protect a friend. "Ms. Hopkins, remember when I told you earlier that I wouldn't let anything happen to you?"

"Yes."

"I meant that."

I glared at him strangely for seconds.

The detective placed his hands on the back of his chair and looked deeply into my eyes. "Did you know Detective Hill before she interviewed you?" he asked with affection. "Had you ever seen her before?"

My eyes fell to my lap. They refused to give him contact. For one, I knew he was falling for me. And two, I didn't want to tell my new admirer a lie. "No," I answered, feeling terrible.

"*You're a lying bitch*," that voice in my head roared. But I blocked it out. I had to. It was time for me to make some changes in my life…making decisions on my own.

"Ms. Hopkins, I can protect you. I promise I can, but I can't if you won't tell me…"

My eyes rose to his pitifully. "Detective," I said, interrupting him, "you said I could have a phone call. Can I please have it now?" I pleaded in an innocent tone.

The detective looked at me for several moments, seeing pain in my eyes. He waited for what seemed like minutes then finally sighed in defeat.

"Alright, I'll take you to make your phone call."

I stood and the detective led me out to the processing area by the crowded bullpen. There was a phone sitting on a long, narrow wooden plank that ran along the bottom of the intake office's bulletproof window. Behind the window at least a dozen uniformed officers milled about conversing, eating donuts, and drinking coffee.

"Only one call, Ms. Hopkins," Spears instructed. "You only get a few minutes, alright?"

I nodded.

The detective took off my handcuffs and walked toward the doorway of the intake office near the uniformed officers. After glancing back at the loud prostitute filled bullpen, I picked up the phone and dialed a number I'd thought I'd forgotten, and there was still heavy doubt that it would actually ring. I hoped desperately for the best but was expecting the operator's voice to say the number had been changed or disconnected. That was the way my luck always seemed to work. Despite my doubts and expectations though, after a few brief moments of silence, the opposite end of the line began to ring. I pressed the phone tightly to my ear and closed my eyes, hoping he would answer...he had to. Finally after the fourth ring he answered. I couldn't believe it. I was so shocked that my mouth was nearly speechless.

"Hello, hello," he said.

I finally spoke up. "Hardy?"

"Zaria?" he uttered in disbelief.

I went totally quiet, not quite knowing what to say to him.

"You've got some muthafucking nerve calling me."

His hostility broke my heart, but I knew I deserved it.

"You're a selfish bitch," he continued. "Not only do you murder my son, but now you bail out on our child. I should've put two bullets in you when I had the chance."

His chastisement nearly killed me. Tears welled up behind my closed eyelids. I knew I was wrong for neglecting my son. I just didn't have a motherly bone in my body unless I had the dad to go with the package. If it wasn't for Devin, my world seemed to be meaningless that is until now that I'd heard Hardy's voice crying out to me. He needed me, yet didn't know it.

"I hope they have a special spot in hell set aside for your ass," Hardy told me. "You need to burn. I mean day and night type of burning. All you do is hurt people."

My knees grew weak, but somehow I forced myself to

remain standing.

Hardy's voice began to crack with sadness. "And how could you do that to Terrell?" he asked with vibrations in his voice.

Hearing him sniffling, I wanted to lie and say I didn't kill Terrell, but something inside my heart wouldn't allow me to.

"That was my little man, Zaria. How could you take him away from me? He never did a muthafucking thing to you."

My eyes finally opened. I leaned my body against the wall shamefully, wishing I could be anyone but myself.

"You destroyed my life," Hardy cried. "You took away Terrell's life. Now, you can't even be maternal enough to be here for your *own* child as he's fighting for his life."

My tears fell to the floor.

"You're not a human being, Zaria. You're a walking plague."

The words stung so hard I winced. Our relationship was dwindling again. "Hardy," I finally spoke softly, staring at the floor, "I'm so sorry."

Hardy was silent.

I needed him to talk to me so we could start over from day one. I knew he could forgive me and maybe we'd be a family again.

"I'm sorry for everything I did to you, baby. I swear I am. If I could take it all back, I would. I don't know why I'm the person I am. It's my upbringing…that's why we've got to do the right thing with our son."

Hardy was still silent, but I could hear his cries. The sound was breaking my heart.

"I just wanted you to love me so badly," I told him. The memory of the very first time he walked into my classroom played in my head, making me wish the both of us could go back to it with a snap of the finger. "I loved you more than I loved myself," I continued, meaning each word from the bottom of my heart. "And I just wanted you to feel the same way about me."

I could feel him inside of me again exploring all my organs with his rod. I could feel myself wrapped in his arms again. I could smell him again. His memory made him feel so nearby.

"Hardy, please forgive me," I begged. "Please say you'll forgive me. I know you'll always hate me. But please say you'll forgive me."

"That'll never happen, Zaria."

"Please, baby."

Someone cleared their throat behind me. I turned to see Detective Spears standing there. "One minute, Ms. Hopkins."

The door that Spears brought me out of opened and a tall, authoritative detective walked out of it. He glanced at me and signaled to Spears to follow him into the intake office. Both detectives went behind the bullet proof glass and began to speak, glancing through the glass at me every now and then. It made me think back to what was actually going on in their investigation.

"Hardy," I said quickly, knowing I didn't have too much time remaining on the phone. My voice was low so no one could hear me. "Look, I have to make things right with you so listen good. I told the police you killed Tyson."

Hardy exhaled into the phone with disgust followed by a long, "What!"

"Listen, Hardy," I demanded. "The police are coming to get you. They know you were at the house that night. But one of the detectives seems to really have it in for you. It's like she knew about you and who you were before I even told her. It's like she wanted to pin you for Tyson's murder even though my prints are on the gun. Something's not right about her. Even the police know something's not right about her." The words were spraying from my mouth like a machine gun. "I also think she killed my cousin Kenneth. I saw her with him the night he was killed."

"Kenneth?" Hardy said questionably as if he knew the name.

"Yeah, she even knows that I saw her with him."

"What's the detective's name?" Hardy asked suspiciously.

"It's Hill. Selena Hill."

"Shit, Zaria. I know that bitch. She's trying to pin your cousin's murder on me."

"You know her?"

"Yeah, but I didn't kill your cousin, Zaria."

"I know you didn't, baby."

Don't call me that, please."

"Okay, I'll stop. Anything you ask, I'll do."

"Well, Selena told me *she* killed him. And since I wouldn't go along with some ridiculous scheme she has going on where she keeps unauthorized immigrants in the country by having someone marry them. She has the police looking for me for your cousin's murder."

It all made sense to me now. This Selena lady was trying to take my son's father away for life. "Hardy, wherever you are, you've got to run. You've got to run now." I was so worried for him.

"Damn it!" Hardy shouted into the phone. "You better watch your back Zaria. She was the one who shot you. She told me."

As my suspicions were confirmed, an idea popped into my head. "Hardy, listen. I have an idea," I spoke carefully. "I'll never see the streets again. They're most likely going to give me the chair for Terrell's murder, but I'm going to tell them that I lied about Tyson's murder. I'm going to tell them you had nothing to do with it. I did it all myself. I'm also going to tell them I killed Kenneth, too."

Hardy listened carefully.

"But the only way it can work is if you do something about Detective Hill. She's the only one who can blow everything apart for us. We need her out of the picture, and pay her ass back for shooting me, the mother of your child."

"Oh my God!" Hardy winced. "My life is so fucked up!"

"Hardy, I've messed up a lot in life, but the son you and I

created doesn't deserve to suffer for it. I'm willing to take the heat on everything if it means he can have his father in his life."

Hardy exhaled.

"Baby, this is the only way."

"I said don't call me that."

"Okay. I won't. But let me do this."

"Alright, Zaria," Hardy finally said with a normal voice. His sniffling seemed to stop. "Don't worry about the detective. I got something that will set her ass all the way straight."

Detective Spears came out of the intake office. "Time's up, Ms. Hopkins."

Knowing I would most likely never get the chance to see or talk to Hardy again, I gripped the phone as tightly as I could and told him I would always love him.

After a brief moment of silence Hardy said, "I know, Zaria. I know." His words were filled with genuine love and compassion. "You take care of yourself in there, alright?"

I told him I would and started making little kissing sounds hoping he was kissing me back.

Suddenly, the line went dead.

I slowly placed the receiver back into the cradle, saddened by the fact that I would never hear his voice again or watch my son take his first step. Spears placed the cuffs on me. As they clicked around my wrists the door at the opposite end of the intake lobby opened. Two cops walked in holding a woman between them with her hands cuffed in front of her. I turned and couldn't believe my eyes.

It was Tayvia.

Tayvia's clothes were ripped, dirty, and wrinkled as if she'd been in a tussle. Her mascara ran down her face filled with sadness. Her eyes were to the floor but rose and widened as she entered the lobby and saw me.

"You bitch!" Tayvia screamed, trying to get to me. She jerked, twisted, and kicked but the officers' grip on her arms were too strong. "You murdering bitch! Tyson loved you!"

At the mention of Tyson's name Detective Spears took

notice. "You know her?" he asked me.

I didn't answer.

"What's her name?" Spears asked the officers over Tayvia's screams.

"Tayvia Roth," one of them announced. "We got her for disorderly conduct, destruction of property, and making terroristic threats down at the hospital. Oh, and for performing a striptease act," the officer joked.

Spears obviously remembered Tayvia's name from somewhere. His face suddenly tightened. She was the witness who said Zaria had argued with Tyson the night of his murder.

Spears unlocked the door to take me back to my cell.

"Noooo!" Tayvia screamed, still fighting. "Detective!"

Spears turned.

"I've got very important information about Tyson's murder!" Tayvia yelled.

"I've got all I need, Ms. Roth. Besides, this isn't the place we would discuss it."

"You don't understand," she said quickly. "It's very important. I guarantee it's much more important than what you've got right now. But I won't tell you what it is unless you let me and Zaria talk."

"Doesn't work that way, Ms. Roth."

"You'll get a promotion for what I'm going to give you, Detective. I swear you will."

Spears stared at Tayvia as if giving it some thought.

"Just let us talk, Detective."

Besides the prostitutes' and crack heads' voices coming from the bullpen the lobby was silent.

Finally Spears told the officers to take Tayvia to the interrogation room. We followed behind them. When we reached the room, the detective sat us both down at the table, closed the door, pressed play on the recorder, and folded his arms.

I eyed Tayvia, hating her. What the fuck did she have to say that was so important?

"What did he ever see in you?" she asked.

I knew she was speaking of Tyson, but remained quiet. After the phone call with Hardy and knowing I would never see freedom again, all the fight was pretty much knocked out of me. The voices in my head weren't even saying anything.

"I'll never understand it," Tayvia continued, her words filled with bitterness. "I'm prettier than you, smarter than you, and have much more going for myself than you."

Spears listened as he leaned against the wall.

"I just don't get it," she continued. "What did he see in a nothing ass tramp like you?"

The words hurt. She was right. She had much more to offer Tyson than I did. For the first time since I'd met him, I now wondered what he saw in me that was much more special than what Tayvia possessed.

"Tyson was supposed to have been mine, bitch," she said, leaning toward my face and pointing like a crazy woman. "You stole him away from me."

Spears finally spoke. "Look, Ms. Roth, I hate to interrupt your little venting session, but what do you have for me? I can lose my job over this shit. Start talking."

"She had an accomplice," Tayvia said eyeing me. "She didn't do it alone."

I saw where this was going. Another woman wanting to blame something on Hardy. I knew I needed to protect him. "She's lying," I blurted out.

"His name is Hardy," Tayvia said.

"We know this already. Give us something else." It was clear that Spears had gotten irritated.

Tayvia rambled as if she had something good. "He and I were supposed to go out on a date that night but he didn't show up. Today at the hospital he told me why."

"She's a liar, Detective. Don't believe her."

"He told me they set the whole thing up. He didn't show up for the date with me because he and Zaria were both busy murdering Tyson. They just needed to lure me away first."

I lunged across the table at her throat. "You lying

whore!"

Spears charged me, wrapping his arms around my mid-section and called for the other officers.

"She's lying!" I screamed as I struggled to break free. "She's lying!"

The other officers opened the door to the room and rushed inside.

Tayvia smirked devilishly. "And just so you know, when they were bringing me in I saw Devin outside with his lawyers," she told me with venom in her tone. "See, my men come for me. He'll have me out of here quicker than you can say, "your pussy stinks."

My heart stopped. *Devin? My Devin? How could he?* I knew that Tayvia knew a lot of guys in the football industry, but I didn't think she knew trainers, too. "You stay away from him! He's mine!" I began screaming. The voices in my head came back for the first time in days.

"*Damn, Zaria. You lose again. That makes you a loser! The only thing you can do now is take Spears' gun and kill everyone. Or of course, kill yourself.*"

The cops were dragging me to the door while I kicked and fought with everything I had. I kept trying to convince myself that Tyavia was lying. She just wanted to get the best of me.

"You're a liar," I blurted.

"*No, she's not,*" the voice in my head spat. "*But, you're a fucking dummy. Kill yourself.*"

"He's paying my bail for me as we speak," Tayvia continued, now smiling and pointing to her neck. "And what about this tattoo. He asked me to get it to confess my love for him."

I paused for just a second to look closely at the tattoo I'd seen hundreds of times. Those initials that I wondered about now made sense. D.T. was for Devin Taylor. She was definitely telling the truth. "Detective," I begged. "Please let me talk to Devin! Please!"

"Take her out," Spears told the officers.

"Don't worry, Zaria," Tayvia said sarcastically as they

dragged me to the hallway. "I'm going to take real good care of Devin for you."

"You stay away from him, you devious tramp!"

Tayvia laughed.

"Detective, I need to see Devin!" I screamed. But the door to the interrogation room shut and faded from sight as the cops dragged me back to my cell.

Maybe I will just kill myself.

Smiley Face. Smiley Face. Can anyone see my Smiley Face, I chanted softly.

HARDY
Twenty-Three

The sound of the window's glass shattering caused me to jump nervously. I took a moment to glance around the back yard's darkness, hoping I hadn't awakened any of the surrounding neighbors. I honestly expected at least one light to come on or the movement of at least one curtain, but thankfully my expectations were wrong. The neighbors appeared to be still sound asleep, allowing me to quickly hop inside.

I knew that what I was hoping for was nothing more than a shot in the dark. It was extremely doubtful that Selena would be stupid enough to keep anything incriminating in her house, but I had no other choice right now except to hope for the best. I needed to find something dirty on her to level our playing field. Right now she had me by the balls. If I couldn't find anything, the only option left for me would be to kill her. The thought filled me with overflowing dread but I was more than prepared to do it if shit came down to it.

After Zaria's call I hopped on the freeway and headed north to Selena's. Only four hours had passed and at least a thousand thoughts had scurried through my head nonstop. Wrapping my mind around the whirlwind of things that had gone on in my life since going to Philly had me overwhelmed. My life was in shambles and it all seemed too far-fetched to believe. The strangest thing happened to be newfound compassion and sympathy for Zaria.

After hanging up with the woman who had destroyed my life, I couldn't help finding myself feeling sorry for her. I couldn't help wondering how things would have turned out if I'd at least *tried* to love her. Obviously it was my own selfishness and cheating ways that sent her completely over the deep end. Knowing that now danced mercilessly on my conscience, especially with her decision to take Tyson's murder rap for me. Her decision to sacrifice herself dimmed my burning hatred for her.

Broken glass crackled and crunched underneath my shoes as I climbed into the dark bedroom and stepped down onto the carpeted floor. My heart was beating loudly as I thought about the gun tucked inside my pants. I hoped I wouldn't have to use it. However, if Selena happened to show up, there would be absolutely no other choice. It would be my life or hers.

I clicked on my flashlight and began to search her expensively furnished home from top to bottom. It always amazed me each time I came to visit her just how lavish her home was. It was filled from top to bottom with shit I knew she couldn't afford on a cop's salary. No doubt it all came from the money she was making from her illegal side hustles. The bitch was as crooked as they came and was living extremely well off of it.

From the downstairs to the upstairs I began to search everything; closets, cabinets, furniture cushions, clothes hampers and dresser drawers. I searched *everything*, careful not to leave a single stone unturned.

The search eventually frustrated me. There was absolutely nothing, I realized as I stood in the center of her bedroom with my hands on my hips. My head swiveled as I looked around the dark but moonlit room, hoping tremendously that I had missed something.

The telephone rang breaking the silence and scaring me half to death. It scared me so bad my heart leapt into my throat and I quickly lifted my shirt, going for my gun.

I remained in the center of the room, calming myself from the fear filled jolt the phone had sent rushing through my body. After several unanswered rings, I then heard a beep and a man's voice began to speak.

"Selena, I've been trying to reach you all day," the man said. "Selena, if you're there, pick up. It's real fucking important. Pick up. We got problems." His voice sounded both anxious and nervous.

I couldn't believe it. This bitch had all types of high tech gadgets and shit along with a nice house, and plenty of money, but still had an old ass answering machine. I shook my head, while continuing to listen.

"Look, Selena," the man continued. "Immigration Services came to see me today. They asked a lot of questions. I think they've caught onto us. I didn't tell them shit. But they're not stupid, for Christ's sake."

I stepped closer to the phone beside the bed.

"Damn it, Selena. I don't know how I let your ass talk me into this shit in the first place. We should've shut down the whole operation after we dumped that Guatemalan bitch in The East River."

My eyes grew wide.

"If Immigration Services is asking questions, it's only a matter of time before Internal Affairs is knee deep in our asses, too."

Another crooked cop. Damn, do they come any other way, I thought to myself.

"This shit is fucked up, Selena. It's really fucked up. Call me as soon as…"

The machine cut him off.

Jackpot, I thought to myself as the man hung up and the answering service beeped. I immediately snatched my cell phone from my pocket, replayed the message into my receiver, and recorded it.

I had her ass for a possible murder, but something inside me told me there was something more I was missing, something in the house. I could just feel it. While standing beside the bed my eyes locked on her Gucci and Prada filled closet. I'd searched it but there was nothing there except clothes and shoes. My eyes dropped to its floor. A questioning possibility popped into my head. I walked into the closet, knelt down, and slipped my fingers between the wall and the carpet's edges. I pulled the corner of the carpet back and shined the flashlight onto the exposed wooden floor. I let my hand slide slowly over the wood. To my surprise, I found exactly what I had been hoping for…loose boards.

I lifted the boards and saw a shoebox sitting beneath them. Anxiously, I pulled it out and opened it. There were two stacks of hundred dollar bills inside and several DVDs in clear cases. The money went directly into my pockets as I stood and walked over to the television. I turned the television on and slipped a DVD into the player. A moment later my eyes couldn't believe what they were witnessing. Selena was having sex with girls who were clearly underage. Some even looked like they were barely thirteen.

My mouth dropped as Selena used dildos and strap-ons on nearly each young girl brutally, their screams and tears only turning her on more and urging her to continue. Each scene I skipped to left me speechless.

Finally, I snatched the DVD out, and placed it back in its case, anxious to get revenge on Selena. As I headed to the window a voice came from the doorway behind me sending my heart racing.

"Got your ass right where I want you," Selena said. "You're dead."

Before I could turn around a gun went off, shattering the room's silence and ending a life forever.

ZARIA

Twenty-Four

Smiley Face. Smiley Face. Can anyone see my Smiley Face? I asked myself not allowing my enemies to see me sweat. Two days had gone by since my initial interrogation at the precinct. Ultimately, my life had been ruined. I'd now been charged and the entire city of Philadelphia and New York wanted me dead.

Destroyed.

And someone had to pay.

I now sat in an examination room at the County Jail dressed in sneakers and an oversized, orange jumpsuit. As I placed the ink pen on the paper confessing to Tyson's and Terrell's murders, I couldn't help but to reflect on the events that had gotten me here. It started with my no- good parents, trickling down to my aunt and other selfish family members who never loved me. Then it moved on to all the no-good men that constantly entered my life, and has now ended with bitches like Milan, Tayvia, and Kelsey who all wanted to hurt me, stealing my style and portraying it as their own. But more importantly, it was time for me to become a no-nonsense bitch only concerning myself with what was important in life.

I thought about Hardy and our son. Memories of their faces brought a smile to my own despite my pain. I knew Hardy still loved me and that's what I would hold in my heart to keep me sane as I did my time. I had visions of him picking me up upon my release, swinging me in the air and deep- throating me for everyone to see.

"Ummmm, you okay," a voice sounded, snapping me from my thoughts.

I remained glossy eyed until he called my name again. "Zaria."

Devin, still fine as ever, stood only several feet away from me with Kelsey standing beside him waiting for me to an-swer. Her arm was in a sling and looked as if she was still emo-tionally trying to move past the blood bath back at Eric's. Her presence gnawed away at me but I didn't let it show. I continued to ignore him.

Turns out, Devin wasn't at the precinct on the night of my interrogation to bail Tayvia's lying ass out of jail. He and his lawyers were actually there to help me. An hour after I had been kicking and screaming like a wild savage back to my cell, De-tective Spears came and got me, saying my attorneys were there to see me. I didn't know anything whatsoever about having an attorney. I'd never hired anyone. The detective escorted me to a visiting room. My eyes grew wide as all out doors when he opened the door and I saw Devin and three attorneys sitting in-side. I extended my arms and thanked God for my man until Kelsey's face appeared. I remembered asking Devin why Kelsey was there.

As Devin's attorneys spoke to me that day, it became dif-ficult for me to concentrate on their words. Since I was so stressed out. the entire visit was spent with me dividing my time between them and the voice in my head. The voice had always been a fuckin annoyance. But that day in front of Devin and the lawyers she chose to show out and go extremely hard on me.

"*You worthless bitch,*" she told me. "*These lawyers can't help you. You're going to burn."*

"I'm not worthless," I remembered saying.

"Yes you are. You've been since the day you were born. The entire world has betrayed you. And now you're going to pay for what you've done."

"I won't!" I remembered saying .

"You will, stupid. You're going to get the chair."

"Why do you always have to call me stupid? I'm not stupid. Stop calling me that!"

The entire room stared at me in utter silence that day, the same as they're doing now.

I guess after witnessing the fallout between me and the voice in my head let my attorneys know that everything they had dug up from my past and my medical history was absolutely true. I was definitely a schizophrenic. Because of that they were able to get my original confession thrown out. Instead, with the confession I signed today, I would be able to plead insanity. The plea would possibly keep me from going to the chair and maybe even get me sent to a special facility for treatment instead of the penitentiary.

"Alright, Ms. Hopkins," Detective Spears said, taking my confession and standing from the table. "You can expect New York authorities to be coming by at some point to take you back to New York to answer for one of the murders you just confessed to."

I nodded, still refusing to speak. My hair was sprawled atop of my head making me look like I'd been stung by a stun gun. Everything seemed so clear to me now. No one mattered anymore but my son and Hardy.

"I'll step out and let you guys talk for a moment," Spears told everyone.

As Spears stepped out of the room my attorneys who had been sitting beside me in expensive suits and Gucci loafers during my signing of the confession, stood and assured me that everything was going to turn out okay.

"Ms. Hopkins, just know that we're going to do our best

for you. You will get the medical help you need."

They shook hands with Devin, grabbed their briefcases and walked out of the room, leaving me alone with Devin and Kelsey.

"Isn't that good news?" Devin asked me with enthusiasm in his tone.

I refused to even blink.

"I still don't see why you're going through all this fuss for her," Kelsey mumbled.

"Quiet," he instructed. "I told you this is something I must do for her."Devin looked at her sternly and sat down across the table from me. "They're damned good attorneys," he assured me. "They're the best in the business, Zaria. They'll get you off."

Smelling his cologne, my eyes were locked on Devin's face. He was still just as handsome and sexy as he was the first time I met him, his frame still muscular, his hair still long and neatly dreaded. His naturally slanted brown eyes still sent sexual shivers through my body which caused me to lick my lips seductively. Kelsey must have saw what Devin's presence was doing to me because she immediately sat beside him and grabbed his hand as if to let me know he belonged to her.

Fucking weak pussied jealous bitch! Why'd he have to bring her any way? What purpose was she serving besides aggravating me like a cockroach begging to be smushed?

"Zaria," Devin began genuinely, "I want to apologize again about the way things turned out between us. I should've never let it start in the first place. I was wrong for leading you on."

Kelsey watched me closely. Her expression looked like a smirk but I couldn't be completely sure. Whatever it was though, her presence was urking me more and more. I wished that Devin and I could be alone. I wished that it was my hand he was holding instead of hers. Above all, I wished Kelsey hadn't survived the shootout back at Eric's.

When I dived into the backseat of the Suburban, Kelsey

and the other woman immediately hit the ground in front of the SUV as the bullets started buzzing by. They escaped being hit, although Kelsey dislocated her shoulder by coming down on the pavement so hard. That's why she was sitting in front of me right now with her arm in a sling, looking like a retarded crippled bitch.

"Cheating on my wife should've never been an option," Devin continued. "No matter what we were going through, I should have been man enough to work things out with her. I pulled you in because I was lonely, and I'm so sorry."

I said absolutely nothing. My head was tilted slightly to the side as I smiled at the happy couple in front of me. Honestly, Devin's words were going in one ear and right out of the other. His words of apology sounded more like he was rubbing my face in the fact that he had gotten back with his wife. Silently, anger burned in me but I knew now was not the time to show it. My revenge would come soon enough. And when it did, I was going to smack that goofy ass smirk directly off of Kelsey's face as I buried her into the ground.

"Smiley Face. Smiley Face," I began to sing as I started rocking back and forth in my chair smiling, and ignoring Devin's voice. "Can anyone see my Smiley Face?"

The song harmoniously came from my mouth over and over again until Devin finally realized his words were falling on deaf ears. He and Kelsey finally left with me silently vowing that we would see each other again real soon. As soon as the door closed a C.O. took me back upstairs to the crowded pod of women, each in orange jumpsuits like mine. As they talked loudly, played cards, and watched an overhanging television, I headed directly to the line of phones and called the hospital to check on my son.

"Ms. Roth," the nurse said after I began to ask for information on little Devin, anxious to hear that he was doing well. "I'm glad you reached out."

"How's my son?"

"He's recovering well. The little guy is a fighter, but has

Department of Children's Services notified you about the latest legal development?"

"No." I wondered what she was talking about. "What latest development?"

The nurse sounded uncomfortable with having to give me the news. "One, the father has legally changed his name. And two, your son is being adopted."

My eyes saw nothing but red. "Adopted by who?" I asked.

"I can't give you that information, Ms. Roth. You'll have to get in touch with Children's Services. All I can tell you is that the woman who's adopting him seems very nice."

I blacked out! Hardy had lied to me. He didn't care about our son. The bastard had only used me to get out of having to answer for Tyson's murder. I slammed the phone and began to pace back and forth angrily. I'd been betrayed and lied to again.

With nothing but vengeance on my mind, I snatched the phone's receiver from its cradle, placed my foot on the wall for leverage, and yanked the receiver several times as hard as I could until it finally tore loose from the cord. With the receiver tightly in my right hand, I marched to a nearby girl sitting at a table playing cards with her back to me. I tapped her on the shoulder. As soon as she turned I sent the receiver crashing brutally into her nose so hard blood splattered her entire face. Snatching her by the shirt and slamming her to the floor, I began to repeatedly bash her face in with the receiver, fracturing and breaking bones with each hit. As my hands grew more and more drenched in blood all I could think about was the revenge I was going to inflict on Hardy, Devin and Kelsey. If they really thought they were going to get away with betraying me, they were sadly mistaken.

Payback is a muthufucka, I told myself.

HARDY

Twenty-Five

My luck couldn't have gotten any better, I thought as I cracked open a cold Heineken and leaned against my kitchen sink, dwelling on my blessings. I guess nearly being killed and just barely escaping prison for the rest of your life would change anyone's outlook on things.

I grabbed the remote from the counter and turned the television on just in time to see Selena's face plastered across the screen for the third time this week. The news stations had been eating her alive all week and I was loving every second of it. But it couldn't have been possible at all if not for Santiago. It was only because of her that I was alive and breathing. Turns out she had been outside the hospital wrestling with her feelings after seeing Tayvia get carried out and leaving me alone. She had been sitting out in the parking lot behind the wheel of her car debating whether or not to stick with me throughout what I was going through. But she just didn't trust me. When she saw me leave the hospital, she followed me to the rental car agency and back to New York. When I reached New York and headed straight to Selena's, she wondered what was going on and assumed she would catch me in the act of cheating.

While parked at the curb with the lights out, Santiago later told me that she circled Selena's house front and back until she discovered that I had broken in from the back. When Selena pulled up unexpectedly, Santiago immediately knew things were going to get ugly. Hearing the television coming from the bedroom Selena crept inside with her gun out, leaving the front door open. When she got to the bedroom and saw me everything changed. I still remembered her words like it was hours ago.

"The thought of killing you for breaking and entering got my pussy all wet," she'd warned.

"Awe nah, Selena. Don't do this. Let's talk," I begged.

As she raised the gun she had no idea that Santiago had crept in through the front door. Seeing that Selena was undoubtedly going to kill me Santiago shot her twice, one bullet to each arm.

Selena survived but only to be released from the hospital directly into police custody. Internal Affairs had already been investigating her and another cop in her department on everything from planting drugs on people, and falsifying paperwork to kidnapping and murder. The movies I had found and the voice message her partner left on her answering service was all it took. Her partner turned on her and told everything to save his own ass. Selena was never going to see the streets again.

As far as me and Santiago, we're good. Seeing her loyalty to me and her willingness to love me when I didn't deserve it showed me what true love really is. These days I understand the value of a good woman. And although my eyes stray occasionally, my mind, body, and heart remain planted in Santiago's arms where I know I belong.

My cell phone rang as I turned the volume on the television down.

"What's good?" Kyle said after I answered.

"Chilling. Just watching this crazy bitch on TV."

Selena was in the back of a squad car trying to disgracefully hide her face behind her cuffed hands from dozens of flashing cameras. I laughed because I could still spot her crazy ass eyebrows.

"Yeah," Kyle laughed. "I'm watching her ass, too."

"I still can't believe she really tried to jam me up like that."

"You got to watch the company you keep, homeboy. I hope you learned your lesson this time."

"Hell yeah," I said in agreement. I truly understood that now.

"You know you can just buy pussy now days, right?" I laughed and just shook my head thinking, not a bad idea.

"So, how things go in court today?"

"They went good. The mediator said she would recommend to the Judge to give Dana joint custody. So, we'll make it official on Friday."

I still couldn't believe the turn of events between Dana and myself. Dana deserved just as much of a chance at finding joy as I did. Terrell's death was my fault. And although I knew nothing could ever change that, I still offered her joint custody of my son as long as I was able to see him freely. With tears in her eyes she accepted and rushed to see Gerald Hardy Junior in the hospital. The paperwork today made it semi-official.

"Was Mario there?" Kyle asked.

"Yeah."

"Y'all talk?"

"Yeah, we good now."

Mario and I squashed our beef. I finally accepted that I had played the biggest part in pushing Dana into his arms. If I had been the man she deserved, she would have never had any reason to go elsewhere. It was my fault.

Kyle and I hung up, promising to get on the court tonight at a nearby rec center for a couple games of basketball. I hadn't been on the court since Terrell's death. It was going to feel good to get back out there.

I exhaled, knowing God had given me a second chance at

love, friendship, and being a father. I couldn't ask for more.
A knock came at the door.

Knowing it was Santiago, I headed to the door, ready to take her in my arms, escort her directly to my bedroom, and make passionate love to her for hours. With a warm smile I opened the door. What I saw standing on my doorstep immediately made my smile disappear and my body stiffen.

"Hey, Sweetheart," Tayvia said, smiling with a gun pointed directly at my face and her finger wrapped snuggly around its trigger. "Told you I was gonna make you bleed."

My hands went up in defense. "Tayvia, what the fuck are you doing?" I asked, totally taken off guard. "How did you know where I even…"

"None of that is important. Now back into the house."

"Tayvia, look."

"I said back the fuck up!" she shouted angrily.

I did what I was told, nearly stumbling over my own feet. Tayvia shut the door and stared at me with rage filled eyes. "You thought you were going to actually get away with hurting me, huh, Hardy?"

"Tayvia, this is the wrong way to handle this." My hands were still raised. "I'm sorry for what I did to you. It was wrong. But this isn't the…"

"You used me, Hardy," she said, interrupting me. "You used me, you fucked me, and then you threw me out of your life like I was a piece of trash."

"Tayvia, I'm sorry for that."

"No, you're not. Men like you are all the same."

"I'm not that man anymore, Tayvia. I'm trying to change."

"Men never change. All of you think with your damn dicks. All of you think it's okay to just play with a woman's heart like a toy."

"Not anymore. Not me. I'm done with that."

"Save it, Hardy," she said, reaching into her purse and pulling out two pairs of handcuffs. She tossed them at my feet.

"Handcuff yourself to that chair over there."

I stepped towards her. "Tayvia…"

She cocked the gun, making me freeze in my tracks. "Do you think this is a game?" she asked. "Do you think I'm playing with you?"

"No," I answered, hoping to God she wouldn't shoot me.

"Now, do what the fuck I told you to do!"

I sat in the chair and handcuffed my ankles to its legs. She pulled out two more sets of handcuffs and cuffed my wrists to the arms of the chair.

"It doesn't have to be like this, Tayvia," I attempted.

"Yes it does. You made it this way. You have yourself to blame."

A knock came at the door.

"Who's that?" she asked, her head quickly swiveling from me to the door.

"I don't know."

She quickly headed to the front window and peeked out. She smiled. "It's your little bitch." She snatched the door open and shoved the gun directly into Santiago's face. "Get your ass in here," she demanded.

"What the hell is this all about?" Santiago fretted, stepping inside with her hands up. " I'm a cop. This isn't a good idea."

"I don't give a fuck what you are," Tayvia responded. "Take your gun out and drop it on the floor."

"Hardy, what's going on?" Santiago questioned me.

"Bitch!" Tayvia screamed. "He's not running shit around here. I am. Now, drop the gun before I blow your head all over this damn room!"

Santiago reluctantly did what she was told. Moments later she was cuffed in a chair beside me.

"So, you're the one that took him away from me," Tayvia told Santiago, the gun still pointed at her. "You're the bitch." Santiago was silent.

"Don't you know he's only going to do the same to you

that he did to me? He's just going to use you. As soon as he's bored with you, he's going to drop you like yesterday's news. That's what he does to all of his women."

"That's not true, Tayvia," I spat.

"Shut up!" she screamed, slapping me across the face with the butt of the gun. "Don't you say shit!"

My mouth ached in pain as I spit blood onto the floor. Tayvia's cell phone rang. She pulled it from her purse and looked at the screen. "Right on time," she mumbled as if expecting the call. She answered.

For several moments both Santiago and I watched Tayvia speak into the phone. Both of us wondered who she was talking to as she made references to us like we were part of some sick twisted plan she and the person on the other end of the line had going. My heart pounded. My body was shaking. I watched her closely, listening to her voice intently.

"Okay," Tayvia finally said to the person on the phone, her eyes directly on us. "I'm going to put you on speaker phone." She took the phone away from her ear, pressed a button, and held it towards us.

"Hey, Hardy," came Zaria's voice.

"Zaria?" I asked, wondering if it was really her voice I was recognizing.

"Yeah," she said. "It's me. You didn't expect to hear from me, huh?"

"Zaria, what is all this about? What's going on?" I could barely hear her with so much noise going on in the background. I could tell she was in prison.

"Oh, you know exactly what it's about, Hardy. You played me. Now, it's time for some get back."

"Zaria…"

"Its over, Hardy! You and your little girlfriend are dead. But before we kill you, we've got something really special planned out for the both of you."

My heart was beating so hard I thought it would explode in my chest. I had no idea what they had planned for us, but whatever it was, I had the strangest feeling it was going to involve a whole lot of pain.

Before I could even blink the sound of a gun went off. I turned to see if Santiago was okay, and could barely make out her face. All I saw was blood as I cried and fainted.

TO BE CONTINUED...
One Night Stand- Part 3 in Stores February 2012

AN EXCERPT FROM

NEXT DOOR NYMPHO
BY CJ HUDSON

PROLOGUE

POW! Diamond's back slammed against the wall. The impact of her vertebrae crashing into the drywall caused her framed, autographed pictures of basketball player, Darius Jones to shatter onto the hardwood floor. Diamond's life flashed before her eyes as she thought back to all the lives she had ruined; all the marriages she had wrecked in her short time on earth; twenty-five years to be exact. The loud thunder clapping through the skies drowned out her agonizing screams.

Her deadly moment had come. The red hot slug from the .357 Magnum ripped through her right shoulder blade, shredding tissue and bone along the way. The crumbling drywall was no match for the angry bullet as it tore through speedily. It destroyed everything in its path, and caused Diamond to fear for her life. Her heart pounded as she tried desperately to reach the .25 automatic tucked down in her purse. To her surprise, it wasn't there. Suddenly, she looked up through tear soaked eyes and saw her assailant holding the missing pistol.

"Looking for this?"

The shooter's haunting laugh sent chills up and down Diamond's spine. Bleeding profusely, she struggled to stand up.

"Who the fuck is you? What the fuck is this shit all about?" Diamond asked hysterically.

"You've stolen something from me that I can't get back, and now its time to pay the piper," a cold voice whispered.

Diamond was sure that she'd heard the voice before but couldn't quite place it. The shooter was dressed in black jeans, a black pullover hoodie, and black boots with a black fedora hat pulled down over one eye. Diamond looked at the floor in amazement as the .25 automatic slid across the floor to her.

"Go ahead, bitch. Pick it up."

Foolishly, Diamond snatched the gun up, pointed it, and pulled the trigger. The hooded gunman's sinister laugh resonated throughout the room.

"And all this time I thought you were smart. But you're obviously a dumb bitch. You really think I would give your ass a loaded gun? All that cum you've been swallowing has made your ass semi-retarded."

Diamond threw the gun down in disgust.

"Fuck!" she shouted.

"Yep, bitch! That's exactly what you are! Fucked!"

As hard as she tried, Diamond just couldn't get a clear read on the voice that was coming at her. Whoever it was sounded very well educated. There was no slurred speech or slang to connect them with the hood.

"What the fuck is that 'spose ta mean?" Diamond asked.

"It means, it's payback time and there's nothing you can do to stop what's about to happen to you."

Diamond's eyes bulged.

"You've allowed your over-active vagina to ruin your life. You fucked the wrong guy, baby. You took away my life and now I'm gonna return the favor. "

Diamond tried to think back, but she'd fucked so many men that she couldn't be sure who the shooter was talking about. Diamond flinched when her assailant pulled something from her back pocket. With a flick of the wrist, a picture sailed across the floor toward her feet. Reaching down with her good arm, she picked it up and stared at it.

"I don't even know this fuckin' kid!" she wailed.

"Well, maybe you should meet him then. The assassin walked stealthily toward Diamond with the barrel pointed at her head. When the hat and glasses were removed, a look of confusion spread across Diamond's face. Then it hit her.

"Wait a fuckin' minute! It's you! But why? You…"

"Your worse fuckin' nightmare, bitch! I would tell you to say hello to him, but he's in heaven. And you're on your way to hell."

Light flashed in Diamond's face as several hollow point bullets were fired. For the first time in her life, Diamond began to pray, and hoped like hell she would survive.

Chapter One

Diamond

<u>How it all Began</u>

"Where the fuck these bitches at?" I yelled to no one in particular.

They always crampin' my style with this bein' late bull-shit. Most bitches like to be fashionably late so they can make an entrance, but not me. I like to get there and scope out the product. That way, if I'm not feelin' the spot, or the men then I got time to go somewhere else, and it won't interfere with my dick searchin' time. I thought about drivin' myself and just tellin' Essence and Angie that I would meet them at the club, but then I came to my senses. Gas in Cleveland had soared to damn near four dollars a gallon. *Why the fuck should I drive and use my gas? Fuck that. Let them hoes drive their own shit, I told myself with a smirk.*

I stopped to laugh while checkin' myself in the mirror for the fifth time in the last twenty minutes. No doubt, I was a sexy bitch. I slid my hand across my short, pixie cut, hair style wondering why people couldn't see a touch of Halle Berry in me. Besides our similar hairstyles, we were both curvaceous, same height, same complexion, just different sized wallets. The only other difference was the fact that Halle once had a sex fanatic on her hands, and I in turn craved sex daily.

It was never hard to get my daily dosage 'cause niggas go crazy over Dream, the nickname I'd given my pussy. Like this one nigga I use to fuck around with. I can't even remember his name… but this nigga was actin' like he ain't ever seen pretty, succulent pussy before. Talk about clingy; I couldn't take a shit without him wanting to wipe my ass. The only way I could get rid of the magnet muthafucka was to have Essence and Angie bring him by the house and act as if I had a surprise for him. I had one for his ass alright. As soon as he walked through the door, he was treated with the surprise of seeing my lips wrapped around another nigga's dick. The look on his face was priceless. Essence and Angie laughed for almost an hour behind that shit.

The worst part by far though was that the lame ass nigga didn't even have the self-respect to get mad. He just stood there cryin' like a bitch, askin' how could I do that to him. Now I know that I'm a bad bitch but damn, show some fuckin' dignity. If that situation taught me anything, it taught me that just because a nigga has a big dick doesn't mean that he can fuck.

Suddenly, I stopped thinkin' and rushed over to the window to look out into the darkness. I got annoyed because I still didn't see my girls, or any headlights comin' down the street. Not content with the view, I opened the door, walked on the porch and looked up and down the street. Still, nothing. Starting to get pissed, I flipped open my cell phone to call Angie.

"Yo', where the fuck y'all at, chick?"

"Keep yo' bra on hoe, we coming." Before I could spit out a comeback, Angie hung up on me.

"Bitch!" I shouted. I'ma get the last muthafuckin' laugh on her ass. That chick owes me ten dollars and as soon as she turns her head tonight, I'ma go through her purse and clip her trick ass. That was a promise. Friend or no friend, I never played when it came to money. I didn't have much, so what I had, I needed..

Knowin' that there was nothing else that I could do besides wait, I went into the kitchen and grabbed a bottle of Mango Alizè that I had chillin' in the fridge. After gulpin' down a few swallows, I decided to call Angie's ass back and cuss her out for hangin' up on me. Just as I started to dial, the phone vibrated in my hand. After checkin' the screen and seeing that it was my boss, Jason Sims, I let it go to voice mail.

As much as I loved havin' his white, eleven inch dick blowing my back out, tonight was girl's night out. Plus, I was sure to get a chance to test drive some fresh dick at the club. Dream needed variety. *Maybe I can catch him at work so we can sneak off somewhere. I really wanna suck him off,* I thought with a devious smirk.

I remembered the last time his pale-lookin' ass came over. Me and my girls were just chillin' out, smokin' a fat ass blunt and watchin' Martin re-runs. But as soon as he walked in with a duffle bag slung over his shoulder, I knew what time it was. Fifteen minutes later my girls were out the door and I was gettin' my ass waxed. Damn, just thinkin' about that night got me hot as fuck. As if it had a mind of its own, my right hand found its way to the top of my off the shoulder, metallic looking dress and dove inside. Ever so slowly, my hand slid over my left breast and caressed my size 34 Double D's.

"Oh shit," I inadvertently moaned as I pinched my now swollen nipple.

After bringin' my left hand up to squeeze my right nipple, I let my right hand drop toward the bottom of my dress. Before I knew it, my finger was attacking my clit. Soon after, two fingers found their way inside my wet love hole. I finger fucked myself until both of my fingers were dripping with pre-cum. Wantin' to bust a nut in the worst way, I slid my fingers out of my pussy and guided them back up to my clit. I pinched, messaged, teased, and flicked my little man in the boat until I exploded.

"Oooo, shit that felt good," I moaned to myself as hot cum ran down my honey colored legs, slightly burning my inner thigh.

A voice sounded.

"Bitch, what the fuck you doing?"

Startled, I opened my eyes to see Essence and Angie standing in front of me with smirks on their faces. As usual, Angie's face was perfectly painted with tons of make-up; different color eye shadows, foundation, blush, and mascara that looked as if it would never come off. Her micro braids were pulled up into a tight ponytail.

"The fuck it look like I'm doin', Angie," I shot back, showin' them that I wasn't embarrassed in the least. "You hoes took so long; so I figured I'd get a nut off while I was waitin'.'"

"Damn, slut. Yo' nympho ass couldn't wait 'til you got back home?" Angie asked with her nose turned up.

"Nympho? Chick, you got a lotta nerve."

"Look, you two can argue in the car," Essence said in her overly proper voice. "Let's roll."

Essence led the way as me and Angie eye-balled each other, headed out the door in search of some hot action.

"And how come yo' ass don't never drive?" Angie had the nerve to ask me.

"Yes, how come you don't ever drive," Essence cosigned.

Jealous-ass hoes, I thought. Just as I was about to make up an excuse, I heard a deep, raspy voice call my name.

"Yo' Diamond, can I holla at chu fo' a minute?"

I turned my head to the right to see my neighbor, Paul, starin' at me with puppy dog eyes. Although this muthafucka was really starting to get on my fuckin' nerves, I smiled to myself at the thought of my pussy being so good that it kept on breakin' these weak-ass men down.

"Damn, girl, that nigga still sweating the fuck outta you?" whispered Angie.

Nodding my head and rollin' my eyes, I asked my friends to wait in Essence's whip. Like I knew those nosey bitches would, they let the windows down so they could eavesdrop. "Damn, you hoes nosey," I said, poppin' my lips. They gave me the finger as I turned around and walked toward Paul.

"What, nigga? Don't you see I'm 'bout to kick it with my girls?"

"Yeah...I mean...I just wanna holla at chu fo a second."

"What you want Paul?" I asked, rubbin' my temples like I was gettin' a headache.

"I'm jus' sayin' Diamond...I mean damn, what the fuck I do? I thought we had a good thing going and you just dropped a muthafucka!"

After lookin' at his screwed up face, I broke out into laughter. I know this sucka for love ass nigga don't call his self gettin' mad. Not when after I cut his ass off from the punanny, he cried like a bitch. After I finally stopped laughin', I put my hands on my shapely hips and went into check-a-nigga mode.

"First of all Paul, I told yo ass from the gate, I wasn't lookin' for no serious type shit. I ain't tryin' to be wifey to no muthafucka."

"I'm just sayin', Diamond, I ain't tryin' ta make you wifey, I just wanna keep havin' a good time wit chu."

I can't lie. I thought about goin' one more round in the sack with Paul, my El DeBarge look-alike. The nigga couldn't fuck worth shit, but his tongue game was on point like a mutha-fucka. I quickly dismissed that thought, knowin' that this nigga would get even more sprung if I gave him any more of my killer pussy. Dream was a beast.

"Look, Paul," I said preparin' him for the lie I was about to spit out. "I didn't wanna tell you this but apparently yo ass need to hear it. The reason I stopped fuckin' you is because me and my ex are gettin' back together. I didn't tell you at first be-cause I didn't wanna hurt your feelings, but you keep pressin' me about the shit." I paused to lick my thick lips 'cause I knew that shit turned him on. "Look, I gotta go. My girls gettin' impa-tient. Plus, I don't want my dude to do a ride by and catch me talkin' to you."

Without saying another word, I turned on my heels and headed for Essence's 2009 Nissan Pathfinder. By the time I jumped in and closed the door, my girls were already crackin' the fuck up.

"Damn, bitch. You got that fool's nose open wider than Essence's legs," cracked Angie.

As usual, Essence didn't get bent out of shape. She just frowned and gave Angie the finger. Her behavior seemed a lil' weird but I didn't say shit. That was her problem. I had my own issues to worry about.

"I keep tellin' you bitches that my pussy is the best thing since hair weave," I said, braggin' on my sweet sex. I took one last look at Paul's sad ass face as Essence pulled off.

Umph...pathetic ass nigga.

Order your copy of Next Door Nympho today!!

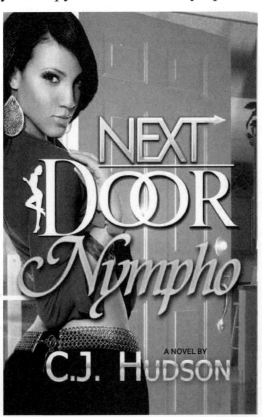

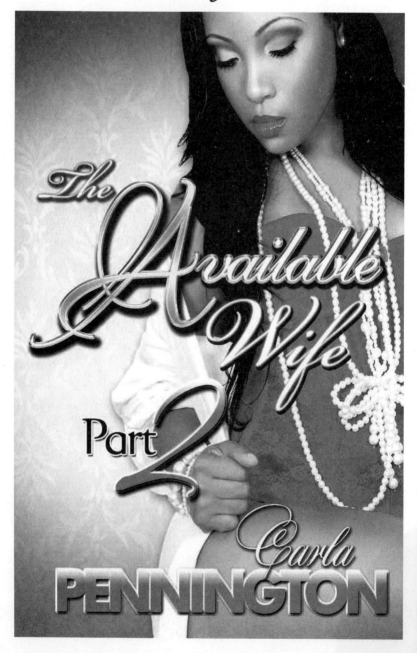

Coming Soon

The Available Wife

Part 2

Carla PENNINGTON

Coming Soon

Wealthy & WICKED

A Novel By CHRIS RENEE

IN STORES NOW

A NOVEL BY BEST SELLING AUTHOR

J. TREMBLE

Bedroom GANGSTA

LCB BOOK TITLES

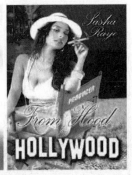

See More Titles At
www.lifechangingbooks.net

ORDER FORM

MAIL TO:
PO Box 423
Brandywine, MD 20613
301-362-6508

FAX TO:
301-579-9913

Ship to:	
Address:	

Date:	Phone:
Email:	

City & State:	Zip:

Make all money orders and cashiers checks payable to: **Life Changing Books**

Qty.	ISBN	Title	Release Date	Price
	0-9741394-2-4	Bruised by Azarel	Jul-05	$ 15.00
	0-9741394-7-6	Bruised 2: The Ultimate Revenge by Azarel	Oct-06	$ 15.00
	0-9741394-3-2	Secrets of a Housewife by J. Tremble	Feb-06	$ 15.00
	0-9741394-6-7	The Millionaire Mistress by Tiphani	Nov-06	$ 15.00
	1-934230-99-5	More Secrets More Lies by J. Tremble	Feb-07	$ 15.00
	1-934230-95-2	A Private Affair by Mike Warren	May-07	$ 15.00
	1-934230-93-6	Deep by Danette Majette	Jul-07	$ 15.00
	1-934230-96-0	Flexin & Sexin Volume 1	Jun-07	$ 15.00
	1-934230-92-8	Talk of the Town by Tonya Ridley	Jul-07	$ 15.00
	1-934230-89-8	Still a Mistress by Tiphani	Nov-07	$ 15.00
	1-934230-91-X	Daddy's House by Azarel	Nov-07	$ 15.00
	1-934230-88-X	Naughty Little Angel by J. Tremble	Feb-08	$ 15.00
	1-934230847	In Those Jeans by Chantel Jolie	Jun-08	$ 15.00
	1-934230820	Rich Girls by Kendall Banks	Oct-08	$ 15.00
	1-934230839	Expensive Taste by Tiphani	Nov-08	$ 15.00
	1-934230782	Brooklyn Brothel by C. Stecko	Jan-09	$ 15.00
	1-934230669	Good Girl Gone bad by Danette Majette	Mar-09	$ 15.00
	1-934230804	From Hood to Hollywood by Sasha Raye	Mar-09	$ 15.00
	1-934230707	Sweet Swagger by Mike Warren	Jun-09	$ 15.00
	1-934230677	Carbon Copy by Azarel	Jul-09	$ 15.00
	1-934230723	Millionaire Mistress 3 by Tiphani	Nov-09	$ 15.00
	1-934230715	A Woman Scorned by Ericka Williams	Nov-09	$ 15.00
	1-934230685	My Man Her Son by J. Tremble	Feb-10	$ 15.00
	1-924230731	Love Heist by Jackie D.	Mar-10	$ 15.00
	1-934230812	Flexin & Sexin Volume 2	Apr-10	$ 15.00
	1-934230748	The Dirty Divorce by Miss KP	May-10	$ 15.00
	1-934230758	Chedda Boyz by CJ Hudson	Jul-10	$ 15.00
	1-934230766	Snitch by VegasClarke	Oct-10	$ 15.00
	1-934230693	Money Maker by Tonya Ridley	Oct-10	$ 15.00
	1-934230774	The Dirty Divorce Part 2 by Miss KP	Nov-10	$ 15.00
	1-934230170	The Available Wife by Carla Pennington	Jan-11	$ 15.00
	1-934230774	One Night Stand by Kendall Banks	Feb-11	$ 15.00
	1-934230278	Bitter by Danette Majette	Feb-11	$ 15.00
	1-934230299	Married to a Balla by Jackie D.	May-11	$ 15.00
	1-934230308	The Dirty Divorce Part 3 by Miss KP	Jun-11	$ 15.00
	1-934230316	Next Door Nympho By CJ Hudson	Jun-11	$ 15.00
	1-934230286	Bedroom Gangsta by J. Tremble	Sep-11	$ 15.00

			Total for Books	$
			Shipping Charges (add $4.95 for 1-4 books*)	$
			Total Enclosed (add lines)	$

* Prison Orders- Please allow up to three (3) weeks for delivery.

Please Note: We are not held responsible for returned prison orders. Make sure the facility will receive books before ordering.

*Shipping and Handling of 5-10 books is $6.95, please contact us if your order is more than 10 books.
(301)362-6508